7-23-14

Praise for the Renaissa

"The Lavene duet ca
whodunit."—*Midwest*

"This jolly series…serves up medieval murder and mayhem."
—*Publishers Weekly*

"[A] terrific mystery series."—MyShelf.com

Perilous Pranks

This novella whets your appetite for the next book in the Renaissance Faire Mystery series - Murderous Matrimony, coming in November 2013. This is a quick fun read. It will keep you turning the pages so you can find out whodunit. The story is well plotted and will keep you intrigued with quirky characters and red herrings galore. Well, Joyce and Jim have done it again - they never disappoint. So if you like your mystery with the fun of a Renaissance Faire, then you should be reading Perilous Pranks.— Cheryl Green

Treacherous Toys

The latest Renaissance Faire Mystery (see Harrowing Hats, Deadly Daggers and Ghastly Glass) is an engaging whodunit made fresh by changing the season as the heroine provides a tour of the Renaissance Faire Village during Christmas (instead of the summer). This exciting amateur sleuth (with Jesse's success rate on solving homicides while risking her life on cases the cops fumble; she should turn pro to pay her bills) is filled with quirky characters as team Lavene provide another engaging murder investigation. By Harriet Klausner

continued . . .

HARROWING HATS

"The reader will have a grand time. This is an entertaining read with a well-crafted plot. Readers of the series will not be disappointed. New readers will want to glom the backlist so they don't miss a single minute." —*Fresh Fiction*

"The Renaissance Faire Mysteries are always an enjoyable read . . . Joyce and Jim Lavene provide a complex exciting murder mystery that amateur sleuth fans will appreciate." —*Midwest Book Review*

DEADLY DAGGERS

"The Lavene duet can always be counted on for an enjoyable whodunit . . . Filled with twists and red herrings, *Deadly Daggers* is a delightful mystery." —*Midwest Book Review*

"Will keep you entertained from the fi rst duel to the last surprise . . . If you like fun reads that will let you leave this world for a time, this series is for you."

—*The Romance Readers Connection*

"Never a dull moment! Filled with interesting characters, a fast-paced story, and plenty of humor, this series never lets its readers down . . . You're bound to feel an overwhelming craving for a giant turkey leg and the urge to toast to the king's health with a big mug of ale as you enjoy this thematic cozy mystery!" —*Fresh Fiction*

GHASTLY GLASS

"A unique look at a renaissance faire. This is a colorful, exciting amateur sleuth mystery fi lled with quirky characters who endear themselves to the reader as Joyce and Jim Lavene write a delightful whodunit." —*Midwest Book Review*

continued . . .

Wicked Weaves

"This jolly series debut . . . serves up medieval murder and mayhem." —*Publishers Weekly*

"[A] new, exciting . . . series . . . Part of the fun of this solid whodunit is the vivid description of the Renaissance Village; anyone who has not been to one will want to go . . . [C]leverly developed." —*Midwest Book Review*

Peggy Lee Garden Mysteries

Pretty Poison
Fruit of the Poisoned Tree
Poisoned Petals
Perfect Poison
A Corpse For Yew
Buried by Buttercups—Novella
A Thyme to Die

Renaissance Faire Mysteries

Wicked Weaves
Ghastly Glass
Deadly Daggers
Harrowing Hats
Treacherous Toy
Perilous Pranks—Novella

Missing Pieces Mysteries

A Timely Vision
A Touch of Gold
A Spirited Gift
A Haunting Dream
A Finder's Fee

Murderous Matrimony

By

Joyce and Jim Lavene

Copyright © 2014 Joyce and Jim Lavene

Cover art by Emmie Anne Studios
http://www.emmieannestudios.com
Book coach and editor—Jeni Chappelle
http://www.jenichappelle.com/
All rights reserved.
No part of this book may be reproduced, scanned, or distributed in any printed or electronic form without permission. Please do not participate in or encourage piracy of copyrighted materials in violation of the authors' rights. Purchase only authorized editions.

Part I

Perilous Pranks

One

Wanda Le Fey was dead.

In the immortal words of Charles Dickens: *"There can be no doubt about that."*

She was also blue—deep blue, a dark shade, not a nice sky blue—from the tips of her toes to the top of her flaming red hair.

I had something to do with the blue part, which was why I was at her cottage in Renaissance Faire Village and Marketplace.

I was wondering why she wasn't screaming and running all over the Village looking for me. She had to know that I was the one who'd put the blue dye-pack in her shower head.

I swear it was non-toxic. It was just a prank—the best prank *ever*—but it shouldn't have killed her.

Was anyone going to believe me?

I studied Wanda again. She was half-in and half-out of the shower. There was a long red gash that looked like a knife, or sword wound, in the center of her chest. Blood was everywhere. I guessed that her attacker must have surprised her as she was getting out of the shower.

Her eyes were still open—those cold, baleful eyes that had driven me crazy the last few years.

Wanda had been the Village nurse, but a meaner, nastier person would be hard to imagine. And it wasn't only me. She seemed to have it in for everyone.

Now it seemed someone had it in for her too.

Pat Snyder, who played William Shakespeare every hour from ten a.m. to six p.m. on the Village Green, peeked around the open door to the cottage.

"Well?" he whispered. "Is she blue? Where is she? Why haven't I heard her cursing you?"

"There's a slight problem. She's dead."

He crept into the bedroom and stared at Wanda's body for a minute while he absently stroked his triangle-shaped beard. It was a pose he assumed quite often as Shakespeare. "This is bad, Jessie. This is *very* bad."

"You don't have to tell *me*. I'm the one who dyed her blue! Who do you think they're going to accuse of killing her?"

"Definitely a *bad* business. You should call the Bailiff, or the police."

"I thought of that." He was no help at all.

"I have to go. The Main Gate is open." He made his excuses. "Visitors will want to see me."

With that, he was gone.

Big surprise. No one wanted to be around Wanda when she was alive. Dead, she was even less desirable as a companion.

Shakespeare was her ex-husband. I'd told him, and a few others, about my prank. That could make them all accomplices.

Standing there with Wanda's dead body made me shiver. It was a terrible death, even though I hadn't liked her. Something about the helplessness of this poor, blue woman in her shower made me realize that she was more than simply evil Wanda Le Fey. She was a victim.

A victim whose killer the police would be looking for shortly. I needed to get out of there!

A white space on her wrist caught my attention. I recognized it as the place she'd usually worn a leather bracelet with a remarkable turquoise-colored stone set in it. I'd always admired it.

I glanced carefully around the bathroom. There was no sign of the bracelet. Yet she had to be wearing it when the dye dropped on her in the shower, or her wrist would be blue too. The showerhead still dripped blue dye.

Curious.

"Jessie?"

I almost jumped out of my skin when Chase Manhattan—Bailiff, Protector of the Village, and my fiancée—called my name. Far worse, I put my hand out and made a big print on the glass shower door.

I was going to pay for that!

"What are you *doing*?" He glanced at Wanda's body. "What happened? I thought you were dying her blue. Did she have some kind of allergic reaction to the dye?"

"Not unless that reaction included a big knife being stuck in her chest." I pointed at the knife wound without moving closer. "I came to see why she wasn't on the cobblestones, shouting for me. The front door was open. I found her like this."

Chase went over and put his finger on Wanda's throat. "No pulse. She's cold too. She's been dead for a while. I have to call the police. Don't touch anything else. We'll wait outside until Detective Almond gets here."

"Okay." I put my hands in the pockets of my long blue skirt. It was meant to mock Wanda's embarrassment at being blue. It should've been the best prank in the world. Instead, it was beginning to look like the prank may have backfired on me.

Chase called the police. We went outside and he hugged me, mussing my short, straight brown hair. "Everything is going to be okay. It was supposed to be a joke. The other part has nothing to do with you."

"I'm not sure Detective Almond is going to see it that way."

Chase looked more like a pirate than the Village equivalent of a police officer. He was six-foot-eight, two hundred and fifty pounds of muscle wrapped in a leather vest and britches. He wore his long, brown hair in a single braid and had a gold earring in one ear.

He was the chief of security for the Village. The Ren Faire could get a little wild sometimes, with 10,000 people a day passing through our Main Gate.

"Even *he* won't think you killed Wanda," he said. "He knows about the pranks that go on here all the time."

"He also knows that Wanda and I hated each other. He's gonna like me for her murder."

"You watch too much TV, Jessie. Detective Almond will look at all the evidence as it comes in and come to a logical conclusion, like he always does."

I wasn't as convinced of that fact as Chase was, but that was a basic difference between us. Chase always looked for the best in people. I always looked for ways to survive around them.

I knew Detective Almond was going to think I killed Wanda. My best defense was trying to figure out who had *actually* killed her.

I had no idea where to start. Even though I couldn't think of anyone who *liked* Wanda, I couldn't think of anyone who disliked her enough to kill her either.

"I have a dress fitting, and I'm expecting my loom today for the museum." I glanced at my wrist, forgetting momentarily that my watch was at our home in the Dungeon.

Those of us who work at the Village—shopkeepers and actors— weren't allowed to wear modern watches or carry cell phones while we were working. The Village was supposed to represent a true Renaissance experience.

I could argue with some of what Adventureland, our parent company, considered 'true' Renaissance, but that was another story.

"I think you should be here if you want to make a good impression on Detective Almond," Chase said. "It's only going to make him cranky if he has to look for you. You know he hates walking around the Village."

I didn't want to tell Chase that I had an awful feeling that Detective Almond would arrest me on the spot as soon as he heard the circumstances of Wanda's death. The only chance I had was to find her killer—before he could lock me up and throw away the key.

Two

Chase and I were getting married in about a month. Despite his belief that I should wait there for Detective Almond, he also knew it could take a while for him to get there. The police didn't like coming out to the Village. They called it 'the crazy place'. That was why they had trained Chase to take care of things.

Playing on my need to go to another fitting for my wedding gown—what sane bridegroom-to-be would deny that?—I promised to come back to Wanda's cottage as soon as he sent one of his security people for me. He kissed me and let me go.

I didn't want to lie to Chase, and technically, I hadn't. I *was* supposed try on my wedding dress again that day at Stylish Frocks, the shop that made all the costumes for the Village. But knowing my time was limited, I went to find Shakespeare instead. I figured if anyone knew who'd killed Wanda, it would be him.

Also, I couldn't quite cross him off of my suspect list. He'd hated Wanda too. Maybe when he'd found out about my prank, he thought it would be a perfect time to kill Wanda and blame it on me.

I liked Shakespeare. I didn't want to think he could kill anyone, but I knew that I didn't kill her.

Minstrels and flower girls were lining up at the Main Gate to welcome our visitors. There would be music and flower petals for at least the first few hundred people at ten a.m. After that, jugglers would trade places with minstrels, and Robin Hood and a few of his Merry Men would indulge in a little swordplay. The day would pass with everyone taking a turn at the gate.

By closing time, there would have been fools, knaves, and varlets waving goodbye to the last visitors and bidding them return soon. We needed them if we wanted to continue our crazy existence.

I knew Shakespeare would be at his place at the podium on the Village Green. He'd be writing an ode with a big quill pen to some pretty girl in a tight, overly-filled bodice. He'd spout poetry and snippets from Shakespeare's plays. He was very good at his role.

But he wasn't at his stone podium when I got there. Mother Goose hadn't seen him, and neither had King Arthur, who was on his way to take the sword from the stone.

Shakespeare was probably afraid the police would want to question him. I didn't blame him. Nearly everyone in the Village had secrets they didn't want dragged out in the open.

I was scared too, even though I didn't have any secrets that would interest anyone. The idea of being in jail on my wedding day wasn't very appealing.

It wasn't a large village, and I knew where he lived. The sooner I spoke with him about Wanda's death, the better for both of us. It's not good to be uninformed when talking to the police.

"There you are, Lady Jessie." My assistant, Manawydan Argall, bowed to me. "I'm afraid the ruffians who have delivered the loom won't allow me to sign for it."

Manawydan (I called him Manny) was fresh out of college with a degree in the arts. He was a short, African-American man with neatly trimmed hair and large glasses. He was always punctual, always knowledgeable, and a snappy dresser besides. His clothes were Victorian rather than Renaissance, but he always looked nice. And he smelled wonderful— like flowers, sunshine, and fresh air.

I was the director of the museum that would feature arts and crafts from the Renaissance. My brand new Ph.D. was in historic arts and crafts, with my dissertation being the Proliferation of Medieval Crafts in Modern Times. I'd studied and apprenticed with almost every craftsman in the Village. I'd made baskets, arrows, hats, glassware and swords.

It was still hard to believe that I had a full-time job working at the Village. I didn't have to teach history classes at the University of South Carolina anymore. I could be with Chase all the time. It didn't get much better than that.

The vertical loom was one of the centerpieces of our new exhibit about tapestry making. It was from Pennsylvania and had been used in the early 1700s. It was made of rough-hewn lumber and would have cost the Village a fortune, but the owner was letting us borrow it. He would also be there for our grand opening where he would be weaving for the visitors.

My hunt for Shakespeare would have to wait. "I'll sign for it. Let's get this over with."

I thought my size twelve feet and long legs would leave Manny in the dust, but he kept up without breaking a sweat. We ate up the space between Shakespeare's podium and the manor houses near the gate at Squire's Lane.

The first visitor through the Main Gate was wearing a gorilla suit. Dressing up in Renaissance style meant different things to different people. Behind him was a high-born lady in a beautiful purple gown with a silver girdle. She was with a knight in full armor.

That was going to get a little hot by the end of the day.

Most people were in Myrtle Beach on vacation when they visited us. They wore what we call street clothes—shorts, jeans, bikini tops, and T-shirts. Some of their sandals could be considered authentic Ren Faire gear. That was about it. Many bought or rented costumes while they were at the Village. It wasn't necessary to dress the part to have a good time, but I thought it helped get into the spirit.

Manny and I walked around a madman in the street. Madmen were respected members of the community. Their entertainment value was tremendous, especially when no shows were going on.

They wore britches and shirts with holes in them, frequently rubbing themselves with sand or dirt. They hit pots and pans together and grabbed at ladies' skirts. Kids loved them.

"You're sitting in front of the museum." Manny pointed out to the madman. "Would you mind terribly moving one way or the other?"

Dave the Madman refused. "This is where the guild told me to be today. Maybe you should take it up with them."

"I'll do that." Manny made shooing motions with his hands. "In the meantime, get away."

Dave grinned. "I'm not going anywhere." He banged his pans together and rolled around on the ground like—well—like a madman. "Good morning, Lady Jessie. Your beauty lights up the day."

I smiled, enjoying the compliment. Visitors were starting to watch us. "Good morning, Sir Madman Dave. How does the morning treat you?"

A pretty lady in a pink brocade gown, holding a matching parasol, dropped some change into Dave's pot and blew him a kiss.

"Quite well, my lady. Please give my regards to the Bailiff."

I liked Dave, even though he was a madman. He might graduate to becoming a knave or a varlet in the same guild, if he stayed for a while. He could even move up into the Forest Guild with Robin Hood or the Magical Creatures Guild with Merlin the Magician, if he played his cards right.

But he was probably only there for a short time, like most secondary characters. The Village was filled with college and high school drama students. Very few stayed permanently.

Manny was patiently waiting near the front door of the manor house in his pointy-toed slippers. "This may look bad for the museum."

"The museum isn't even open yet. Even if it was, seeing madmen and musicians on the cobblestones is part of the experience."

"I see." He nodded. "These circumstances are a bit *unusual*."

"You'll get used to it." I patted him on the shoulder. "You might even want to *be* a madman someday."

He shuddered and opened the door for me. "I think *not*."

The four burly men, who'd carried the large old loom from the parking lot to the museum, were waiting. They didn't look happy about it either.

The delivery men moved the heavy loom into place. It was a difficult process to get the loom where it needed to be.

Manny wasn't much help. He expected the legs of the loom to fit exactly where we'd made the chalk drawings for them.

If looks could have killed, Manny would certainly be dead.

I signed the document for the four men after examining the loom to make sure it was still in good repair. "Thank you, gentlemen. Please stay on at the Faire if you can, as my guests. We appreciate all your hard work."

"Are you kidding me?" The biggest of the four, and the one who seemed to be in charge, glanced around the museum. "This place looks like the loony bin to me. I had a buddy who visited here one day with his girl. He *never* came out again."

It sounded like the end of a bad horror story.

I inclined my head in what I hoped was a graceful and ladylike gesture. "It happens frequently that visitors decide to stay with us, sir. For many, our lives here are better than the ones in the real world. What, perchance, was your friend's name?"

"His name was Ralph. I think he calls himself Rafe now. He's a pirate, or something."

"Yes. Rafe is the king of all the pirates on the Queen's Revenge. I shall tell him that you asked about him."

"Whatever." He looked around again and gestured to his helpers. "Let's get out of here."

While Manny documented the receipt of the loom, I admired it and the rest of the tapestry exhibit we'd managed to put together so far. There was a great richness and history to what we were trying to do. It was different than the rest of the Village. People could learn here, as well as enjoy themselves.

I ran my hand along the rough wood of the loom, thinking about the hands that had worked on it. I imagined the tapestries that had been produced on it.

Beside the loom were glassmaker's tools that had been donated by Roger Trent from the Glass Gryphon, a shop in the Village. He was also one of the Village craftspeople who would demonstrate his skills at the museum when it opened in November.

His wife, Mary Shift, was a Gullah basket weaver. She'd promised to spend a day here too. I'd learned to weave sweet grass baskets with her.

My foot scuffed something on the hardwood floor. I looked down and saw a glint of color where it didn't belong.

It was Wanda's missing bracelet.

Of course, there was blood on it, and I'd put my hand into it. The smell of fresh blood made me want to vomit.

It looked like the real killer was trying to frame me for Wanda's murder.

Three

"Who else has been in the museum this morning besides you and the loom movers?" I tried not to panic as I wiped my hands on a handkerchief in my pocket.

"The museum was empty when I came here this morning," Manny said. "The loom movers came later, and then I went to find you. Why? Is something wrong? What *is* that smell?"

Manny and I were the only ones with keys to the museum. He was new to the Village. I had no reason to suspect that he might be involved with what had happened to Wanda. The killer probably came in while he was gone and hid the bracelet because he or she knew I could be blamed for Wanda's death.

"Nothing is wrong." I looked at the bracelet and wished I had a plastic bag to put it in. The only thing I had was my free drink mug that all employees carried. When you presented it at any of the eateries in the village, you got a free drink.

Could I ever drink out of the mug again if I stored Wanda's bloody bracelet in it until I could give it to Chase or Detective Almond?

I wasn't sure, but I couldn't walk around with it in my hand either. Grimacing, I dropped the bracelet into the mug. That was that. I'd have to get a new mug.

"Blood." Manny sniffed again, moving closer to see what I was doing. "*New blood.* What did you find?"

"Nothing. I-uh-cut myself shaving this morning." I didn't want to discuss this with him. I knew how the Village gossips worked. One word and everyone would know.

"Really?" His dark eyes gazed into my face as though trying to discern the truth. "It doesn't *smell* like you, Lady Jessie."

That was weird.

I took a few steps back from him and put my hand across the top of the cup. "I have to go. You have to go too."

"Why? I have a lot of work to do here today. I can't leave."

I nudged him out the door. "Yes, you can. Consider it your day off." I closed and locked the museum door behind us. "Don't set foot inside until tomorrow, or when the police tell you to."

"The police?" He put his hand lightly on top of mine, the one that was covering the cup that held Wanda's bracelet. "You can trust me with your secrets, Lady Jessie. What has happened?"

"I can't talk about it yet. I'm sorry." I jerked my hand, and the cup, away from him. "It's not that I don't trust you, Manny. I'll tell you later. I promise."

He peered at me with such intensity in his eyes that I thought lasers might come out of them. It was scary. I thanked him for his help, as I always did, and ran down the stairs to the cobblestones.

I knew Detective Almond would want to look over the area where I'd found the bracelet. Clearly, the killer had been in there. Maybe he or she had left some fingerprints behind. They could probably get something from the blood on the bracelet too.

I stopped in at Merlin's Apothecary, which was uncomfortably close to the First Aid Station where Wanda would normally be. Her cottage was only a few hundred feet from there too. Chase was probably there, talking to Detective Almond about her death.

Merlin could be a little wacky sometimes, but he was a good friend. His purple wizard's robe had a tendency to fly open, even when there was no breeze. Most of the ladies in the Village knew to look away. He also wore a large, pointed hat that matched his robe.

His apothecary was full of stuffed birds, jars of bugs and worms. He sold colored powders and liquids, magic tricks, and wands. It was one of the most visited shops in the Village, though I couldn't say why. Maybe it was the name.

The first thing anyone saw as they walked inside was a motley moose head Merlin called Horace. It was disgusting, but kids loved it.

"Lady Jessie." Merlin bowed regally to me as I entered. He held his pointed hat on his scraggly gray hair. "To what do I owe the honor?"

What most people didn't know, even those who'd lived in the Village for a while, was that Merlin was the CEO of Adventureland. I wouldn't have known either, but Chase told me. Merlin lived here because he said it helped him keep up with his work.

I knew better. The man loved the *weird*.

"I have a big problem I need to discuss with you."

"That sounds serious. I could make an appointment for day after tomorrow."

"It has to be now. Wanda is dead, and it looks like I might've killed her. I didn't. But it *looks* like I could be guilty."

His blue eyes widened comically above his gray beard that didn't look too much better than Horace's fur. "That is *quite* a problem. Have you told the Bailiff yet? Has anyone called the police?"

We sat down in his shop, and I spilled everything—from the blue dye prank to finding her coming out of the shower.

"Well, the prank was a long time coming after she glued your gown to the chair at the Lady of the Lake Tavern," he mused. "I was beginning to think you weren't going to get her back—that maybe you were too caught up with the wedding plans and the museum. *That* part I understand."

"This was more than a prank. It looked like the killer caught her right after the dye had come out of the showerhead. It was awful."

He nodded in what I suspect should have been a wise manner. Instead his hat almost toppled from his head. He came close to falling out of his chair as he tried to catch it.

"And what can I do for you in regard to this matter?" he finally asked.

"I was wondering if you could tell me anything about Wanda's life that might be helpful. Was she seeing anyone? Had she broken up with someone? Blades are used in crimes of passion, Merlin. Was there someone she felt passionate about?"

He stroked his beard again and gazed toward the ceiling. "It seems to me that she was seeing someone. Yes! A younger man, I believe. Shakespeare had some words to say about that. I remember hearing them argue night before last. They were divorced, you know."

"Yes. I knew they'd been married." Maybe Shakespeare had killed Wanda *and* set me up. The prank made me look guiltier than anyone else I could think of, including him.

"Well, then you may also know that Shakespeare was paying Wanda alimony, unheard of in this day and age, but apparently he'd strayed during their marriage and had no choice but to pay up."

That was news to me. No one in the Village made much money. How could Shakespeare afford to pay Wanda alimony?

Maybe he couldn't. Her death *would* mean the end of that extra expense. It was a strong motive.

"What about the younger man?" I asked. "Do you know his name?"

"No. I might know him if I saw him. He works here—a knight, I believe."

"Thank you, kind sir." I got to my feet and sketched him a slight curtsy when I noticed visitors coming into the apothecary.

The visitors applauded and smiled. This was one reason why the people who lived here were 'on' the whole time the Main Gate was open.

"You are very welcome, lovely lady." He bowed, keeping one hand on his hat.

I left the apothecary, headed for the castle to see if Shakespeare had run for sanctuary there.

Ginny Stewart, the owner of the Lady of the Lake Tavern, was standing beside the Hanging Tree, watching the police outside Wanda's cottage. She was a tough, older woman with ragged white hair—the epitome of what anyone would think of as a female tavern owner from the Renaissance.

She always wore the same, slightly dirty green dress as her costume, her enormous bosom barely contained in it. "What's going on over there?" she asked in her rasping voice.

"Wanda is dead. Murdered," I informed her.

"Oh." She turned away. "A lot of fuss about a trifle then."

Ginny and I weren't particularly friends either. I wasn't surprised by her attitude, though it was cold. I couldn't think who she *was* friends with in the Village either, besides the men.

One of Chase's security guards saw me. Detective Almond had arrived and was requesting my presence. My time to find possible alternatives to me being the killer was up.

I knew there was nothing else I could do. I followed the security guard. There was an ambulance, a coroner's car, and a police vehicle in front of Wanda's cottage. It wouldn't be long before everyone knew what had happened.

It was always so odd to see vehicles here, especially emergency vehicles. It felt like poking a stick in the wheel of normal Village life. You could almost forget the real world was out there, until something like this happened.

Detective Don Almond was a chubby, middle-aged man who always seemed in need of a haircut, and he wore his pants too tight. His heavy chin rested above a dirty collar and a shirt front always stained with whatever his last meal had been.

When he saw me, he bowed slightly. “Look who’s here. Welcome, my lady. Have you come to answer for your crimes?”

Four

Detective Almond and I have had our moments—not many of them good. He seemed to love Chase like a son and equally disliked me.

So I knew what he saw when he appraised me in that brief moment: thirty-something, ex-associate history professor, six-foot, blue eyes, and straight brown hair.

A little on the weird side, maybe.

"Jessie isn't responsible for what happened to Wanda." Chase stepped in to defend me like the chivalrous knight he was.

"Except that she had a long-term disagreement with Miss Le Fey, which had led to several confrontations that I know of—not the *least* of which was dyeing the dead woman blue. How could I possibly *not* think that Jessie was responsible for this murder?"

That hadn't gone so well. Chase glanced at me. He hadn't given up.

Before he could have another go at telling Detective Almond that I was innocent, I stood up for myself. "Yes, it's true. I put the blue dye in the showerhead to get back at her for gluing my skirt to a chair in the tavern. But she was expecting it. That doesn't mean I killed her. She was dead when I found her."

"Another point *not* in your favor." Detective Almond's smile was smug. "I'm guessing that was your handprint on the shower glass too."

"I know." I produced my mug. "Someone also put Wanda's bracelet at the museum to set me up. I locked the door before I left, so you can go over the scene in case the *real* killer left some clues."

I explained about the white spot on Wanda's arm where the bracelet had been—in case he hadn't noticed.

He took the mug from me, glanced in it, and then handed it off to an officer. "I really appreciate your help, Jessie. Maybe we should start with where you were at around six a.m. this morning."

"She was with me," Chase volunteered. "We were together all night."

"Since you're the constable of this place, it might be better if you don't get involved personally in the investigation," Detective Almond told him.

"Okay—I quit. If being Bailiff for the village means I can't defend Jessie then I quit."

I knew Detective Almond didn't want that to happen. He wanted Chase to stay where he was. If he left, that would mean Myrtle Beach would have to assign another trained officer to take his place.

"Let's not be hasty. I know you love your job here. We just need to be unbiased."

"Maybe you should take that to heart," Chase shot back. "I don't think immediately pegging her as the killer is unbiased either."

Detective Almond gave in. "Fair enough. I'm going to question other possible suspects. You have to admit, your girlfriend looks to be on top of the list. She had motive. She may have had opportunity. And if I remember correctly, she's pretty good with a sword, which my assistant medical examiner tells me is probably the weapon used by the killer."

"First of all, she's my fiancée. You know that. We're getting married in a month. And second, I told you she was with me all night. You can take opportunity *off* that list."

They were talking about me like I wasn't even there.

"Excuse me," I interrupted their debate. "I don't think we got up until seven a.m. and the showerhead prank was set up yesterday afternoon while she was working. Someone told me she took showers in the morning before work."

"How did you get into her home?" Detective Almond demanded.

"Everyone knows she leaves her door open while she's at the First Aid Station. It only took me a few minutes to get the dye ready."

He was writing down what I'd said in a small notebook and glanced up as I finished. "And you set this up by yourself? No help from anyone else?"

I thought about Shakespeare, who was a big help in relaying Wanda's habits to me so I could make the prank happen. He wasn't actually at the cottage while I was putting in the dye pack, but he was there right after me that morning.

I wasn't giving him up, at least not yet, not until I had a chance to talk to him.

"I was alone. It wasn't hard to do," I responded. "Are you going to arrest me?"

"No." He put away his notebook. "Not right now anyway. Show me where you found the bracelet."

We walked down the path that took us past the castle and Mirror Lake where the pirate ship was in the process of sailing toward the Lady of the Lake Tavern.

The Hanging Tree was beside it. Public hangings of unfortunates happened at least once a day here. It was always surprising to me how many visitors *wanted* to be publically hanged. They signed up for it as they entered the gate, and even paid extra for the privilege.

Of course it was all staged, like the stocks where visitors threw squishy vegetables and fruit at each other for supposed wrongs—and almost everything else in the Village.

We walked past Eve's Garden where they sold live plants and herbs used for food and medicine during the Renaissance. There was a tour and a tasting. It was never as popular as I thought it should be. There were some interesting plant poisons used during that time.

As we reached the mermaid lagoon at the far end of the lake, Detective Almond's eyebrows shot up. "Where are the mermaids?"

Usually, the mermaids would have been sunning themselves on large rocks in the water. They'd flick their tails and giggle as they waved. They each wore long blond wigs that covered their shoulders, and left plenty of cleavage showing from their bikini tops.

But it was November and the hot days of summer were behind us. The mermaids would be back again in May.

"It's too cold," Chase explained. "Everyone asks about them."

I watched dozens of people make a sharp turn to the left to visit the mermaids after entering the Main Gate. Their looks of disappointment mimicked Detective Almonds'.

"I've always liked the jousting," he finally said, turning away from the empty lagoon. "I caught part of one of the Templar Knight horse shows earlier this year. They're amazing horsemen."

I knew deep down inside, Detective Almond liked the Ren Faire. He had a hard time admitting it. He'd been the first bailiff when the park had opened. It was probably still in his blood.

"I thought I caught a vibe this morning." Former police officer Tom Grigg shook hands with his ex-boss. "I heard Wanda Le Fey was murdered."

Grigg had been assigned as an undercover officer at the Village. He'd gone native and stayed on as Tom, Tom the Piper's son, but now he sailed on the Queen's Revenge and had a tattoo and gold tooth to prove it.

"Yeah." Detective Almond tried not to look at his former contemporary—now in torn, black pants with a dirty white shirt tied around his waist. "She was dyed blue," he glanced at me, "and *someone* shoved a sword through her heart."

"Have you heard anything that could help?" Chase asked Grigg.

Grigg shook his head, his once super-short hair now down to his shoulders. "Nope. Sorry. She was at the Lady of the Lake a couple of days ago with a sweet young knight. We left them alone during the raid. Last time Captain Rafe went to her for a bad sprain, she wrapped it so tight—it almost cut off the circulation to his leg. We don't mess with her if we can help it."

This was the second time I'd heard about Wanda's young lover. "Did you recognize the young man she was with?"

"Nope. Might not live in the Village." There was a loud rumble as the pirate ship prepared to fire off one of her cannons. "Gotta go. Plunder calls!"

"Arrgh!" Chase did the expected pirate fist pump. Grigg saluted him, and was gone.

'Are they still pretending to kidnap visitors at the tavern?" Detective Almond gazed toward the ship in disgust. "They should've stopped that years ago."

"We tried." Chase shrugged his broad shoulders. "We got a lot of complaints. People love the pirate raid."

Robin Hood, Maid Marion, and Little John were dressed in forest green with little green hats perched on their heads. They were battling the evil Sheriff of Nottingham for the attention of hundreds of visitors on the cobblestones. They repeated this, with some variations, every hour or so. Robin Hood always won, and led his men back into Sherwood Forest.

We walked past the spectacle quickly, and were almost to the manor house where the museum was being set up, when I heard a call from behind us. My twin brother, who was officially the promoter and web designer for the Merry Men, ran to catch up with us.

Tony looked a lot like like me, except with brown eyes—and male parts. He favored our father in appearance and disposition. I was more like our mother.

I had to admit he'd been more reliable in the last year since Robin Hood had put him to work. I hadn't loaned him money in months.

"Hey! What's going on, Lady Sis?" He grinned at Detective Almond and Chase.

"We're on our way to the museum," I told him. "Detective Almond thinks I murdered Wanda."

Tony didn't look surprised. "Was it the blue dye?"

"How many people in the Village knew about this prank?" Detective Almond asked with a snarl.

"Probably fifty or more." Tony shrugged. "Someone even put it on the Internet. It was a super *awesome* prank."

"Not so super *awesome* for the dead woman," Detective Almond reminded him.

"I suppose not. But she had it coming. She knew it." Tony stared at me. "What happened to her, if it wasn't the dye?"

"Someone killed her with a sword." I filled in the blanks.

"But not you?" he asked. "You wouldn't do something that crazy, right? Unless she attacked you *because* you turned her blue. I'll bet a lawyer could argue that issue."

"We don't have time for this," Detective Almond said. "I want to see where you found the bracelet."

Tony grinned. "Are you talking about that bracelet Jessie always loved? I remember her saying how she'd like to take it from Wanda."

I sighed. "Thanks, Tony."

Five

I pushed on for the manor house before my brother totally incriminated me. He'd managed to score another point against me in Detective Almond's notebook.

I opened the front door to the museum, and a cold breeze swept past me, pushing around in little whirlwinds up and down the stairs.

I shivered. It was eighty degrees outside, and hotter in the building. Our ceiling fans weren't on yet. *Where had that come from?*

We went inside, and I showed everyone where I'd found the bracelet. Detective Almond called the crime scene team to go over the museum. I asked him to be careful— some of the older tapestries, the loom, and woodwork items were irreplaceable.

"Of course." He held out his hand. "I'll take the key to make sure this stays closed until the investigation is over."

"Sure." My hand shook as I gave him the key that represented my future in the Village.

"You've landed on your feet here." He walked around and studied the vertical loom and Roger Trent's glass-making equipment. "I hope you didn't mess it all up for some stupid prank."

If I'd thought it would help, I would've crossed my heart and sworn that I didn't kill Wanda. That might've worked with some of my friends, but only time—and the end of this investigation—would remedy the situation. I needed to find Shakespeare. Maybe between us, we could prove that neither of us killed Wanda.

Chase put his arm around me, and I leaned into him as we walked back down the stairs to the cobblestones.

Around us, life in the Village played out. Fred the Red Dragon was growling at kids and making them shriek. The Green Man wobbled on his stilts, clothed by his tree costume, as visitors vied to have their pictures taken with him. Sam Da Vinci coaxed pretty women of all ages to allow him to draw their portraits. A young apprentice knight called out the time between jousts at the Field of Honor.

"It's going to be okay," Chase promised with a hug and a kiss on the forehead. "You have plenty to do getting ready for the wedding, right? Just concentrate on that right now. Wanda's death will sort itself out."

"At least Detective Almond didn't arrest me."

"That's the spirit!" He hugged me again. "Let's grab some lunch."

We stopped for lunch at Peter's Pub. Peter Greenwalt, the owner, waited on us, even though the pub was busy. His thick mutton chops, long hair, and heavy beard distinguished him. He was a nice man and a good shopkeeper.

"I've heard about your morning, Lady Jessie." He smiled and bowed his head a little to show respect. "What would you like for lunch? On the house."

"Thank you so much, kind sir." There were dozens of visitors around us, snapping pictures and listening to our words. "Doth thou have a cheeseburger, and perhaps fries?"

He nodded. "Also a large Coke. And for you, Sir Bailiff?"

"I require the same fare, shopkeeper." Chase regally inclined his head. It was expected of him to be a little aloof since he was only below the king and queen in Village status.

"Very good, sir. Your food will be out shortly."

Sometimes it's difficult living your life on a stage where hundreds of people are hanging on your every word, watching you, and taking pictures that are immediately posted to the Internet.

This was one of those times. I wished I could be alone to feel ragged by myself.

"You could hole up in the Dungeon today," Chase suggested as though he was reading my mind.

That's only one of the many reasons I love him. "I probably will after I go for the dress fitting."

He raised one brow. "I thought you were going there this morning? I can't believe you lied to me." He sighed and shook his head.

"I wasn't lying." I tried to repair the damage." I thought it might be more important to find Shakespeare. He knew about the prank, and came to Wanda's cottage right after I found her dead. I went to look for him, but he wasn't at his podium when the Main Gate opened."

"I'll have people keep an eye out for him. You think he was involved with Wanda's murder?"

"I don't know. I didn't to begin with, but now with him disappearing . . . I guess it's possible."

"Okay. Just don't worry about it. Pat has been playing Shakespeare here since the Village opened. He isn't going to walk off the job. We'll find him."

"Thanks." I managed a smile, but I didn't have the same confidence he had. If Shakespeare had killed Wanda, he could be long gone by now.

"There she is," a familiar voice bellowed across the pub.

Daisy Reynolds was the master armorer for the Village. She was a large woman with muscled arms, badly dyed blond curls, and a kewpie doll smile she enhanced with scarlet lipstick. She wore a formidable breast plate with the image of a phoenix on it.

"Good morning, Master Armorer." I stood and greeted her with a head nod, as was proper in this case.

"Never mind that crap." She threw her big arms around me and almost hugged the breath out of my chest. "I'm proud of you finally taking care of that she-witch. I heard she was blue from head to toe. Great prank, Lady Jessie!"

"Hey! Save some of that for me." Bart Van Impe was a giant of a man who made Chase look small. He was Daisy's lover and one of the Queen's Guards.

He hugged me even tighter than Daisy had, until my feet couldn't reach the floor. The breath woofed out of me, and my head felt dizzy.

Both of them shook hands with Chase and then pushed into the booth with us.

"It's not as good as it sounds," I told Daisy and Bart. "Wanda is dead, killed by a sword."

Daisy frowned. "But not by your hand. I don't believe it."

"Of course not," Bart added. "Just because Wanda died after someone stuck a sword in her chest, and Jessie is one of the swordswomen in the Village, no reason to think that."

I sighed. "Would you mind *not* telling the police that?"

Daisy and Bart ordered lunch. Peter's sister, Maude, brought our drinks. Everyone in the pub was staring at us. A few brave visitors asked to take Daisy's photo.

Even though Daisy worked with swords and knives, and was considered one of the best sword-smiths on the Ren Faire circuit, she was also good-hearted and generous. She and Bart both stood to have their pictures taken. I was afraid for a moment that the tiny woman visitor with the camera might faint.

When it was over, they sat back down with us.

"They don't really think you killed her in that obvious, *stupid* way, do they?" Daisy asked.

"I think they don't have another suspect," Chase answered.

"I dyed her blue. And I was the person who found her. And we had a long standing history of problems. Detective Almond knows all of that—and the part about me knowing how to use a sword."

"When you put it that way." Bart shrugged his huge shoulders. "I might think you killed her too."

Daisy nudged him hard with her elbow. "Jessie didn't killer her! But someone did. Let's try to think of another suspect or two to throw the cops off."

"I heard the queen yelling at Wanda yesterday," Bart said. "But that's an everyday occurrence. They didn't get along well. Did *anyone* get along with Wanda?"

"Wasn't Shakespeare married to Wanda at one time?" Daisy frowned. "Where is he anyway? I heard Sir Reginald complaining to Gus Fletcher at the castle this morning.

Shakespeare hasn't been at his podium. Don't ask me why, but plenty of visitors come to see him."

"Maybe he ran off," Bart said. "I'd leave if I killed her."

"I heard Wanda was dating a young knight before she died," I said. "Have you heard anyone talking about that?"

It was unusual for people not to know who was dating who around here, but Daisy and Bart hadn't heard anything about it.

They both promised to let me know if they *did* hear anything. Our cheeseburgers and fries finally arrived, and we were quiet as we ate.

Chase was called away to an emergency at the Merry Mynstrels Stage before he could finish. A visitor had jumped up on the stage and was insisting he should be allowed to play his violin with Susan Halifax and her harp.

Bart had to go back to the castle to escort Queen Olivia on her daily amble through the Village. Now there was the baby, Princess Pea, to consider as well. That meant at least twenty guards, courtiers, fools—and a few parasol holders.

"I have to get back too, Jessie." Daisy left a generous tip on the thick, wood table. "Ethan is a big help now that I've got him trained right, but he takes off a lot. I think if I could find him a good woman, he'd settle down and be more regular. See you later."

Ethan was Daisy's son who helped out at her shop, Swords and Such, which was part of Armorer's Alley. Enchanted Armor and Splendid Shields were there too.

I thought about young, *eligible* Ethan. If I wasn't arrested for killing Wanda, I might have to find a lady for him. Everyone in the Village knew I was the best at matchmaking. I'd been the one to put Bart and Daisy together, among others.

That left me on my own again. I didn't feel up to handling the crowds and the fall heat waiting for me on the cobblestones. I needed time to think about what had happened and what I could do about it. I felt sure Detective Almond was in the Village figuring out all the little things that could have lead me to kill Wanda.

I left Peter's Pub, keeping my head down, and made it back to the Dungeon. Chase and I shared the apartment above the fake prison cells in the bottom of the structure.

It had been unnerving at first, walking into the special effects area that made it look like fake prisoners were being tortured. Their shrieks and pleas for mercy could be heard outside. Eventually, you get used to anything.

I went upstairs and opened the door to the apartment. It wasn't very big—two rooms, a very small kitchen area, and bathroom. There were only two of us so it didn't matter. It was one of the nicest places in the Village. Most village housing had no air conditioning and there were communal showers.

The window overlooked the stocks where Vegetable Justice was meted out. Chase presided over the vegetable punishment twice a day, wearing a white wig and black robe. When there were no visitors signed up, he went out and conscripted village residents for the job. It was very popular with visitors, not so much with residents.

There was a knock on the door. It obviously wasn't Chase.

"I'd like to talk to you, Jessie. I hope now is a good time." Detective Almond glanced up at the wall where my sword and Chase's were crossed. "Nice swords."

Six

"Thanks." I stood back and let him into the apartment. He'd been following me, or having me followed. I was sure he knew I was here without Chase. "What's on your mind?"

"You know I meet here with Chase sometimes, and I was thinking about those swords. Mind if I hold one?"

"No. Not at all. But if you're looking for a murder weapon, you must think I'm pretty stupid. No one would use their own sword to kill someone." I took both swords down from the wall.

I handed him Chase's heavier broadsword first. "As you can see, the wound in Wanda's chest would've been much bigger if someone had used this sword on her."

"I appreciate your wisdom in these matters, Jessie. But I hope you won't mind if I have *both* of them tested."

I looked at my lighter, silver sword. Daisy had been specially made for me, balanced and constructed for my height and strength. "I don't think it matters if I mind or not, does it?"

"Sure it does. If you don't agree voluntarily to have it tested, I'll have to get a warrant."

I handed him my sword. "There you go. Easy peasy. You don't even have to ask twice."

He looked around the tiny apartment, filled now with mine and Chase's stuff. "You two are kind of crushed in here since you gave up your job in Columbia, huh? Once you get married, you might even have a few little ones. It would be nice io have a bigger place, huh?"

"We'll see." I shrugged. "We're not having babies yet."

"Village housing is at a premium unless you're a shopkeeper. Even I know that." He snapped his fingers. "Oh *wait*! There's an opening at the other end of the Village, with Wanda being dead and all."

I managed a brave but probably foolhardy smile. "That would be a stupid reason to kill Wanda. Chase and I have standing in the Village. We could live at the castle anytime. Try again. I *didn't* kill Wanda."

He nodded. "Okay. Just trying to work my way through all of the craziness. Don't get defensive. Chase technically works for the police, just like I do. We'll figure it out."

I didn't have anything more to say to him. He'd ruined my peaceful hideaway. I opened the door. He took our swords and left the Dungeon.

I wanted to slam the door behind him, but I didn't want him to realize how upset I was. I fell back on the bed and pulled the pillows over my head.

I was scared. This didn't seem like it was going to end well for me, just as I was starting my new life.

It had always been my dream to live at the Village. I hadn't wanted to depend on Chase supporting me. The opening of the museum, with me as salaried director, had come at almost the same time as Chase's marriage proposal. I thought my life was going to be perfect.

I closed my eyes and tried to think about something else—*anything* else. I must have fallen asleep because the door to the apartment suddenly blew open. I knew I had to be dreaming.

Like old Jacob Marley come to haunt Ebenezer Scrooge, I knew I wasn't alone.

There was a deep sighing followed by unmistakable laughter that chilled my soul. "Lady Jessie Morton. What are you doing up here? Why aren't you out on the cobblestones looking for my killer?"

I sat up quickly, my heart pounding. No one was there. It was just a nightmare.

A bright blue face came right up in front of mine, and a British-tinged voice said, "Think I'm a nightmare, do you? Think again, dearie."

You know how you wake up from a dream and you *think* you're awake, but you're not? And then you wake up again, and this time it's real.

I fell back on the bed again, hoping that was about to happen to me. I closed my eyes and kept repeating, *"Wake up, Jessie. Wake up."*

"Yes, indeed. Wake up, you lazy slattern. My killer is running free in the Village while you're in here getting some beauty sleep. It won't do, you know. Ugly is as ugly does."

I sat up and scooted down to the end of the bed. The door to the apartment was closed. I took a deep breath. *It wasn't real.*

I put my hand on the doorknob. *I was only dreaming.* It was all the talk about who had killed her and seeing her dead, that's all.

Wanda's head came right through the door, followed by the rest of her deep blue, naked body. "Here I am, ducks. Didn't think I'd leave so soon, did you?"

I was out of there. Her cackling laughter followed me down the stairs and into the fake dungeon area where I scared two teenage boys who seemed to think I was part of the exhibit.

I didn't care. I ran out into the sunshine where hundreds of people were walking up and down the cobblestones. Tom, Tom the Piper's son was chasing a piglet while a group of visitors laughed and followed him. The Lovely Laundry Ladies were calling out bawdy remarks to the people passing by. Everything seemed perfectly normal.

"Still here."

I glanced to the side where a large swing hung from the branch of an old oak tree at the corner of the Dungeon. "*Wanda*?" I could hardly force her name from my lips.

My hands were shaking, and my thoughts were scrambled. *How is this possible?*

"That's right. Who were you expecting? Was there some other dead woman you dyed blue today? Did you think that would be it?"

"I'm pretty sure there's a rule about pranks not going beyond the grave." I turned and started walking quickly down the cobblestones toward the Stage Caravan where scantily clad young men and women were undulating to the music of pipes and flutes. "You stay here. I'll go look that up."

Before I'd taken more than a few steps, she was beside me like some kind of horrible blue plague.

"Where are you off to?" Wanda's voice screeched in my ear.

"To find your killer. Or a psychiatrist. Or both." I started walking faster. "Go away or I'll have you exorcised."

"I don't think you *will* do that, sweetie. I think we're new best buds. I'm sticking to you until you find my killer."

"What if I leave the village?" I was trying to think of all the stories my grandmother used to tell me and my brother about ghosts. It seemed like they couldn't cross running water and they were allergic to garlic. *Maybe.*

"I don't care if you leave the planet. I'm staying with you." Wanda stopped at a big mirror that was captioned as a looking glass into another world. "*Gad*! Will you look at me? Not only am I dead, I'm naked as a jaybird, and the same color. What did you *do* to me, you little black-hearted witch?"

"It's just some dye. It's non-toxic. People use it with costumes at Halloween. It would've worn off in about a month—if you were still alive. Maybe it will wear off anyway."

She glared at me. "I hate you. I've always hated you. I wish you were blue and dead instead of me." She tried to smooth back her red hair that was streaming over her shoulders. "But too late for that. I'm the one who's dead. Now find my killer or you'll be sorry!"

"Will that make you rest in peace or something? Will you vanish and stop haunting me?"

"Perhaps. I'm not sure yet. I can tell you one thing. *You* will never know a moment's peace until you find out who killed me. I *need* to know. I need *revenge*."

My legs felt wobbly. I wanted to drop down on the hot cobblestones and not get up again until she was gone. I blinked my eyes several times, but she was still there when I opened them. How was this possible?

"Okay." I smiled and curtsied at the two visitors that were dressed like Snow White, and Prince Charming. Their children were dressed like three dwarfs, complete with beards. "I'll find your killer. I was looking into it anyway. I don't know about the revenge part. Maybe you could haunt them and that would take care of it."

"Jessie?" Chase came up behind me. "Who are you talking to?"

"Wanda," I whispered. "She's come back."

He looked at the refection of him and me in the big mirror as he put his arm around my waist. "I don't see anyone else. Wanda is dead. She's not coming back."

I squinted hard. There was no sign of Wanda anywhere. "I didn't imagine it. At least I don't *think* I imagined it. She came into the apartment after Detective Almond left with our swords. She was furious."

Chase didn't seem to comprehend what I was trying to tell him. "Detective Almond took our swords? I can't believe he didn't say anything to me about it. Are we working together or what?"

"Now he thinks I killed Wanda because I wanted her cottage for us and our babies."

Chase looked blank. "*Babies*? Is there something you need to tell me?"

"I'm not pregnant with even *one* baby right now. He was planning our future for us."

Was that a sigh of relief I caught from him?

"You *want* to have kids at some point, right?" I asked in case there had been a miscommunication.

He kissed me. "You *know* I want to have kids with you. Maybe not right now, but sometime. We *don't* have to live in Wanda's cottage."

"That's what I told him."

We started walking past the Dungeon. The boys I'd scared were long gone. I hoped Wanda was too. I hoped she was a figment of my guilt. I hadn't meant for her to die. It wasn't my fault that someone else had killed her.

"Maybe not, dearie," she whispered near my right ear. "But you're gonna help me find the knave who did it."

Seven

I jumped away from that side, my back against Chase's sturdy frame. "Did you hear that? She's not gone yet."

"I didn't hear anything, Jessie." He glanced around. "Is she standing next to you *now*?"

"No. She whispered in my ear."

Lovingly, he said, "This has been a strain. You should rest."

I laughed. "Like I can rest with her shoving her big blue face at me all the time."

"Maybe we should go have a talk with Madame Lucinda."

"Madam Lucinda?" I searched my brain. I thought I knew everyone in the Village. "Who's that?"

He tucked my arm through his, and we continued walking. "Madame Elizabeth retired. Madame Lucinda is taking her place."

"The fortune teller? How is *she* going to help?"

"Everyone says she's really amazing. If Wanda is haunting you, maybe she can help."

I was sure Madame Elizabeth didn't have any special powers—I didn't think her replacement did either. I'd spoken with the old Madame a few times. She mumbled a lot—it was difficult to understand her. Maybe that was why very few visitors ever went to her small, purple and gold tent close to the Honey and Herb Shoppe.

I was always surprised when I left, and came back months later from the university, that the fortune teller was still there. Adventureland could be ruthless when it came to cutting out exhibits that didn't pay. For some reason, that had never happened to the fortune teller.

Maybe that was her *real* magic.

As we reached Madame Lucinda's tent with its bright gold dragon flag flying, Chase got a call about a big food fight happening at The King's Tarts Pie Shop at the other end of the Village.

"I have to get over there. That new pie shop owner has been a handful."

"I know. You miss the sexy sisters, right?"

"At least they knew how to treat their customers." He smiled and kissed me. "Go in and talk to Lucinda. I don't know if she's amazing or not, but Hephaestus down at the Pleasant Pheasant swears by her."

I grinned back at him. "So she's young and attractive then."

"Just try her. Who knows? Maybe she can see Wanda too."

I almost didn't bother going inside once I saw Chase cut through the alleyway between the museums. I didn't need a phony Madame with 'powers'. I needed the police to finish their investigation into Wanda's death, tell everyone that I was innocent, and re-open the museum. If all that happened, I'd be just fine.

"The only way you're going to be fine is to get justice for me." Wanda popped out of nowhere.

That was enough for me. I ran into the cool, shaded interior of the purple tent.

I didn't see anyone for a moment. My eyes were still adjusting from the bright sunlight. As I got used to the darker space, I began to make out a small table with a crystal ball in the center of it.

The room was filled with strange and unusual artifacts—antique knives, charms, carved wooden sticks. One of the most prominent was a dog-sized green dragon with glowing yellow eyes. It was perched on a shelf as though it might fly away at any moment.

It was so lifelike—I reached to touch it.

"Good day, and welcome, young woman." A stooped gray-haired woman in a purple robe greeted me in a cheerful voice. She walked slowly, painfully, across the room and stopped before she reached me.

"Good grief! What is that dead blue creature that has attached itself to you?"

I grabbed her hand in excitement and gratitude. "You can *see* her? Can you make her go away?"

"From here, yes." She lifted her hand, and Wanda screeched as she flew back out of the tent as though pulled by invisible wires.

"*Yes*! Does that mean I don't have to see her again?" I was in awe at what Madame Lucinda had done. Amazing wasn't the word for it.

"Don't be ridiculous. When the dead become part of our lives, we are the *only* people who can make them go away." She was staring at the space *beside* me rather than at me. "In this case, I'd say she needs you."

I slumped down in one of the chairs at the table and the crystal ball lit up. "You don't understand. She made my life miserable while she was alive. I'm pretty sure that's what she wants to do now that she's *dead*."

Madame Lucinda slowly sat opposite me. "Trust me, Jessie. Wanda needs your help. She can't move on until her killer has been brought to justice. She thinks you're the only one who can do this. Maybe it has something to do with her being blue. Maybe it's a return for that indignity. What is it you all call that type of dishonor here?"

I sighed. "A prank. Turning Wanda blue was a prank. It would've gone away in time."

She patted my hand on the table. "She'll go away in time too. Never fear. Even the strongest haunting can only last so long."

"How long is that? Days? Weeks?"

"Oh, usually not more than a hundred years. If you're still seeing her after that, you're probably only glimpsing a shade of her."

"*A hundred years?* I'll be *dead* then too. Isn't there anything you can do for me?"

"I'm afraid not. Wanda and you are bound together until you find her killer. It's as simple as that."

That wasn't the news I'd wanted to hear. I gave her a couple of dollars. She refused, and said that the next time I came I could bring her something silver. I walked to the front of the tent and glanced toward her with one last question.

The dragon was now perched on the table, close to where I'd been sitting. Madame Lucinda was stroking its long neck and it was making purring sounds like a cat, but much louder.

Forgetting the question and everything else but the need to escape, I ran out into the sunshine. I took a deep breath to steady my nerves.

Of course, that wasn't a *real* dragon. This was the Renaissance Faire! Things like that happened here, but they weren't real.

"Right. Well, that was a bit odd, wasn't it? Where are we off to first?" Wanda fell in step with me, although her feet didn't touch the cobblestones.

I didn't jump this time. I was making some progress.

"Okay. I get it now. Because my prank was the last thing you experienced, I have to make it up, like karma, by finding your killer."

"I think you've got it finally. You always were a little thick, Jessie."

"Good day, Lady Jessie." A handsome, well-dressed lord from the castle tipped his hat to me and smiled.

"Good day, Lord Simon." Wanda curtsied a little and acknowledged him.

"Good day, Lord Simon," I repeated so he could hear it.

"I am dreadfully sorry about what happened to you this morning." He took my hand in his gloved one. "Terrible bit of luck there."

"It's about time someone said it," Wanda returned. "I have been maligned, you know."

"Thank you for your sympathy, my lord," I replied.

"On a lighter note, I received an invitation to your upcoming nuptials to the Bailiff. Good show! Looking forward to it."

I nodded modestly, as was proper, and Lord Simon went on his way.

"I don't believe it!" Wanda lashed out. "I'm standing here, *dead*, and he wishes *you* well on your wedding."

"He can't see you," I reminded her. *I wish I couldn't see you.*

"This is some serious mess you've gotten me into."

"Me? You've been nasty to everyone for as long as I can remember. Everyone hates you—hated you. I'm surprised it didn't happen sooner."

She glared at me—I'm talking big dead face, open red mouth, and evil green eyes. "That's just too bad for you, isn't it? If the fortune teller was right, the only way to get me off your back is to figure out what happened to me. You'd best start figuring."

I was getting used to her shock value. I barely trembled at her terrible face. "Okay. As I was saying, we have to figure out who killed you. What's the last thing you remember before you . . . *um* . . . died?"

"Don't be shy about it." She raised her head and screamed. "I'm dead."

Her voice was a hideous shriek that was heard above the racket made by daily life in the Village with ten thousand visitors. It frightened the seagulls perched on the top turrets of the castle, not something easily done.

I noticed a few people in the crowd passing by turned and stared as though they could hear her. *Just a few of the lucky ones like me.*

I decided to take this conversation off of the cobblestones. I walked behind the Dutchman's Stage where a raunchy puppet show, with naked puppets wearing crowns symbolizing them as Queen Olivia and King Harold, was taking place. It was very funny, from the laughter of the crowd.

I sat on a carved wood bench. Wanda kind of sat beside me.

"Look, I'm sorry you're dead," I told her, only half lying. "You were a great pranker, and probably a good health professional. For *some* people. But we have to work together to find out what happened to you. What do you remember last? Was anyone with you this morning?"

She seemed to think about it, rolling her eyes around until only the whites of them were showing. "The last thing I remember is realizing that you'd found a way to turn me blue. I took off my enchanted bracelet before the dye could reach it and threw it on the floor. I was very angry and already thinking of all the terrible things I could do to you during your wedding."

"Wait a minute. *Enchanted* bracelet?"

"That's right, dearie." She tossed her head and her neck gave way, leaving her head dangling to one side. Her smile only made it worse. "I saw you staring at it when you were around me. Everyone did when they saw it. They all coveted it, including *you.* It was spelled for me years ago by a passing sorcerer."

"Wanda, I know you may *think* that what you're saying makes sense. And maybe it does from your vantage point, being dead and all. Like maybe you *think* you look good with your head hanging off like that and your eyes all white."

She straightened her head and her eyes were kind of normal again. "Sorry. I didn't realize. Is that better for you, love?"

"Yes." I smiled. "Thanks."

She totally lost it at that point. It was like her whole body started falling apart. Her eyes were rolling around and her tongue was hanging out.

"It's too bad for you that you have to see me this way. I don't care. I'm barely forty, and I'm dead. Suffer."

"Barely *forty*? In your dreams."

Her hands came toward me like talons. "Some nerve you have speaking to me that way. If I weren't a ghost, I'd rip your face off."

I admit my heart bumped a little at that moment. Apparently she couldn't rip anything off. She could threaten. She could scare. But she couldn't gouge. I was starting to understand her parameters.

"I know you hate me. I pretty much hate you too. Let's get through this, shall we? You were blue except for your enchanted bracelet, which you threw out of the shower. What happened next?

Eight

"I turned off the water and started to get out of the shower myself." Wanda frowned. "I don't know what happened after that. Someone was there. I can't remember who. I felt a terrible pain in the center of my chest. I thought I was having a heart attack. Then nothing."

No matter how I felt about Wanda, it was hard not to be moved by the sorrow in her voice. I was going to have to adjust my attitude toward her. It wasn't *her* fault that she was dead. She might have been annoying in life but certainly didn't deserve to be murdered.

"Did you have anyone there with you the night before you died?"

Her face took on a dreamy quality—well as much as her horrible countenance *could* anyway.

"Yes. It pains me to leave him more than anything." She smiled and pointed toward the Field of Honor. "He's the queen's new champion, Sir Marcus Bishop, late of Atlanta. When he kisses you, you know you've been kissed. He's so tender and kind. I'm sure some of that is his age, as he's under thirty. But some of it is just *him*. His eyes are so blue, and his lips are so sweet, and . . ."

"I get it." I stopped her before she went on to any other body parts. "Maybe he's the one we should see first."

"But he left me late last night, well before I was murdered. Marcus certainly had nothing to do with what happened to me."

"Let's go and talk to him anyway. Maybe he saw something. They should be finishing up the last joust. I'll head that way. You try not to talk to me when other people are around. I don't want everyone to think I'm crazy."

Her laugh was vicious. "Too late for that, sweetie. The only reason anyone tolerates you here is because the Bailiff loves you. Remember that in future."

That was depressing. I didn't expect anything else from her. It was one reason, out of many, that I never spent any more time with her than I had to. She *always* ruined my day.

"What about Shakespeare—Pat?" I asked before we left the quiet spot behind the stage. "He was there right after I found you this morning. Now he's vanished."

"He was always a coward. He was probably sneaking a peek at Marcus and me. I wouldn't worry about him. I would appreciate it if you found my enchanted bracelet. The sorcerer who gave it to me—another excellent lover—said it would give me immortality."

"Guess he had that wrong."

"Or the killer was able to take my life because I'd removed my bracelet. Think about *that*, Jessie. I'm going to freshen up. I'll meet you at the field."

When she was gone, I took a deep breath. It felt good to be alone.

But I was getting a handle on this. Wanda was dead. I was helping her. I understood what I was supposed to do. All I had to do was figure out who killed her, and everything would be fine.

I was hurrying past the Monastery Bakery, the delectable smells of coffee and fresh cinnamon rolls enticing me to stop, when I heard a *psst* sound coming from behind some bushes. I got off of the cobblestones and went to investigate.

"Is she *here*?" Pat/Shakespeare asked in a trembling voice.

"What are you doing back there? I've been looking all over for you."

He peeked out from behind the greenery. "Is she here? Have you seen Wanda?"

I knelt on the grass and glanced around before I answered. "You mean dead Wanda?"

His voice, usually melodic and smooth, was a gasp. "*The ghost of Wanda.*"

"Yes. I guess she's appeared to both of us."

"She's hideous. *Terrifying*. I have to get away from the Village. I'm trying to keep her from following me."

"Good luck with that. I've spent way too much time with her today. She wants me to help find her killer. Did she ask you to do that too?"

"I don't know. I don't know why she appeared to me."

"You might as well get out of there. If she wants to find you, she'll find you. She's a ghost. She can go anywhere and do anything. She stuck her head through my door."

He wept, covering his face with his hands. His little triangle-shaped beard quivered. "You have to help me get away from her, Jessie. I have a bad heart and arthritis. I'm not a young man. I can't take the strain."

"I don't know anything I can do to help you. I can't get rid of her either. Maybe since she's following me, she won't bother you anymore."

Shakespeare shook all over. “She’s *following* you? You’ve led her right to *me*.”

Sure enough, there was Wanda. She was doing her new trick of seeming to dislocate all her body parts at the same time. I felt impervious to her horror as I watched her scare him. Shakespeare went screaming and running toward the castle.

Wanda laughed. “That was fun. Wait until tonight.”

“Whatever. I’m going to the field now. Are you coming?”

We walked through the crowds. Wanda literally walked *through* them.

Chase was holding court for vegetable justice with a big crowd of visitors. He didn’t need any residents for the stocks. A pretty young woman, dressed like Robin Hood, was throwing half rotten tomatoes at her boyfriend who kept asking her to stop.

I saluted Chase as I walked by, smiling at his serious expression under his white wig. He nodded and turned back to the job at hand.

“You know you’re lucky to be with him,” Wanda said. “He’s one of the most honorable men I’ve even known. Do you know how hard I worked *every* time you went back to university, trying to find someone who’d get him to cheat on you? He never even noticed. If I’d been younger, I would’ve done it myself. A word of advice?”

I was angry and miserable already. “Sure. Why not?”

“Don’t marry him, Jessie. He’s *too* good. Once you put that ring on his finger, he’s going to stray. Mark my words.”

I gritted my teeth and started walking faster. I couldn’t find Wanda’s killer soon enough.

We found Sir Marcus Bishop cleaning his armor in the stable near the Field of Honor. He was indeed a handsome young man with his lean body, brilliant blue eyes, and flowing blond hair.

He smiled as I approached him and got to his feet. "My lady." He put one hand across his heart and bowed to me. "To what do I owe the honor of this visit?"

"Isn't he the best?" Wanda sighed. "He's so handsome and so sweet. I could just *eat* him up."

She ran her fingers through his hair and stood close to him, whispering in his ear. Lucky for Sir Marcus that he didn't appear to hear or feel her.

"I don't know if you're aware yet that Wanda Le Fey was found dead at her cottage early this morning." I glanced at his dirty sword. "She was killed with a large blade of some kind."

His eyes followed my gaze. "And you think *I* had something to do with it?" His blue eyes appeared truly wounded that I would suggest such a thing. "I would *never* have hurt my lady, Wanda."

I nodded, trying to avoid watching Wanda's ghostly flirting with the knight. "I appreciate that. Any idea who might have wanted to hurt her?"

Two young wenches, whose job it was to get the crowd excited during the joust, approached Sir Marcus. It seemed Wanda wasn't the *only* one who wanted the young knight's favor.

"Is there *anything* we can do for you, Sir Marcus?" One of the girls, a buxom blond, giggled.

Wanda kept rubbing her blue body up against his. He didn't seem to feel it at all. He put aside his armor and invited both pretty young things to sit on his knees.

"I am feeling a little hungry and thirsty after the joust. Perhaps you could fetch me some food and drink while I finish cleaning my armor."

Both girls kissed him and ran to do his bidding. It appeared to be a normal circumstance for them. I knew it wasn't unusual for the knights to have groupies. They were very popular in the Village.

"I'm sorry, Lady Jessie. I have no idea what could've happened to Wanda. I shall mourn her passing."

I could tell.

"I know. So many people will." I tried harder to ignore Wanda's antics. My stomach was churning, watching her. "Just for the sake of asking, where did you go when you left Wanda's house last night?"

His brows rose. "Have you been following me, lady? I have heard rumor that you are marrying the Bailiff. Are you looking for a last fling?"

Knights also have *very* large egos. No doubt due to all the attention given to them and the groupies willing to do anything for them. I knew the kind of hero worship that went on.

Chase had started in the Village as a knight and gained his reputation fighting for the queen's honor. I'd heard rumors about him, too, after we'd met. I made *sure* I knew what he was doing, even though we weren't together for years after that.

"No, Sir Marcus. I'm not looking for a fling. But I assume you have more than one lady you dance attendance upon. I'm not a stranger as to how knights live."

He shrugged and put one leg up on a bale of hay, knee bent as though he was posing for a photo. "Of course. Most knights aren't exclusive. There are so few of us to go around."

"*What*?" Wanda stopped trying to touch him. "What are you saying, Marcus? You never told me there was someone else. How could you betray me that way?"

I'd never seen Wanda cry, at least not while she was alive. Big fat tears rolled down her blue cheeks and her lips quivered. I felt sorry for her. Obviously she'd thought the young knight was hers. It was too late now to do anything about it.

She couldn't make the knight feel her presence, but she could whip up an errant breeze that moaned through the stable rafters, shaking pigeons from their perches and rattling the windows. Hay flew everywhere in small whirling devils that blew up dust on the knight's armor.

"What's going on?" He spun around as the swirling hay pelted him.

"Who else were you seeing?" I raised my voice to be heard over the gust of wind.

"I don't know." He slapped at the hay. "A few others."

"Last night," I persisted. "Where did you go after you left Wanda's cottage last night?"

"Ginny Stewart at the Lady of the Lake invited me over for a drink." He was fighting off the hay as it began striking at him like small arrows. "I went over there. Then I went home. What's happening? Why isn't the hay hitting *you*?"

Nine

I curtsied and left him there with Wanda haunting him. Ginny was a likely candidate for an affair with the knight. She'd always flirted with Chase. She wasn't as obnoxious as Wanda, but she was annoying.

Walking away from the Field of Honor, Wanda finally joined me again.

"Ginny Stewart?" she fumed. "*Really*? He was seeing that cow behind my back. I can't believe it. I thought he loved me. It never occurred to me that he was cheating. I'll get him for that."

"Is that how you plan to spend your afterlife—tormenting your ex-husband and making Sir Marcus pay for being with other women? Don't you have something important you should take care of? Shouldn't this be a spiritual time for you?"

"Don't be stupid. I'm dead. Spiritual things are all I have. That, and revenge for anyone who has ever wronged me. We have to go talk to Ginny. I think I need to throw a few pewter mugs at her. I can't believe Marcus spent time with her. The woman must be sixty years old or better. What was he *thinking*?"

"You know how the knights are, Wanda." I stopped to admire some jewelry being sold out of a handcart on the side of the cobblestone walkway. I hoped that would obscure what would be viewed as me talking to myself. "They go after anyone who shows them any attention. Do you feel any better about those two young girls being with him?"

"Oddly enough, I do feel a bit better about them. Thinking Marcus left me to go to Ginny makes me feel dirty." She stared at me. "Do you think he killed me?"

"Did he have a reason to kill you?"

"No. I was as good as gold with him, gave him everything he wanted."

"Well then, let's not consider him."

"He has a sword," she whispered. "He could have killed me and taken my enchanted bracelet. Perhaps you should alert the police so they can take a peek at him."

"Okay. I'll call Detective Almond."

"And what would you be calling me about?" Detective Almond's familiar voice—speaking around a roasted turkey leg—said from behind me.

I turned around quickly and smiled. "I was just talking to the young knight that Wanda was sleeping with. They were together last night. He said he left her before she was killed, but he does have a sword."

He wiped his hands on a napkin. "And you think this man may have killed Wanda? Or is this someone who can get *you* off the hook?"

"I'm not *on* the hook. I know it looks like I had a part in this, but I didn't."

"Who were you talking to just now, Jessie? Guilty conscience?"

"No. I'm in contact with Wanda. She wants me to help her look for her killer."

He laughed and then almost choked on a large piece of turkey he tried to swallow at the same time. "This place can do funny things to people. Have you finally lost it?"

I raised my head and held my chin high. "I haven't lost anything. The knight's name is Sir Marcus Bishop. He was at the Field of Honor. Maybe *you* should talk to him."

"And maybe *you* should let the police investigate this matter."

I started walking away from him. "I would—*if* you were investigating someone besides *me*."

"Watch your back, Jessie. We might be coming for you."

I ignored him and raced back toward the Main Gate. I thought Detective Almond would talk to Marcus. Chase was probably right about him being a good man, although I questioned him being a good detective. At least in the Village, he frequently had Chase do his work for him.

"Lady Jessie." The Tornado Twins—Diego and Lorenzo—bowed and swept their red, plumed hats from their heads. The brothers were similar in appearance—both black- haired and dark-eyed, short and thin. They weren't twins though. That was only their stage act.

"Twins," I responded as I patted their pig that was on a gold leash. "It's a wonderful day at the Faire."

"Indeed it is," Lorenzo agreed. "News of Wanda Le Fey's death has reached our ears. Forsooth, we are devastated—and *intrigue*d. Did you truly slay the lady?"

"No. I just dyed her blue."

Both men started laughing so hard that their pig squealed and ran away.

"Go get him," Diego said to his brother.

"No. I got him last time," Lorenzo retorted. "You go get him."

Diego looked up and stared directly into Wanda's scowling blue face. "I would, brother, but there's a dead woman standing in front of me. I am afraid I have soiled myself."

"*You* can see her?" I asked him.

"No, he can't see dead people," Lorenzo said. "I've been telling him that his whole life—no dead people. Excuse us, Lady Jessie. We must catch our pig."

Lorenzo ran after the pig to the laughter of the nearby visitors. Diego didn't follow him right away.

"Be careful," he warned. "Wanda looks *mad*."

"He can *see* me," Wanda shouted as he ran away.

"I don't think he *wants* to see you," I told her.

"I don't care." She began following Diego. "I know you can see me," she yelled at him. "I can see you too. Let's have drinks."

I was starting to get a headache. Being followed by the ghost of a woman you couldn't stand when she was alive could do that to you. I saw Chase quelling some kind of disturbance at the Fractured Fairy Tales tent and went to see what was happening.

It seemed that Cinderella was having an issue with Prince Charming regarding their latest breakup. The evil stepfather (this kind of thing is what makes the fairy tales fractured) was egging them on, even offering his short sword to Cinderella.

Chase grabbed the short sword and put it into his belt. The crowd of visitors cheered and shouted *Huzzah!* as the tableau ended. The stage emptied with Cinderella and Prince Charming still bickering.

"There you are." Chase saw me and put his arm around me. "What happened with Madame Lucinda?"

I shrugged. "She told me I have to help Wanda find out who killed her and then she might go away."

"Not what I was hoping for, but I guess you've been trying to figure that out, right?"

"Yes. I don't think I'm any closer to knowing who killed Wanda." I told him about Marcus and Shakespeare. "I gave Detective Almond Marcus's name. He still thinks I did it."

"He'll figure it out. Have you been over to Stylish Frocks yet? Portia was looking for you. Beth needs you to come over for a fitting."

"I don't think I can do that with Wanda hanging around. She kind of puts a crimp in my life, like she always did."

He hugged me. "Is she here now?"

"No. She wandered off following Diego because he could see her."

"Interesting. I wonder why some people can see her and others can't."

"I don't know. Sir Marcus couldn't see her. I wish *I* couldn't see her."

"Well maybe now would be a good time to head down to Stylish Frocks," he suggested. "I'm headed that way myself. There's trouble at the Frog Catapult."

I shuddered, having worked at the Frog Catapult one year. It was an awful job. Throwing slimy rubber frogs should be banned.

"Maybe I'll do that. I'm my way to talk to Ginny Stewart about her and Wanda sharing the same knight."

"You know you should leave this to Detective Almond and me. I'll talk to Ginny. You shouldn't be involved."

"That's fine, except I'm the one with the evil blue ghost following me around. I need to figure this out."

We stopped walking, and Chase studied my face. "This will all be over soon. Don't forget that whoever killed Wanda might be willing to kill you too. Let me talk to Ginny. Don't go into that blindly. Okay?"

"Okay." I hugged him. "You talk to Ginny and let me know what she says. I'll go let them stick pins in me again. I'll be glad when the wedding is over."

"Me too. I love you. Be careful until we catch the killer."

We split up in front of Sherwood Forest. I went to Stylish Frocks, and Chase headed toward the Frog Catapult.

Portia was leaning her head on her hand in the costume rental window, as usual. She was Beth Daniels's assistant and she hated her job. Beth was the head costume designer and seamstress for the Village.

There was a long line of visitors waiting to rent or return costumes. Most residents got their costumes early in the morning each day. This left the costume shop free to handle the requirements of visitors who wanted to dress as woodcutters, high-born ladies, knights, and other characters.

"It's about time," Portia called out as I waved to her. "Beth has been looking for you. Go around back."

In the shop, hidden from visitors, were dozens of seamstresses at buzzing sewing machines. Many times, they worked around the clock to keep up with demand.

Beth was attending to the details on a beautiful green silk gown for a visitor who was planning to be at the Ren Faire the following week. The work was demanding, but the fees for special orders like this made it worthwhile.

My wedding gown was on a mannequin dummy. I lifted the dust cloth that covered it. The split-skirt pink gown was simple—high-waisted with a low cut bodice. I would be wearing a white silk chemise beneath it. The gown was trimmed and laced in gold threads. I'd also bought a white corset for the ceremony that was done of handmade lace.

I'd opted not to wear white. It wasn't a good color on me. The deep pink was so much nicer. Beth was making a six-foot, matching train for the gown that would be carried by several children who lived in the Village.

"There you are," Beth addressed me when she'd finished the green silk gown. She was a very plain-looking woman whose personal style never showed what marvelous creations she made each day. "I was beginning to think you'd lost interest in your gown."

"I've been a little busy."

"So we've heard." Andre Hariot was the Village hat maker who was dating Beth. "You finally got Wanda back for her prank at the Lady of the Lake. I'm guessing her death was something you hadn't planned on."

I'd apprenticed with Andre at his hat shop. He was a dapper hat designer in his fifties who'd once been a hat maker to the stars in Hollywood before coming to the Village. He was a small man but he had big style, especially when it came to hats.

The hat he was wearing that day was bright blue and held three peacock feathers in the wide brim. Of course it matched his outfit and the shoes he wore.

He'd been accused of murder—once in the Village and once before he'd left Hollywood—exonerated in both cases. I figured he understood my position better than most.

"I only wanted to dye her blue. Now her ghost is following me, wanting me to find her killer. The only thing worse than Wanda alive, is Wanda dead."

Andre and Beth exchanged disbelieving glances.

"Well." Beth cleared her throat. "Let's get this fitting over with. Is Wanda here now?"

"No. She's out in the Village looking for people who can see her, people she can scare. Death hasn't made her any nicer."

I stepped behind the beautiful tapestry Beth used as her fitting screen and removed my loose white blouse and blue skirt. Beth came around the back, and with the help of one of her assistants, she lowered the wedding gown over my head.

"I'm not sure about this inset." Beth played around with one of the darker pink panels in the skirt. "Why doesn't Wanda know who killed her?"

"I don't know. She says it happened too fast for her to see a face."

Andre walked around the tapestry. "I saw a ghost once. It was Errol Flynn. That was a man who liked his hats, on and off screen. I'd been working on a hat for him. He died, and I set it aside. A few months later, I went to my shop, and there he was—trying on the hat. He gave me a quick salute and vanished."

"Did he take the hat with him?" I asked.

"No, but I took that to mean that he approved. He would've looked *fabulous* in it!"

"What about you, Jessie?" Beth's hands were on her hips while her assistant measured the hem of my gown. "Do you plan to wear a hat for the wedding, or a veil?"

"You should let me design the perfect hat for you," Andre offered. "You have great cheekbones. Hats look good on you. I'm thinking of something in plum, with a three-foot brim, and a large plume. We could attach a nice veil as well. You'd look *splendid*."

"Aren't you making a hat for Chase?" I asked.

"Yes. It's going to be *astonishing*," Andre said with enthusiasm. "A handsome man like Chase shows off a hat to its full advantage."

"Then I guess I'll wear a veil. Two hats seem like a lot to me. I don't want to crash my big hat into his hat as we take our vows."

"I agree with Jessie," Beth said. "Two hats are too much. We can do a great veil that will stream out behind you with your train."

"What about a tiara?" Andre asked. "That might work."

That was one of the big side effects of everyone knowing we were getting married. They had an opinion on what we should and shouldn't do. I loved weddings at the Ren Faire and had dreamed of one for years. I didn't want to give mine up. I just had to hang tough on what I did and didn't want.

"No tiara," I said. "I'm too tall."

"Flowers?" Beth asked as she checked the inset on the dress again. "Flowers would look nice."

"I don't know about flowers." I noticed my reflection in the mirror. It didn't even seem like me. "I might start sneezing."

Andre looked at my reflection too. "Have you thought about shoes? I know a shoemaker who makes wonderful shoes out of spun glass."

That was it for me. Beth's assistant had finished pinning the gown. I stripped it off—after Beth shooed Andre from behind the tapestry. "I have to go."

"Your wedding is going to be wonderful," Beth reassured me. "People are going to talk about it for years."

I thanked her and left Stylish Frocks. Being remembered for years could also be a curse. Kind of like the Hindenburg and Superstorm Sandy.

It wasn't always a good thing, and that's why I was determined to keep my wedding what I wanted for as long as I could.

Ten

I was glad to be out of Stylish Frocks. I watched the Queen's Revenge on the glistening lake water as Captain Rafe shouted orders to his crew.

I'd spent a summer once on the pirate ship. Probably the best summer of my life. It had represented freedom to me. Now I had the responsibility of the museum—not to mention a husband, and possibly children in the future.

It seemed my wedding gown wasn't the only thing I needed to make happen my way. There was a whole new life ahead of me. What was it going to look like? How would it be while I was living it?

Robin Hood aka Toby Gates was walking back toward me along the path from Hangman's Tree and the Lady of the Lake.

"What ho, Lady Jessie! Remember to save a dance for me at your wedding." He grinned. "And save several glasses of mead for me too. I'm looking forward to the event. Marion is out now perusing dresses for the party and depleting Sir MasterCard."

"It's good to see you, Robin Hood." There were dozens of picture-taking visitors on the path around us. "I am looking forward to you and your good lady dancing at my wedding."

He surprised me by putting his arm around my shoulder and urging me into a fast walk back the other way that he'd recently come.

"I wanted to get you alone." He bent his fair head next to mine. "I heard about Wanda. Terrible news. Are there any suspects?"

"I'm probably the best one." I briefly described what had happened. "After me are probably Shakespeare and then Sir Marcus."

He frowned, puckering his forehead. "Sir Marcus, the knight?"

"Yes. Apparently they were lovers. He was with her the night before she died."

"That *is* a bit odd. I know for a fact that Marcus has been keeping time with Ginny Stewart at the tavern. Hard to believe those two ladies would share *anything*. They were always rivals."

"Marcus told me he only went to have a drink with Ginny after he left Wanda."

"Is that what they're calling it these days?" Robin laughed and slapped his thigh. "That's what happens when you don't keep up with the slang."

"I was on my way over to see her. I'm not looking forward to it. She and Wanda both disliked me. They had that in common."

"You're kidding, right? Ginny wants Chase. She doesn't like, or not like you. You're just in her way."

"I suppose she would've been okay setting me up for the murder at the museum then."

"No doubt," he agreed.

I thought about my run-ins with Ginny. There was an unscrupulous aspect to her nature that frequently showed itself. Yet, she was one of the unchangeable aspects of the Village.

I knew she flirted with Chase, but many women did. I'd learned to overlook it. As Wanda had said, Chase never flirted back.

"Let me come with you. You shouldn't try to do this alone."

"I'll be fine. Chase is going over there too. It's not like Ginny is going to try to kill me."

Robin Hood stopped and smiled at me. "Okay. Time for the big farewell. Are you ready?"

"Oh yes, Sir Outlaw."

He raised his voice for the benefit of the crowd, as was his job. "Adieu, my lady." He swept me a handsome bow and kissed my hand. "Don't forget that evil Prince John will be fighting the Merry Men from Sherwood Forest at three p.m. today, near the Main Gate."

"Fie on thee, Robin Hood, for flirting with me. Where is Maid Marion?"

"Marion awaits! Good day to you, Lady Jessie."

The crowd loved it. They snapped dozens of pictures and applauded as Robin went back toward Sherwood Forest. He was the more interesting of the two of us. The visitors followed him eagerly.

I had to wait for three horse-drawn carriages to pass before I could continue toward the tavern. After that, I scooted across the walkway and waved to Master Archer Simmons, at The Feathered Shaft. I'd apprenticed with him years before.

I wasn't much with a gun, but I could shoot *anything* with an arrow.

There wasn't a big crowd at the Lady of the Lake. Ginny started to greet me as I walked out of the hot South Carolina sun.

As soon as she saw who I was, she turned away with a scowl. "What do *you* want?"

"I want to talk to you about Wanda's death."

"Send Chase. I'll talk to *him*."

I looked at Ginny's tough features and her long, wrinkled gown. She smoothed her unkempt white hair, and I noticed something on her arm. She pulled down her dress sleeves too quickly for me to tell what it was.

I'd seen her pull a knife on a few people who'd rubbed her the wrong way. She was fast and smart. But thinking about her killing Wanda was another thing.

Was she capable of something like that?

Wanda chose to join us at that moment. Despite myself, I was startled and made a small *whoofing* sound as the air abruptly left my chest.

"It's about time you made it down here," Wanda scolded.

"Don't faint in my place," Ginny cautioned, misinterpreting the sound I'd made. "I'll boot you outside."

Two of a kind. Not a good kind either.

"As I said, I don't know if you talked to the police, but I'm trying to help find Wanda's killer."

Ginny cackled. There was no other word for it. "You mean to shake them off your tail, huh? The police were here to talk to me all right—about why *you* killed Wanda. I told them I saw you over there working on your stupid prank."

I counted to ten and tried again. "I was wondering if you saw or heard anything over there this morning when she was killed. I didn't kill Wanda, but I have a powerful motive to find out who did."

"You mean besides saving your own ass?"

"Yes. I mean Wanda's blue ghost haunting me everywhere I go."

Wanda laughed as she swept some napkins and menus from the counter to the floor.

Ginny hunkered down a little and gazed furtively from side-to-side across the tavern. "Where is she? That little trollop deserved to die. She wanted to take my lover away from me."

"You mean Sir Marcus?"

"What do you know of it?" Her claw-like hand with thick, dirty nails grabbed at my throat.

Lucky that she was so much shorter than me. We could have had one of those comical fights where I hold my hand on her head and she takes her best shot but can't connect.

Yet as she reached for me, the long green sleeves of her dress fell back from her wrists again. The material had been covering a *particular* patch of blue.

There was no way Ginny could have had that shade of blue on her—unless she'd been there when the dye was fresh and it had stained her arms.

I stepped back from her. "You killed Wanda!"

"She did?" Wanda turned to stare at her. "Oh my God! I see it all now. She came in as I was trying to get away from the dye coming out of the showerhead. She was standing there with my enchanted bracelet in her hand. The next thing I knew, she'd buried her sword inside me. Let me at her."

Wanda did her best to make Ginny see her. She pummeled the older woman with her fists and kicked at her. Ginny couldn't see or hear anything. She pulled down her dress sleeves and produced a long, sharp knife from her pocket.

"That's right, Little Miss Know It All." Ginny used the knife to point toward the back of the tavern, her strong hand digging into my shoulder. "Nice and easy. No tricks—or you'll be dead with her."

I knew where she was headed. The pirates kept a cave under the tavern where they staged their raids from the ship. It was little more than a rough opening with a trap door and stairs leading up into the tavern.

I'd been there before. It was a while ago, and a long story.

The pirates raided the tavern several times a day when they made berth on that side of Mirror Lake. They went inside with a lot of sound and fury—not to mention fake pistols. If visitors were lucky, the pirates kidnapped one or two of them and gave them a ride on the Queen's Revenge. It was something every visitor longed for.

Ginny told me to pull up the trap door as she stuck the knife to my side. "Be quick about it too."

I peeked around us. There were no residents in the tavern. Even the visitors who were there didn't seem interested in what we were doing. My dawdling caused Ginny to prick me through my blouse with the knife. It hurt, and I felt a drop of blood slide down my side. I knew she was serious.

"I said get a move on it, Jessie!" Ginny hissed.

The staircase was narrow, but she managed to keep one arm around my middle with the knife threatening to rip my gut. The trap door fell closed above us. We were alone in the cave overlooking Mirror Lake.

The cave was filled with props that the pirates used—smoke bombs, fake pistols, and swords. There were plastic skeletons hanging from the ceiling and pinned to the walls as a warning to trespassers who might stumble upon the space. A few visitors had done that in the past, mostly teenagers.

Ginny pushed a fake skeleton out of the hangman's noose that was always drooping down from the ceiling. "Use that rock and haul yourself up there, my lady. The pirates aren't due back for at least thirty minutes. By the time they find you, you'll be another ghost to add spice to their legend. People will think you hanged yourself because you killed poor Wanda."

"They'll think that because *you* tried to frame me with her bracelet!"

"What of it?" She prodded me forward with the knife again. "Everyone knows the two of you were headed for a showdown. It was only a matter of time."

I stared hard at her. "I've known you for years, Ginny Stewart. You might be scared right now, but killing me won't help. Who do you think the police will ask about my death? And even though the visitors upstairs didn't seem like they were paying much attention, when Detective Almond and Chase question them, they'll remember what they saw."

"Is that the best you can do?" Wanda demanded. "Fight for your life. Rush at her. She might cut you up a little, mostly because you're a slow moving giantess, but you'll probably survive. I need you to tell *my* story."

"Aye." Ginny wielded her knife with skill, and she was strong. "I know you, too, Jessie Morton. Always standin' between me and the Bailiff. He would've been mine years ago, if not for you. I have a lover now, but once you're gone—and you've taken those infernal wedding plans with you—who knows but that Chase and I might enjoy a spell together."

"*You* do something, Wanda." I looked right into her anxious blue face. "Maybe you can't make her see you, but I know you can make her see other things."

"Bah!" Ginny poked me again with her knife. "You can't scare me with any hocus-pocus. Get up there on that rock, and put your head in the noose."

"Oh! I know what you mean." Wanda's grin was frightening. "I can *do* something, all right! Hold on, dearie."

Eleven

I climbed up on the rock and steadied myself. If Wanda didn't do anything to help, I figured I could kick Ginny in the face the next time she came close to me with that knife.

I didn't have to worry about it. Suddenly, it was as though the cave was alive. The noose began swinging as though storm winds were affecting it.

Ginny looked up and paled. "What's going on?"

I shrugged. "I told you Wanda's ghost is here with us, and she's *really* mad."

Ginny reached for me. I kicked the knife out of her hand and climbed down off the rock. Now we were on a more level playing field.

Wanda set the fake skeletons whirling like demons in the air about the cave. Ginny shrieked and ran for the ladder to go back upstairs. The skeletons converged on her and pulled her down to the cave's rocky floor with their fake, bony hands.

"I'll teach you to use a sword on me, hussy!" Wanda's face and voice were thick with emotion.

"Mercy, please!" Ginny called out, trying to get to her feet.

Wanda would have none of it. The swords that were left by the pirates suddenly jumped up and set in a challenge stance around her, as though invisible hands held them. They poked and prodded.

Wanda howled—the sound echoing off the roof of the cave. Even Ginny heard that. She dropped to her knees and put her hands over her face, moaning piteously.

"I didn't mean to kill you, Wanda," Ginny explained in a terrified voice. "I only meant to scare you away from Marcus. You were bending down to get your bracelet when you opened the shower door. The sword was there waiting for you. God help me."

I sneaked past them and up the stairs to the trap door. I heard more ghostly sounds and actions going on behind me. I didn't look back.

Once I was out of the cave, I locked the trap door. Ginny could get out of the cave from the front but it was a steep walk down and I didn't think Wanda would let her go that easily.

I took out my cell phone, thankful for once that I had it with me, and called Chase. I apologized to the surprised visitors around me. I figured this warranted a break in protocol.

Then I waited at a rough wood table, thinking how many times Chase and I had eaten here. The food was pretty good. Ginny never gave discounts for the residents like most of the other Village eateries. I certainly wouldn't miss her, but it was the end of an era.

Chase showed up at almost the exact minute that Detective Almond and two of his uniformed officers walked into the tavern. I explained everything as the officers asked the visitors to leave. More officers waited outside to take their statements.

"Are you okay?" Chase eyed my blouse where blood had saturated the material. "You should go to the hospital and have those cuts looked at. You might need stitches."

"I'm fine," I told him. "I was lucky to have Wanda with me."

Did I say that?

We watched Detective Almond's men escort Ginny up the stairs from the cave. She was crying and calling out for help.

"What's wrong with her?" Chase watched her walk by.

I nodded to Wanda who accompanied her. "Ginny can't see her, but Wanda can be pretty annoying even when she's invisible."

He shrugged. "I'll have to take your word for it."

"Be glad you can't see her." I shuddered. "She's not a pretty sight. And she's learned some really disgusting tricks."

"I heard that," Wanda yelled back at me. "Don't forget. You owe me, Jessie Morton. I saved your useless life."

I waved to her. Chase laughed at me. "What's she saying?"

"She's promising to make my life miserable, as usual."

We got to our feet and I put my arms around him. "The day is turning out much better than I was expecting. Let's go and get a cinnamon roll. I could use a triple shot mocha too."

#

Chase and I were summoned to the castle as the Main Gate was closing that evening. It was bound to be something about Wanda's murder and Ginny's arrest. I thought we might even get some kind of Royal Decree for doing such a good job.

Or a Royal Censure for pranking Wanda, though their Royal Highnesses usually ignored such things.

The police were long gone, with Ginny in tow. Detective Almond had released his hold on the museum, and it continued to move toward its opening day. Everything felt like it could get back to normal now. Wanda's memorial at the Village was scheduled for two days later.

Chase had been the purveyor of that last information. I wasn't eager to attend Wanda's memorial, but it was going to be a Village-wide service held at sunset for residents only. I could hardly refuse to be part of it, especially given our relationship while Wanda was alive. I knew everyone would be waiting to see if I'd be there.

I didn't want to disappoint them.

"Any other messages from Wanda since you found her killer?" Chase asked as we approached the castle.

"Nope. I'm hoping she's gone now. Maybe she can rest in peace. Or at least make some other person's life miserable."

He laughed and took my hand. "I'm sure everything will be fine. We're getting married in less than a month! Life is good!"

Princess Isabel was waiting at the side gate with Master at Arms, Gus Fletcher. She welcomed us to the castle, and we followed her inside.

The Village had been rife with rumors about a romance between the princess and Gus. This followed the birth last year of Queen Olivia and King Harold's new daughter, Princess Pea, who would no doubt take up Isabel's princess responsibilities at some time in the future.

I thought Gus, who was a former wrestler, was a good match for the spoiled princess. Everyone didn't agree. After all Gus wasn't a lord or even a knight. Some residents thought it seemed inappropriate.

I thought they took Village life a bit too seriously.

Isabel led us through the large entryway to the king and queen's private quarters, past the seating area for the King's Feast that happened every Sunday night. There was jousting in the Great Hall on those nights—along with singing, dancing, displays of valor, and Cornish hens.

It was a great time for one and all, according to the ads on TV.

"Greetings Sir Bailiff, Lady Jessie." King Harold seemed happy about something. He was unusually jovial and friendly. "How goes my kingdom?"

Chase glanced at me. "We have seen Wanda Le Fey's murderer taken into custody. A good day's work, sire."

King Harold glanced at Queen Olivia in much the same way that Chase had looked at me.

"I had no idea such dreadful events were going on," he protested. "Pray tell who this foul killer was."

"It was Ginny Stewart, sire. She confessed to killing Wanda, but said it was an accident."

"An accident?" King Harold roared. "By God, I ought to—"

"Now, now, dear." Queen Olivia laid her hand on his arm. "That is not the reason we summoned this couple to us."

"Quite right, my love." King Harold smiled at us again as he strove to regain his composure. "We have a wonderful surprise for the two of you. It gladdens my heart to be able to tell you personally."

"We're very anxious to hear what you have to say, Your Majesty." I was starting to get a sinking feeling about this.

"We have news this day that more than two hundred and fifty couples will be joining you on your day of wedded bliss. Adventureland is making it a theme day for the Faire. Consider this our gift to you for years of dedicated service, Sir Bailiff."

Two hundred and fifty other couples getting married at the same time?

It was like some horrible nightmare. The king and queen gushed on about how exciting it was, and all the revenue it would bring into the Village—not to mention worldwide television and Internet exposure.

Our thoughts and feelings on the subject were unimportant. Adventureland was going to make our wedding day one to remember for people we didn't know, who would never know us.

Chase grabbed my hand and squeezed. "Thank you, sire. We're sure this will be a wonderful day."

"Yes, indeed," I agreed with less enthusiasm than I'd ever had lifting a wet frog for a small child to catapult across the game booth. "A day to remember."

I heard Wanda's raucous laughter echo through the castle. It seemed finding her killer hadn't made her disappear into the hereafter either.

Maybe we could elope.

Part II

Murderous Matrimony

One

"I have a bad feeling about today, Jessie."

The ghost of Wanda Le Fey began humming *Bad Moon Rising* from Creedence Clearwater Revival as she inspected her nails.

I put my hand to my head and sipped my triple shot mocha, but there wasn't enough caffeine in the universe to help with this situation. My usual breakfast, a handmade cinnamon roll, sat forgotten on a tiny brown napkin.

Wanda had only been dead about two weeks. It seemed much longer. I'd played a small part in her death—I dyed her blue as a prank before she was brutally murdered.

That left Wanda spending almost all of her time with me. Ghastly, blue, and naked—she was even worse dead than she'd been alive. She was free to wander wherever she chose—which was usually wherever I was. She'd been in the shower with me that morning, and stood behind me in the bathroom mirror as I brushed my teeth.

I'd had to plead exhaustion or a headache every night with my fiancée since she'd died and come to stay with us in our tiny apartment. I knew he was wondering what was wrong with me.

It was hard to kiss him knowing she was there laughing and making fun of everything we did. When we started cuddling, she made retching noises or stared close up with those terrible, burning eyes.

"Is your cinnamon roll not to your liking, Lady Jessie?" Brother Carl asked as he started past my rough, wood table at the Monastery Bakery.

Traffic at the Monastery Bakery in Renaissance Faire Village and Marketplace was brisk for nine a.m. The Main Gate wasn't open yet. That meant the only customers were half-asleep residents, trying to get themselves together enough to cope with the ten thousand visitors who would walk the cobblestone paths that day at the theme park.

Brother Carl was head of the bakery—and the Brotherhood of the Sheaf—a monk-like guild that believed in the power of baking bread. They lived at the Village, along with a few hundred lords, ladies, fools, knaves, knights, and shopkeepers.

And me—Jessie Morton—former assistant history professor at the University of South Carolina, Ren Faire lover, and miserable wretch.

Like all the other brothers in his order, Carl wore plain, black robes that were usually covered in flour. His face was nondescript, somewhere between thirty and fifty. He was medium height, and his dark hair was cut military short.

"I'm sure it's fine, brother. Thank you."

He sat with me. "Is there anything I can do to help?"

"I don't think so."

"You are about to embark on a new life, Lady Jessie Morton! You're marrying the man of your dreams, and living here at the Village. Aren't these things what you've always wished for?"

They were *exactly* what I'd always wished for. I couldn't deny it. The problem was that those things came with a ghost in my bed, and The Great Wedding Fiasco.

It was less than two weeks until The Great Wedding Fiasco. Yes, Village Bailiff Chase Manhattan, the love of my life, and I were finally going to be married. I had a beautiful dress with a six-foot train, and a handmade lace veil. Our friends and family would be there—and so would at least a thousand strangers.

Because Adventureland, the parent company of Renaissance Faire Village and Marketplace, saw a golden opportunity with our wedding, they'd invited another two hundred and fifty couples to take their vows at the same time.

Those two hundred and fifty couples had family and friends. There were so many of them that the Village would be closed to the public that day.

Adventureland had sweetened the pot for all of the people who'd planned to have their wedding that day, including me and Chase. The cake was free. The flowers were free. The venue, on the Village Green under sapphire blue Myrtle Beach skies, was also free.

So were the television and Internet opportunities for the theme park. It was the chance of a lifetime—at least it was presented to me and Chase that way.

"Stop whining," Wanda said in her Americanized British accent. "You get the man. You get the wedding. What more do you want?"

Brother Carl seemed to agree with Wanda, even though he couldn't see or hear her. "You would be churlish not to appreciate the gift given to you, Jessie."

"I wouldn't want to be *churlish*," I muttered.

I didn't want to seem ungrateful, especially since Adventureland had also hired me to be the director of their new Renaissance Arts and Crafts Museum in the Village. They'd paid me nicely to get the museum set up.

Working at the Village, and being with Chase, was everything I'd ever wanted. But sharing my perfect day with a thousand strangers—and the ghost of a woman I didn't even like when she was alive—was almost too much.

"Does Chase mind?" Carl asked. "If not, why do *you*?"

I agreed with him, and excused myself. I'd had this internal debate for the last two weeks. I didn't want to be churlish. I didn't want to be selfish. I only wanted a simple wedding to the man I loved—and to get Wanda out of my life.

She followed me out of the bakery, floating above the cobblestone walkway that circled the Village.

"Why don't you find someone else to torment," I suggested. "I know I'm not the only one in the Village who can see you. You've managed to run off several knights, knaves, and ladies—not to mention scaring the crap out of your ex-husband every time you see him."

She smiled. It was a horrific thing. "Yes, dearie. It's the little things in death that give me so much pleasure. Did you know that animals can almost always see me? I've experimented with Bo Peep's sheep. I have great plans for the elephants and camels."

"I don't suppose it would do any good to remind you that people could be hurt if you scare large animals."

"None whatsoever. But thanks for telling me. I have an appointment on top of the rock climbing wall with whoever would like to take tea with me. Bye-bye, Jessie."

Wanda hadn't been a nice person in life. In death, she was far worse than I could have ever imagined.

These were the only moments of respite that I'd had since Wanda died. The Village's resident fortune teller had told me that Wanda would disappear as soon as I figured out who killed her.

I'd checked that off my to-do list, but Wanda was still there every time I looked up. Chase couldn't see her, though he was nice and didn't say he thought I was imagining her.

It was time to take action—about my fouled wedding plans, and Wanda. I straightened my backbone and lifted my chin. Life was good.

Lady Godiva rode her white horse past me at a fair clip. "Have you heard the news?"

"No. What's up?" I called back.

"There's been another murder—this time at the Arts and Crafts Museum."

Sometimes life has a way of slapping you back down.

Two

My assistant director was already at the museum. Manawydan 'Manny' Argall was a short, African-American man with close-cropped black hair and large glasses. He was always punctual. He was always knowledgeable. I wasn't sure how I would've managed to open the arts and crafts museum without him.

He dressed impeccably, even though that usually meant a Victorian costume. I'd tried explaining the different time periods to him. He either didn't get it or he didn't care. I wasn't sure which. I couldn't complain. He always looked good, and he smelled like fruit, spices, and flowers.

Chase Manhattan, my fiancée, was beside him.

Chase was six-foot-eight, two-hundred and fifty pounds of tan skin and taut muscle. He was the law and order in the Village. He was magistrate at Vegetable Justice, a squishy vegetable throwing form of vengeance, and kept the peace between residents and visitors alike. He'd been trained by the Myrtle Beach Police Department to be the Bailiff—a constable-type position.

He was wearing his usual costume which included leather britches and a free-flowing, white cotton shirt under a tied, leather vest. His long brown hair was braided, and there was still a gold earring in his ear from his days as a pirate.

Chase had performed in almost every position in the Village. He'd been a jouster, a knight, and a stable hand. He'd also been a member of the Queen's Guard. That was part of what made him so good at his job. He always knew what to do.

"Is it true?" I was breathless after completing the rest of the way to the museum at a brisk jog. "Someone was killed?"

Manny solemnly nodded. "I'm afraid so, Lady Jessie. He's at the top of the stairs. I think the poor creature was seeking help when he was struck down."

"Manny called me and we waited for the police." Chase glanced at the police cars on the cobblestones. "I think he was killed by a crossbow."

"Why didn't someone call *me*?" I admit it was a small matter, but I *was* the director of the museum.

"I tried," Manny said. "Your phone device didn't work."

"I was already out here." Chase put his arm around me. "You've been sleeping so badly, I thought I'd give you a few extra minutes. There was nothing you could do anyway. Detective Almond is up there looking things over."

"Who was it?" I whispered.

Manny shrugged. "It was the panhandler from the street. You called him Dave, I believe."

"Madman Dave?" I couldn't believe it. He worked the area around the museum, banging his pans together and entertaining visitors to the faire. "That's awful. Who would want to kill him?"

"I'm sure I don't know." Manny flicked an invisible speck from his embroidered vest. "He was here at the museum door when I arrived."

"Not Dave!" Wanda joined us, though no one else could hear her. She cackled at the circumstances. "I'll bet your man there killed him. They were *always* arguing, you know."

She was right. Manny had given Madman Dave a hard time since we'd started working on the museum. It bothered him to have Dave out there. He felt like it wasn't '*seemly*'.

Of course Manny didn't shoot Dave with a crossbow. They'd exchanged a few heated words. It wasn't a big deal. I hoped the police wouldn't make it into one.

"Any ideas about what could have happened to Dave?" Chase asked. "Have you seen anyone unusual hanging around since you started the museum, Jessie?"

I thought about it. "No. Nothing unusual. Dave has been working this area for a while. I saw him yesterday. He was here when I left last night."

Manny—who always had to point out the details—cleared his throat. "I should probably say that I strenuously opposed the man sitting out here on the ground. He and I have had a few debates. I don't understand the whole madman routine. I have threatened to take him to task for blocking the sidewalk, and pulling on ladies' gowns as they pass."

Chase shook his head. "You can't go around threatening people because you don't like what they're doing. Did anyone *hear* you threaten him?"

"Possibly only Lady Jessie." Manny held his head high, not a bit regretful. "I didn't shoot the man with a crossbow, if that's what you're asking."

"You should have told me there was a problem." Chase said. "That's why I'm here, and why the Village pays for fifty security guards to be here every day with me."

"I'm sorry." I intervened. "I suppose we should have said something. It didn't seem that important."

"It might be now." Chase nodded as Detective Almond beckoned to us from the concrete landing at the top of the stairs.

"A word of advice," Chase warned Manny. "Keep that story to yourself if you want to stay out of jail."

"All right." Manny didn't look particularly nervous. "I'll do as you say, Sir Bailiff. Thank you."

Chase and I went up the stairs to talk with the police. Manny stayed behind on crowd control as visitors walked by on the cobblestones, gawking at what was going on.

"Chase." Detective Almond greeted him with a handshake and a smile. "How's my favorite bailiff today?"

"Sorry I wasn't here, Don. Someone set one of the elephants free. The poor thing was scared to death. We have a new animal handler who was just as scared."

I glared at Wanda. She covered her blue mouth with one hand. "*Oops*!"

She disappeared again—thankfully—though at least when I could see her, I knew what she was doing.

"That's okay." Detective Don Almond was a chunky man whose chin hung heavily on his chest. He always wore his pants too tight, and had a food or drink stain on his clothes. This morning it appeared to be blueberry muffin on his white shirt.

Chase and I both looked at the sheet-covered form of Madman Dave. Who'd want to kill him? He was a good guy, and an excellent madman.

Detective Almond sniffed. "It could only happen *here*. Someone shot an arrow into the man's heart. I think you said when I got here that you thought it was from a crossbow?"

Chase explained about the different sizes of arrows. "A crossbow arrow is really a bolt. It's shorter. This bolt looked like an antique to me, or something homemade."

The police around us were dusting everything for fingerprints. They measured the concrete landing, and squinted up at the roof—probably checking the trajectory of the bolt.

"What was he doing here so late?" Detective Almond stared at me for answers. "Was this place open? Isn't there a curfew or something?"

"I don't know why he was here," I answered. "He usually works close to the museum, but the Village would've been closed. The madmen aren't usually out after everyone goes home, at least not professionally. But he could've been on his way to eat or something."

"What time does the assistant medical examiner think he died?" Chase asked.

"Probably around midnight." Detective Almond watched the curious visitors go by on the cobblestones for a moment. "Looks like it was an inside job then."

"Inside?" I questioned.

"A resident," he translated. "Not a visitor."

It seemed odd to me that Dave was lying under that sheet, and there was very little blood on the landing around him. There wasn't much blood on the stairs coming up there either. "Where do you think he was shot?"

His eyebrows arched. "Why not right *here*?"

"Not enough blood." I shrugged. "Someone must have killed him elsewhere and then brought him here.

"That's good, Jessie." He scratched his chin. "Better watch it, Chase. She may be after *your* job."

"She's good, Don." Chase grinned and put his arm around me.

"To put your mind at ease, we found the spot right down there by the walkway. There's plenty of blood. The bolt didn't kill the man right away, and he probably crawled up here looking for help."

It was sad to think that Dave had laid out here and died with no one to help him. "So that's what happened?"

"We don't know for sure *yet*." Detective Almond looked at his notes. "What about your assistant, Jessie? Manny, right? Have him come up here a minute."

I motioned to Manny to have him join us.

He *knew* about what had been happening with Manny and Dave. We couldn't get around it. I should have known better. Detective Almond might seem inept sometimes, but he always seemed to know what was going on.

Manny stepped up and introduced himself. "A pleasure to meet you, Detective."

"I heard you've had a problem with Mr. Olson regarding his . . . *occupation*."

"The matter was resolved to our mutual satisfaction."

Detective Almond shifted his stance. "A few people overheard you threaten Mr. Olson. Is *that* true?"

Manny shot me a quick glance. 'I'm afraid that is true. I only meant it as incentive to get the brute moving."

"But as he said, everything turned out okay." I tried to get past this awkward moment. Manny was dense sometimes, but he wasn't a killer. "Dave was healthy, and walking around the last time I saw him."

"Which was?" Detective Almond's pencil poised above his notebook.

"About five p.m. when I left for the night."

"And you, Manny? When was the last time you saw Mr. Olson alive?"

"About the same time."

It took a few more minutes of Detective Almond's pencil scratching on the paper to write down what he wanted. "You know how to shoot a crossbow, Manny? Because I have no idea."

"Of course! Where I come from, we learn early how to hunt with a bow. I was *very* good at it!"

How exactly was that keeping his mouth shut?

"Detective Almond, Manny knows how to use a crossbow. So do I. So does Chase, and a hundred other men and women who live in the Village. That doesn't mean he killed him."

"Don't get so worked up, Jessie." Detective Almond glanced at Manny. "If he's willing to come to the station and give us a statement—with some DNA and prints for comparison—that will go a long way toward making me believe he wasn't involved."

Manny looked at me for guidance.

"Of course," I answered for him with my hand on his arm. "He has nothing to hide."

"Good deal. We'll be glad to give him a ride there and back. It shouldn't take too long." Detective Almond nodded at Chase. "If you think of anything else, give me a call."

Manny accompanied a police officer down the stairs and to a waiting squad car.

"I hope you know what you're doing, Jessie." Chase watched Manny slide into the backseat. "He should've had a lawyer."

"He didn't do this. You know Manny. He wouldn't risk getting blood all over himself. Besides, it was just a few arguments. Whoever did this had a bigger beef with Dave, don't you think?"

"Maybe." Chase was still troubled. "But Manny has no idea what's going on with our legal system. You can tell that he doesn't know when to shut up. That could be a bad mixture."

I had confidence in Manny. He might say too much, but he had nothing to hide. It was better to get this over with so the police weren't coming back to talk to him every day until they found another suspect.

"You wouldn't have done it," Chase murmured.

He was right, of course. But that was different.

Detective Almond approached us again. "I'm gonna have to close off the museum until the crime scene people are done here. Sorry, Jessie. I'm sure you have plenty to do with your wedding coming up and all. I think my wife sent you our RSVP. I'm not dressing up, but we'll be here."

"Is there anything else I can do to speed things up?" I knew from personal experience that an investigation could take weeks.

Detective Almond shrugged. "Hope you're wrong about Manny and that he *did* kill Mr. Olson? That would speed things up!"

"Maybe something else."

"I don't think so, but thanks anyway. Chase will keep you updated."

"Thanks."

Two burly officers stood at the walkway to warn visitors away. Their blue uniforms looked out of place in the Village. They could at least have found them some Ren Faire outfits.

"That went badly," Chase said when we were alone with on the cobblestone walkway. Two of the three police cars were slowly driving out of the Main Gate.

"It was terrible. He has Manny—and the museum has to be closed."

"You gave him Manny," he reminded me.

"I thought it would help get through this faster if he could cross him off the suspect list right away. We know he's not guilty."

Chase was right. Where had my brain been? I'd had to explain to Manny about money. He'd told Adventureland that he didn't want to get paid. The police were going to eat him *alive*!

"I can't believe this is happening—especially right after Wanda's death—and two weeks before our wedding." I shook my head. "What can I do to help him?"

I watched the Green Man, a walking tree, performing on his stilts. He had to be new. A small child could've knocked him over. He wouldn't make it through the day, at least not upright.

"It's going to be fine." Chase put his arm around me. "Like you said, he's innocent, right? If the worst happens and they keep him, we'll get him a lawyer. He'll be okay.

"We have to start looking around. Someone in the Village saw what happened—or has some idea why it happened."

"That's why I'm here. I'll figure it out, Jessie. They pay me to do this kind of stuff." We stopped walking and he kissed the engagement ring on my finger. "You've been under a lot of stress lately. Maybe this would be a good time for you to relax and take it easy."

Relax? That was almost as bad as my advice to Manny!

His radio buzzed and he glanced at it. "I have to go see what's up at the rock climbing wall. The kids have been falling backward when they get to the top. One of them said a ghost is up there." He kissed me. "I'll call you later about lunch."

"Probably Wanda. She enjoys the 'sport', as she calls it."

"I wish she'd move on. She's starting to give the Village a weird reputation!"

I watched him walk away, cutting across the Village Green, and the King's Highway.

I knew Chase meant well, but the Village kept him moving seven days a week. It was all he—and his fifty security guards—could keep up with. They might never figure out what happened to Dave by themselves.

I knew how this worked. If I wanted Detective Almond to leave Manny alone, and re-open the museum, I was going to have to find out why Dave was killed.

"Oh dear," Wanda sighed as she stood next to me. "I told you this was going to be a bad day."

Three

It seemed to me, since I was now temporarily without employment, that my first move should be looking up Dave's records here at the Village. I didn't even know what his last name was until Detective Almond said it. I wasn't sure how long he'd worked here. I thought it had been for a year or so, but I couldn't be sure.

Everyone knew him, or at least recognized him. Madmen were the clowns of the cobblestones. They'd do anything for a reaction. There were a lot of madmen, jesters, knaves, and so forth, in the Village. It was impossible to personally know them all.

But someone else could tell me where he lived, and what kind of things he was into. He was bound to have shared his past with a resident over a glass of beer one night. Everyone who lived here seemed to have secrets about their past that he or she was hiding. I was sure Dave was no exception.

Employment records, and other official business, were kept at the castle. I passed the Main Gate on my way there. It was teeming with visitors coming in for the day. They were being entertained by minstrels, and good-looking lords and ladies with wonderful costumes. Jugglers and singers welcomed them into this magical place as scantily clad fairies tossed petals at their feet.

The visitors were no slouches where costumes were concerned either. Just in the first few hundred, I saw a centaur, two Greek goddesses, a man in a Batman costume, and a woman with shoes that were at least a foot tall.

I passed Mermaid Lagoon. It was closed for the year. No one had been able to convince the mermaids that they should splash around in the water during the cold months. It was too bad. The mermaids were one of the most popular attractions. Several young men were already standing at the edge of the lagoon, and mourning that they had missed them.

The smells of a hundred different kinds of food—from pizza and turkey legs to roasted corn and stew—assailed my senses. Across the Village, cooks were getting ready for lunch, and the hearty appetites of the visitors who kept all of us here. The cool November breeze wafted the aromas of baking bread and funnel cakes to tease the senses.

There were so many choices: Baron's had beer and brats, Three Pigs had several variations of barbecue. Polo's had pasta and pizza. There were pretzel carts and pickle carts. It was almost impossible not to find something you wanted to eat.

I ran into an old friend as I walked toward the castle. Rita Martinez was the head of the enormous kitchen staff there. She was a hardworking, older woman with gray-streaked black hair, and dark eyes that didn't miss a thing.

I'd worked for her when I'd first come to the Village. We hadn't exactly been friends then, but after we'd known each other a while, that had changed.

"I can't believe Madman Dave is dead." She shook her head. "You just never know."

I told her that the police were questioning Manny. "I know he wasn't responsible, but his arguments with Dave look bad."

"So what are you gonna do about it?" She used her work-roughened hand to shield her eyes from the sun as she talked to me.

I was at least a foot taller than her. I leaned a little closer. "I'm going to find out what I can about Dave. Maybe someone had a grudge against him. He wouldn't be dead otherwise, not like that anyway."

"Too much of *that* going on." She crossed herself. "Look at what happened to Wanda just two weeks ago! We'll probably never find another qualified nurse to work here."

I couldn't help but feel some responsibility for Wanda's death. Chase was right about that, but I didn't think it was what had drawn her ghost to me. "I know."

"Don't get all down in the mouth about it." She flicked my chin. "Yes, you dyed her blue, but you weren't the cause of her death. Poor thing—going through eternity that way."

I stopped walking and stared at her. "Can you *see* her?"

She gave an exasperated sigh and kept walking. "How could I see her now? They buried her last week!"

"Rita, her ghost has been with me since she died. I know it seems like it can't be true, but it is. I don't know if Chase really believes me either."

"Do you see her right now?" She surveyed the people around us.

"No. She comes and goes when she wants to. It's been crazy for me and Chase. She was doing this weird trick—

turning her eyeballs inside out—two nights ago when Chase and I—"

"Hmm." She smiled knowingly. "That explains the expression on the Bailiff's face for the last two weeks."

"Two weeks before the wedding—and I'm pretty sure he thinks I don't love him. I don't know what to do."

We continued walking past Mirror Lake. I watched the pirate ship *Queen's Revenge* sailing toward her berth near the Main Gate. Her full white sails picked up every stray breeze against the clear blue sky.

The cannons were being fired onboard the ship—as they were every day at ten, twelve, four, and six p.m. Large plumes of gray smoke accompanied the thunderous sound. There were children standing beside the lake with their parents, fist-pumping and yelling *Huzzah!* at each blast.

"You've got the shakes, Jessie, that's all," Rita said. "Everybody gets them right before they get married. You're seeing blue ghosts—I saw giant meatballs! Once the wedding is over, you'll be fine!"

I looked at my unique engagement ring. It had originally belonged to Chase's grandmother. He'd had it changed from a plain gold band with two ruby hearts to a dragon holding two ruby hearts. It was perfect.

I loved the ring, and I loved Chase. Maybe Rita was right. Just getting married was a big deal, without the Village adding in their ideas about publicizing it. I never wanted that, but what was good for the Village was also good for me and Chase.

"Thanks. You're right. I was a mess without Dave getting killed right outside the museum. Only two more weeks. That's all I have to keep it together."

"You can do it, Jessie. The two of you have always been perfect for each other. I'm so glad you're staying in the Village."

Rita and I walked quickly through the dew-damp green grass, admiring a juggler who was balancing eight flaming sticks in the air. Not far from him was a trio of musicians, getting their instruments tuned for the day.

"You know, I don't get the hanging tree." She walked up and stared at the big tree. Why would anyone want to pretend to be hanged?"

"I don't know. It's popular. Hundreds of people sign up to be hanged every day. Chase tried to get it closed down once after a fight broke out. Adventureland wouldn't hear of it. It makes money for the park."

"Do you think those people have a death wish or something?" She shook her head. "I think it's crazy!"

"People wear a collar that protects their necks. No one gets hurt. Well, not often anyway, and not too badly. People come here to escape reality. They want to do things they might never do again."

"Would you do it?" Rita asked. "Have you done it?"

"No." I stared up into the almost naked branches of the gnarled old oak. There were only a few yellow leaves left that hadn't fallen. "But I live here. I don't need the excitement."

That brought us to the Lady of the Lake Tavern. It had been empty for two weeks with the loss of its owner, Ginny Stewart. I'd heard some chatter on the cobblestones that her niece or sister was coming from Baltimore to re-open it.

The sign outside—half girl/half fish, holding a sword and tankard in her hands— looked forlorn. I glanced through the small panes of glass that made up the windows on the ground floor. It was dark and eerie inside. All of the benches and tables were empty. It looked like a ghost house. Maybe it would be a good place for Wanda to live.

I knew the pirates hated that the tavern was closed. Kidnapping visitors from the tavern each day was a highlight for them, and the people they kidnapped. It was a very hands-on experience that led to an exciting sail across Mirror Lake in a pirate ship for some lucky visitors. I'd done it more than once when I'd first come here. Pirates were the best!

"You know," Rita continued as we started up the hill to the castle entrance. "I've heard that assistant of yours is a *real* prince from another country."

I'd heard this story before. According to Manny, he was the heir to a kingdom in a country I'd never heard of. People in the Village tended to exaggerate. It wasn't anything new.

"I don't know. Maybe he is. Doesn't everyone have some secrets?"

"There are secrets," she said. "And there are *secrets*! What do you think?"

"Manny *is* a little odd. He doesn't have a cell phone. He claims that he's never watched TV. All I know is that he's a good person, and a wonderful assistant director. I'm sure he didn't kill Dave, and I'd be lost without him at the museum while he's gone."

"I guess we'll have to see then. Sometimes those old secrets come up again, don't they?"

We'd finally reached the tall, bulk of the castle.

It had once been the runway tower for the Air Force facility that had been here for many years. Some turrets had been added, and concrete had been used to create a fairy-tale structure that towered above the lake. It was the one building you could see from everywhere in the Village.

Here, King Harold and Queen Olivia resided with their new daughter, Princess Pea. Harry and Livy, as they used to be known, were Adventureland's top salespeople at one time. They'd been rewarded with their positions here—a royal lifetime of lords, ladies-in-waiting, minions, and servants. They presided over feasts, and had all their needs attended to.

It was a sweet gig.

Master at Arms, Gus Fletcher, a former professional wrestler, was waiting at the castle gate. He was a large man whose prime was well past, and yet his strength and girth made him legendary.

Pinching ladies' butts as they passed his guard post had made him infamous as well. I wasn't sure how many times he'd been slapped. I knew he'd been reprimanded at least twice for the practice. He couldn't seem to keep his hands to himself.

"What ho!" He greeted us at the gate. His wide shoulders and narrow waist were accentuated by his green and gold armor that gleamed in the sun. "Lady Jessie. Mistress Rita. Welcome! What seek you here?"

"I'm going to work," Rita said in her no-nonsense tone. "Good luck, Jessie. Just hold on. Everything is going to be fine. You'll see."

Gus reached for her backside as she walked into the castle. Without turning around, she said, "Touch me and lose your eating privileges for a week! Keep your hands to yourself!"

He laughed.

I always made sure to keep myself turned *toward* him so those roaming hands couldn't find my butt. Mostly, he left me alone because he was friends with Chase, and didn't want to end up on his bad side.

There was a large crowd of visitors coming out the castle. Only the best Ren speak would do for now.

"I seek an audience with Sir Bart, Master at Arms." That was our way of letting Gus know we needed to use a phone, fax machine, or computer.

Bart would have Dave's personal information, or know how to get it. We needed to act fast if we wanted to find out who'd killed him. For all I knew, the killer could have already left the Village.

"Of course, my lady." Gus bent gracefully from the waist, with the help of his staff. "Sir Bart is able to speak with you. Please go in."

"A formidable warrior," I heard one visitor whisper as she passed him. "They are fortunate to have someone like this guarding their village."

"I'd be more fortunate if he'd keep his hands to himself." I smiled as I said it and backed away from Gus until I was too far for him to reach.

Chase had spoken to him many times, as Bailiff, about watching his hands. The problem was that Gus was related to the queen. No one wanted to get her riled up.

I went into the office, which was the main hub of the Village. Everything, and everyone, was documented and filed here. Orders were made for what the Village needed from food to building materials.

At the center of it sat a giant of a man. Bart Van Impe was almost seven feet tall and weighed more than I cared to think about. He was strong too. He could pick Chase up in his arms like a baby.

He was as good-hearted as he was huge—and he was smart. Bart was single-handedly putting years' worth of the Village's paper records into the computers with a software program that he'd created.

"Hello, Jessie!" He got up and hugged me, lifting me easily off the floor. "What brings you by today? I hope it's nothing to do with Dave the Madman."

"Why? Don't you have that information?"

"I do. But you should leave this to the police."

“The police wouldn’t know what to do with the information if they had it.”

“Don’t you have enough to do with your wedding coming up?” Bart didn’t move to answer my request.

“Why is it everyone seems to think the only thing I can do is get ready for the wedding? Honestly, there isn’t that much to do since Adventureland is taking care of it.”

“Detective Almond told me not to give you any information.” He shrugged. “I’m sorry, Jessie.”

“Me, *specifically?*”

“Looks like you have a problem, Jessie, my pet.” Wanda’s laugh raced through the castle. “They beat you to it!”

Four

"Bart—you know I can do this! I know the Village better than the police. I'm the one who found your brother's killer."

"I can't help you under fear of penalty of law." He frowned. "Detective Almond said he'd arrest me for being an accessory if I tell you anything about Dave."

Detective Almond wasn't going to stop me that way!

I glanced around the office. "Bart, I need to make a few copies of things for the museum."

"Jessie. I can't help you!"

"It's only copies." I crossed my heart. "There's nothing wrong with copies, right?"

"Copies, huh?" He grunted and heaved himself out of his specially built chair. "All right. I'm going to get some coffee. I never saw you. Don't be here when I get back."

"I won't." I kissed his cheek. "Thanks, Bart!"

When he was gone, I sat down at the computer and looked in the file for Village employees. I'd sneaked into the office once before, and looked at as many files as I could while Bart was gone. I hadn't been looking for Dave's file at the time, but then he wasn't dead.

"*Ooo*, look!" Wanda sat on top of the monitor. "Everything you've always wanted to know about everyone here. Wish I'd seen this before."

"Good thing you didn't. No telling what kind of things you would've done to them."

"Nothing you wouldn't have done too! I think I am a monument to that truth." She stood up, blue and naked, and floated around the room. Papers hit the floor and maps of the Village flew off the walls. "I'm becoming rather good at this, aren't I?"

"Wonderful." I tried to ignore her and get the information before Bart got back. I knew he wouldn't really do anything to me, but I didn't want him to get in trouble either. If anyone else from administration found me here without Bart, it would be bad.

"Found it!" I said out loud. "David Olson, thirty-eight. Graduate of UCLA. Degree in drama and theater."

"And still he ended up here playing a madman," she mused. "What a pity!"

"It says that he wasn't married. No close family. He was reprimanded twice for gambling by Roger Trent." I frowned. "I didn't know he'd been here that long."

"Oh, I could have told you *that*!" Wanda said. "I remember him being here almost since I came."

I felt bad about that, but the truth was that there were so many people who lived and worked here—or stayed for a season, left and came back—it was hard to keep up with them. Hundreds of high school seniors and college students worked here on and off. I only knew the main players who were here all the time.

But Roger might be a good person to talk to about Dave. I definitely knew Roger since I'd apprenticed with him at his glass shop, The Glass Gryphon.

I hurried and shut down the screen as Wanda tried to take another peek. I didn't know what she could do with the information, but I didn't want to find out either.

"Well, that wasn't very nice!"

"Sorry. I think someone's coming!"

It was Bart coming back with an egg biscuit and a cup of coffee. "Want one? There were some left over after breakfast this morning. None of those skinny ladies-in-waiting eat around here." He smiled at me. "I think it's time for you to go."

"No biscuit, thanks, but I appreciate your help."

"What help?" He sat back down. "I just went out for coffee. You were making *copies* when I got back."

"Yeah. See you later. I have to figure out what happened to Dave before my wedding."

"Good luck with that." Bart waved.

Workmen were putting up big posters on the castle walls where visitors would wait to get into the King's Feast on Sunday night. They were advertising my wedding, along with the "full day of fun festivities" on local and cable channels.

Merlin, our resident wizard, had said the 250 or so weddings that day would be seen world-wide.

I tried not to think about it.

I heard a scream behind me. It was followed by the sound of a tray hitting the stone floor. There was also some breaking china. No doubt it was Wanda, frightening a chamber maid.

Sometimes it was possible to be calm and rational about things. But I didn't know what to do about Wanda. She was causing havoc everywhere, as Chase had said. No one seemed to know how to stop her.

I decided to give Madame Lucinda, our resident fortune teller, one more try. She could be on my way to see Roger about Dave. What could it hurt? Imagine if I could find Dave's killer *and* get rid of Wanda before my wedding. That would be something worth celebrating!

As I left the castle, I saw a group of archers practicing outside The Feathered Shaft. I hadn't even thought to ask Master Archer Simmons for his take on Dave's murder-by-arrow. He might have some good suggestions too.

"Jessie!" Master Simmons hailed me from outside his shop. "Just the lady I was hoping to see."

Master Simmons never seemed to age. He was a jovial, round-faced man with laughing eyes. He'd been one of the first craftsmen signed up for Renaissance Faire Village. I'd apprenticed with him when I'd first started working on my dissertation, and I learned a lot.

"Good morning. How goes your life, good sir?"

There weren't many visitors headed our way yet, but I liked to stay in practice. You never knew when someone was standing behind you with a camera.

"Things are good, Lady Jessie. I have great news for you. I received permission from the king and queen to have twenty archers each send a flaming arrow into the sky at the end of your marriage vows to the Bailiff. Exciting, eh?"

"Very exciting," I agreed with him. "We appreciate your tribute, Master Archer."

"Oh yes." Wanda was there beside me, yawning. "So exciting I almost forgot to be awake. Fiery arrows? I'm all a'quiver. What will people think of next?"

I was glad only a few people in the Village could hear her. Since Master Simmons didn't so much as blink when she spoke, I knew he wasn't one of them.

When anyone actually saw or heard her, they ran away. I'd read a few accounts of ghost watching here by visitors on the Internet. The ghost stories probably enhanced attendance, but made for some disappointed visitors when they didn't see a ghost.

Yet another reason to get rid of Wanda—beyond my personal issues with her.

I ignored her, and clasped his hands. "Thank you so much for being part of our special day."

He snorted. "Me and about a million other people, huh? Now *that's* exciting. I hope my team of archers will be asked to perform at other venues, maybe the Super Bowl."

We laughed, and he gave some direction to his practicing archers.

"Master Simmons, have you heard about Dave the Madman? He was found dead at the museum early this morning. There was a crossbow bolt in his chest."

He frowned. "Most unpleasant!"

"It's possible it was an antique. There's one in the weapon museum next door to the arts and crafts museum. I saw it when they were first setting up."

"That would be mine," he acknowledged. "I donated it, at least for a time, to the museum."

"Do you have any bolts that go with it?"

"I do. I don't think anyone could have used the crossbow to actually shoot a man. I donated it because it's not in good repair. They told me they only wanted to hang it on the wall, so it was fine."

"Could I see one of the bolts for it?"

"Of course!" He told his archers that he was going inside for a moment, and to continue their work.

As usual, The Feathered Shaft was littered with bows and arrows. Some of them were in the process of being created, while others were waiting to be picked up by buyers. Feathers for the nock end of the arrows flowed colorfully across the wood floor. Tips were even more apparent.

"Pardon the mess," he joked as he always did.

But I knew he loved the shop exactly as it was. He wouldn't have changed a thing.

"Here's one of the bolts that go with that crossbow." He held it up, and we looked at it. "As you can see, not the straightest thing in the world. I only had four with the set. I lost one. There are two at the museum, and this is the last. You'd have to be a better archer than you or I, my girl, to hit a target as small as a man with it!"

I could see that what he said was true. It didn't help my case. "I'll see if Chase can get a good look at the bolt—after they examine Dave. In the meantime, I'll see if your crossbow is still at the weapon museum."

"I'm sorry I can't be more help." His smile faded and he whispered, "I'd rather have my name left out of this if it's all the same to you, Jessie. I have a little *background* with this sort of thing. I hope the police don't think to drudge it up."

"Of course," I replied. But I wondered what kind of trouble he'd been in. "I wish you well, sir. Good day."

Three visitors behind me laughed and applauded. They asked us to pose for a picture with the archers outside and then we each took pictures with them. Most players here understand the excitement and enthusiasm of our visitors, even if we don't always share it.

The Templar Knights were impressing visitors with their horse tricks by the time I reached the Main Gate again.

Dressed in full armor, with their eye-catching red and black shields, they could make their horses dance. One of the knights flipped a penny right in front of another rider, and the horse came to a stop immediately. Another horse and knight crouched down, and a rider jumped over the top of them. It was amazing power and control, considering the size of the animals. It scared me watching them.

I was headed to Madame Lucinda's tent again. I knew she had the answer for what I could do to get rid of Wanda. I decided that I wasn't asking the right question. But what was the right question? How many different ways can you frame, 'How do I get rid of a ghost?'

I couldn't really knock on her purple and gold tent. How do you knock on material? I kind of announced myself, and parted the folds of the tent.

"Hello?" I looked around the darkened interior and didn't see anyone. "Madame Lucinda? It's Jessie Morton. I need to talk to you again about Wanda. Are you here?"

I'd been to see her several times in the last two weeks. She was probably getting tired of me, especially since I'd never paid her anything. She'd asked for silver, but I didn't have any real silver except an old bracelet and some earrings. I would have gladly parted with them if she could take care of the problem.

Technically, her advice was part of the ticket price at the Village. However, I would certainly be willing to overlook that if she'd help me. I had some change in my pocket, but it was doubtful any of it was silver. It was hard to remember to bring jewelry with me. Usually I saw her, spur of the moment, from desperation, like this.

"Madame Lucinda?" I stepped a little further into the tent.

It was an amazing place. I had no idea where she'd collected all of the artifacts that hung on her walls. I believed most of them were genuine—a grouping of medieval weapons and everyday items that had been used for survival at one time. There were priceless statues from every corner of the world, and gold cloth that seemed to have been spun by spiders.

But how are they hanging on these flimsy tent walls?

Being in the tent produced a feeling that nothing existed anywhere but here. How could a piece of tent material totally squash all the noise from a loud faire going on right outside?

There were too many oddities about this place, and yet I was attracted here. I could hardly keep myself from walking inside when I passed it.

Before I could call out again, the principle wonder of Madame Lucinda's tent walked in front of me and stopped, taking up a challenging stance.

"*Nice dragon.*"

I know. There was no way the dragon was real. It defied everything I had ever learned. It wasn't a puppet. It wasn't a holographic image. It wasn't a person in a costume, like Fred the Red Dragon. I'd checked out all those possibilities.

The dragon was the size of a large terrier, the head seeming too large for the body. It was shiny green, the scales variegating from green to blue. It had yellow eyes that were fastened on me. Its mouth showed rows of sharp teeth. I'd seen it spit fire before.

Though it seemed impossible—even here at the Ren Faire—I was pretty sure the dragon was *real*. I didn't know how, but I had no other answer for it.

When I'd mentioned it to other residents of the Village, they were all fine with the idea that there was a dragon inside the purple and gold tent. No one even seemed to question how a *real* dragon could be here. Many actually thought dragons had always been real, like dinosaurs, and had convincing arguments why this should be true.

Of course, residents of the Village are not always the most logical, practical people in the world. Let's face it, we live in a fantasy land where visitors from outside come to be immersed in another time and place. We're encouraging people to use their imaginations.

My imagination was having a hard time wrapping itself around this very real-looking dragon, confronting me like a guard dog. I feinted one way, and he followed me. I was definitely in his sights.

"Oh. It's you, Jessie." Madame Lucinda suddenly appeared in the quiet darkness of the tent. "I'm sorry about Buttercup. She doesn't like surprises, or unannounced visitors, for that matter."

"Buttercup? It's a *girl* dragon?"

Madame Lucinda laughed daintily as though my ignorance was amusing. She was an older woman, almost hunchbacked, who always wore a long purple robe. She had a difficult time walking. I thought maybe she was crippled, or in some way deformed, since she hid herself in here all the time, even after the Village was closed at night.

She moved her long, gray hair away from her face as she sat down carefully in her chair. Before her was a tiny table with a glowing glass ball resting on it. "Actually, in their fight to survive, dragons have learned to be flexible in their gender. Buttercup is a female right now. She may be a male someday. She's not old enough to mate as yet. We'll see when the time comes."

I moved quickly as Buttercup jumped on a shelf where she usually perched above Madame Lucinda. I took the chair opposite the fortune teller at the table.

"Are you telling me Buttercup is a *real* dragon?" I said it with all the authority that a master's degree in medieval history could bring. "Because you know dragons were only mythology. They weren't like dinosaurs where they existed and went extinct."

I looked up at the dragon as it made a kind of purring noise on the shelf above us.

I wanted to hear her say it. I don't know why since I probably wouldn't believe it.

"What do you think, Jessie? What does your heart tell you?"

"I don't know about my heart, but my eyes tell me the dragon is real." I shook my head. "But I know it can't be."

"Mythology is hard to define," she said in a gruff voice. "One person's mythology is another person's truth."

"That doesn't really answer my question."

"You aren't here to ask me about Buttercup anyway, are you, Jessie?"

"No." I tried to clear my mind and accept that the dragon was a grand illusion that the fortune teller wasn't giving up. I didn't blame her. If I had an illusion so lifelike and difficult to ignore, I wouldn't either.

"I'm here about Wanda again. She's ruining what's left to ruin of my wedding. She figured out she can scare animals now, and doesn't care if she hurts anyone, including children."

"Regrettable."

"And I can't *be* with Chase knowing she's looking on and laughing. I have to find a way to get rid of her. Please. You have to help me." I hadn't meant to say so much, so quickly. It kind of poured out of me before I could stop.

The fortune teller sighed. "Our options are limited. Therc are spells that can scrape a spirit away from another, but that would mean wishing Wanda on someone else. Are you prepared to do that?"

I thought about it—I *really* thought about it. How could I wish an evil, naked, blue dead woman on someone else and ruin their lives? At least I understood what she was all about. She could make someone else have a heart attack, or worse.

"I can't do that, as much as I might want to. Isn't there something else?"

Madame Lucinda smiled at me. "I can't do anything more for you, but there might be someone who can. I'm expecting him soon, in fact, he may be here already."

"Who is it?" I tried to think of anyone who could help with the Wanda problem. My list of friends and family, even on Facebook, didn't include someone with Ghostbuster qualifications.

"He is a powerful sorcerer. Your friend, Wanda, met him long ago. He gave her a trinket that she cherished until she died. He won't leave it here with anyone else. He'll be back for it, and when he comes, you can ask him to take Wanda away. He'll know what to do."

The whole sorcerer angle of that plan left me a little unhappy. I'd known sorcerers since I'd started coming to the Ren Faire when I first got out of college. As far as I could tell, they specialized in BS, and trying to get free meals and rides out of town. I didn't believe there was one who would take Wanda anywhere with him.

"Well, thanks anyway. I guess I'll keep looking into it." I got up from the little table. It's not like I hadn't asked her before, and the answer was never forthcoming. She might have a dragon, but she either didn't know how to get rid of a ghost, or she wasn't telling.

"Do you have the trinket, Jessie?"

"Oh! I have some change that might have some silver in it." I reached into my pocket. There was an older silver dime in there.

Her eyes got big and greedy when I held it out, and she snatched it from my hand.

"Thank you." She smoothed back her hair and wiped her hands on a small towel as though she'd just eaten. "But I was referring to the trinket the sorcerer gave to Wanda. Is it in your possession?"

"If you're talking about Wanda's enchanted bracelet, I have it. I have all of her personal possessions. The police gave them to me because there was no one else to take them. We weren't friends, but I hated to just throw them away."

She nodded and smiled. "Then the sorcerer will find you. When he does, he'll ask if you wish a boon for the return of the trinket. You know what to say."

It was hard not to believe in the dragon. She was sitting right there looking at me like I was a snack. But a sorcerer? Not so much.

"Don't make the mistake of treating this request lightly," she warned. "He is powerful, and will take what you say quite literally."

"Sure." *So much for her help*. "A sorcerer is coming to take Wanda away." *Yeah, right.* "What's his name?"

"That I cannot say. He rarely uses the same name or form twice. I dare not speak his real name. I cannot afford the cost."

I thanked her, and eyeballed the dragon one more time. As much as I loved the Renaissance world, there were definitely some whackos in it.

I walked back outside into the blinding morning sun. Chase was approaching the tent. Someone was playing a dulcimer at the Main Gate, and a few of our bawdy ladies were welcoming visitors into the Village.

Fred, the Red Dragon, was pretending to breathe fire and giving out tickets to a fire eater's show at the Dutchman's Stage. I shivered thinking about Buttercup.

"You'll never get rid of me, dearie," Wanda purred. "I'm with you like snakes in the gutter. You'd best get accustomed to it."

I stared hard at her, and wished I could shoot her with an arrow. Maybe it was mean, but I was really frustrated. And it wouldn't have mattered anyway. I could shoot her with a hundred arrows and they would pass right through her. *Arrgghh!*

"Are you okay, Jessie?" Chase hugged me and gave me a lingering kiss. "You were staring really hard at Fred. Is something up?"

I held on to him tightly and closed my eyes. I wished it could always be this way—just me and him. Nothing bad could happen and Wanda could never get between us.

I wasn't sure he believed me about Wanda. He hadn't said he *didn't* believe me, but he kind of didn't treat it as seriously as I wanted him to. He didn't seem at all nervous or uncomfortable about the idea that she was watching us when we were alone together.

"I went to see Madame Lucinda about Wanda again."

"Oh. What did she say?"

"She said she couldn't help me—again. But a sorcerer is coming who can help." It suddenly struck me that Wanda had told me about her sorcerer/lover who'd given her the bracelet. How had Madame Lucinda known about it?

I decided that I'd probably given it away to her in my emotional blathering and didn't realize it. It had been a difficult two weeks.

There was one question I could clear up right away. "Could you do me a favor?"

"Anything." His strong arms stayed at my waist, and his handsome, arresting face was close to mine.

"Can you look in the tent and tell me what makes that dragon tick? I can't figure it out."

"I've never noticed a dragon in there." He gently smoothed a few flyaway strands of hair out of my face. "Let me check it out."

He stepped inside the tent. I could hear him talking to Madame Lucinda. I waited impatiently for him to come out. Wanda was gone, thank goodness, although that meant she was terrorizing someone else.

"Well?" I asked when he was out of the tent again. "What do you think?"

"You mean the dragon statue? That's the only dragon I saw in there."

I looked at him, thinking about all the things I loved about him. Chase was intelligent, sensitive. He was a history buff, and loved horses. He worked as a consulting patent attorney who researched patents for his wealthy clients in his spare time, mostly after the Village closed in the evenings. He worked hard and played hard. He was a good friend to the residents of the Village, and stood up for them when it was necessary.

But at that moment, I was too annoyed to care. "Dragon statue? I'm talking about a living, fire-breathing, small dragon." I ducked my head back into the tent. There was Madame Lucinda wearing her enigmatic smile, and petting Buttercup's head.

I looked at Chase. "It's right in there. How could you *miss* it?"

"I don't know, Jessie. I only saw a statue. It wasn't alive, and didn't breathe fire." He kissed my forehead. "You haven't been sleeping, and you've been upset about this thing with Wanda, and the wedding. You should get some rest while the museum is closed."

"In other words, you think I'm imagining it."

"I didn't say that."

The tension between us kept ramping up. I couldn't explain it, and I couldn't do anything about it. "I'll talk to you later, Chase."

"Sure. Lunch?"

"That's fine."

Two giggling teenagers dressed as spiders ducked inside the fortune teller's tent. I wondered what they'd find inside.

Five

Police officers still stood guard at the Arts and Crafts Museum across the cobblestones. Crime scene people were working around the front door, and at the site where Detective Almond thought Dave had been killed in the grass.

I wondered how Manny was doing at the police station. If I hadn't been so angry, I could have asked Chase to call about him. I'd lost that opportunity until lunch.

Staying focused wasn't easy. I couldn't worry about Manny, or anything else, if I wanted to find Dave's killer.

The two police officers glared at me, folding their arms across their chests. I wasn't welcome in my own museum.

But there were no police officers next door at the antique weapon museum. I walked inside the door under the guise of wondering how the exhibit was progressing.

I knew the man putting together the exhibit. Phil Ferguson was the owner of The Sword Spotte, a fine maker of swords. He was another old-timer at the Village.

His swords were coveted around the world. He was a nice man too. Although I had considered that he had access to the weapon museum, with the antique crossbow, and could have killed Dave. I rejected the idea as soon as it crossed my mind.

There were a dozen workmen there, putting up shelves and installing glass cases. I figured I might as well go ahead and see what they were doing—maybe ask a few pertinent questions. I wandered in and looked around.

"Jessie!" Phil saw me and came over. He had a clipboard in his hand, and was wearing jeans and a T-shirt instead of Renaissance gear. He was very short and studious looking, more like a librarian than a sword maker. "Come to check out the competition, eh?"

I laughed. "I don't think of you as competition. There are plenty of visitors to go around."

"I suppose that's true. I think of our museums as catering to different clientele too. The men and teenage boys will come in here to look around while the ladies drag the girls and small children to *your* place."

"I don't think it will be like that." I defended my museum. "We'll have something for everyone."

"And what's your first exhibit? Tapestry weaving! That's right! Every man's dream."

I was starting to get a little hot. I reminded myself that I wasn't here to argue with Phil. We'd never argued before. There was no reason for it now. Time would tell.

"I stopped by to take a look at the crossbow and bolts that Master Simmons donated to the museum. Would that be okay?"

"It would," he agreed. "If something hadn't happened to them the day after they were installed." He pointed to a blank space on the wall. There was a page of information about crossbows next to where the crossbow should have been.

"Were they stolen?"

He shrugged. “I don’t know. Chase and his men have looked everywhere for them. They would be worth a fortune to the right collector.”

I glanced around. “What about the workmen?”

“It happened at night when the workers were gone and the Village was closed. The doors weren’t locked yet—I didn’t expect a thief. Adventureland is giving me a hard time about it now too! They weren’t covered by insurance because the exhibit wasn’t open.”

I thought it was odd that the theft had happened right before Dave’s death. “Did you contact the police?”

“I let Chase take care of that stuff. As it is, we’ll be lucky to make our grand opening deadline. Master Simmons doesn’t have another crossbow like that one to donate. We’re gonna have to purchase one. It won’t be cheap, unless we go with a new one.”

“I see.”

“What are you looking for, Jessie?”

“We think Dave was killed with a bolt. Maybe not from *that* crossbow. The police are still working on it.”

“Poor old Dave.” He shook his head. “He was a good guy. Bad poker player, but a good sport. I’ll miss him.”

“You didn’t hear or see anything unusual last night, did you?”

“I wasn’t here after the gates closed. My sister had a new baby. My wife and I went to see her at the hospital.”

"That's great! Congratulations, Phil!"

"Thanks."

"There's something else." He glanced round. "I probably shouldn't speak ill of the dead, Jessie, but I know Dave owed some money to a bookie in town. He loved gambling on just about everything, you know. And he lost all the time."

"A bookie. Do you know who it is?"

"His name is John Healy. He runs most of the gambling that goes on in Myrtle Beach. I owed him money once. I didn't pay off on time, and he trashed my car. He said I'd be next. I managed to pay him off, and I stopped gambling."

"Did Dave owe Healey a lot of money?"

"He owed *everybody* money. He owed Healy more money than he could pay off in the next ten years. Dave was scared too. There just wasn't anything he could do about it."

"Thanks. Maybe I can do something with this. The police thought my assistant, Manny, could be guilty."

"That *lump*?" Phil laughed. "I don't think so! Dave could have beaten him off with his pots and pans that he loved to bang around."

I didn't think of Manny that way, but he was welcome to his opinion.

"Good luck trying to figure out what happened to Dave." Phil watched the workmen around us. "Be careful, Jessie. Healy is dangerous. You don't want to mess around with him."

I promised that I would be careful, and left the museum.

It was hard to believe a bookie would follow Dave into the Village and kill him here. But then what did I know about the thousands of strangers who visited each day? Any of them could have been killers, blackmailers, and bookies. Anything was possible.

It was clear that whoever had killed Dave was familiar with the Ren Faire, and had chosen his weapon well. I wondered how much Dave had owed Healy.

Chase was waiting at the foot of the stairs. "The queen said she saw you going in here. I thought I'd pick you up for lunch."

My heart melted at his beautiful smile. I couldn't stay mad at him. "What a nice surprise!"

"Is Polo's Pasta okay with you? I have to go over and talk to him anyway. I thought it could save me a few steps."

"That's fine. What's up over there?"

We started walking across the Village Green where musicians were playing, and children were throwing coins into the Good Luck Fountain. Smells of onions frying, and corn roasting were filling the warm, humid air—the scents of lunch from around the world at the Renaissance Faire.

"It's probably not a big deal. You know how the people at Polo's take everything personally. They want me to arrest Merlin because he refused to pay for lunch."

"Maybe he thought it was free lunch day."

Chase frowned. "You know they *never* do that kind of stuff at Polo's. They never even let the residents eat leftovers for reduced prices after the Village closes."

"Is Merlin there now?"

"He's waiting. You know he's not upset about it. Nothing bothers him."

"And they want you to sort it out?"

He shrugged. "That's my job. I'm sure I'll end up paying for his lunch, and I'll have to be reimbursed. I thought we might as well eat while we're there."

We left the lush green grass and got off on the cobblestones at Polo's Pasta. It was a small restaurant dedicated to the travels of Marco Polo, serving Italian food at the highest prices in the Village. But I had to admit, it was always a good meal.

Merlin was there with the owners, Lynda and Morris Bell.

Merlin was our resident wizard. He wore a purple robe with gold stars on it and a matching cone-shaped hat. He looked like you'd expect a wizard to look. His gray beard was scraggly, and his head was a little grizzled. He had a large nose and inquisitive brown eyes.

He was also the CEO of Adventureland, though most people who lived in the Village didn't know that. I only knew because Chase had told me. Merlin looked much different in a suit and tie.

He loved the Village more than anyone else I knew. I think he liked living there because he could truly be who he was—that and the occasional chance to flash people with his robe.

"I'm glad you're here, Sir Bailiff." Merlin held himself erect and brandished his staff. "These people are accosting me. I wish them removed."

Chase was nothing, if not diplomatic. "Hail, good wizard." He also had to be aware of the crowd of visitors in the restaurant. "Let us adjourn to the back room to work out a solution to this problem."

"There *is* no solution, Bailiff," Morris Bell stated flatly. "This is twice he's tried to stiff me on his lunch tab. I want my money. It's hard enough to make a living here."

"I am simply eating for all the other residents of the Village who would occasionally appreciate a free or reduced price meal. Can I get a *Huzzah!*?"

He turned to the people around him who resoundingly yelled, "*Huzzah!*"

This was something no one liked to have happen in the Village. It was worse than asking visitors for Lady Visa or Sir Master Card. It took them out of the mystery of traveling to another time and place.

The odd thing was that the visitors loved it.

"Get him out of here!" Morris, a short man with a mound of curly black hair on his head, yelled at Chase.

The restaurant crowd continued to chant, "*Huzzah! Huzzah*! Give them food!" They pounded on the wood tables and stamped their feet. The situation was rapidly getting out of control.

Morris shoved Merlin, and Lynda went to hide behind an empty table. Merlin retaliated by striking Morris in the chest with his staff.

To make a bad situation even worse, Wanda decided to find out what was going on. I saw her come through the gondola at the front of the restaurant. She laughed out loud as she did what she could to make matters worse.

Cups, bowls, and plates began to fly through the air. They smashed against the walls along with glasses, silverware, and pasta.

At first, no one seemed to notice—or they thought the tiff had become a food fight. It didn't take long to realize that food and eating utensils were *independently* taking flight.

"What the—?" Morris first looked angry and then fear took over. "Is this *your* doing, wizard?"

Merlin was just as mystified. He watched, open mouthed, as the restaurant seemed to come alive. "I can't do anything like this. I'm not a *real* wizard, you fool."

Wanda laughed as visitors began to run from the restaurant. Her abilities had increased. She was able to lift a man and toss him through a window. She didn't have to touch him to do it either.

Morris picked up a broom and held it before him like a sword. "I've heard people talking about this kind of thing today. They think the Village is haunted. It's just a trick. There is no such thing as ghosts."

"Oh no?" Wanda grabbed a large, metal coffee urn and smacked him in the head with it.

Morris dropped like a rug. Lynda ran to his side.

"I'm out of here." Merlin grabbed his hat and ran out the door. "Take care of it, Chase."

"Yes, Chase," Wanda urged. "Take care of *me*, won't you?"

Luckily Chase couldn't hear her. He ducked a hot plate of spaghetti that she threw his way when he ignored her.

I grabbed his arm and pulled him outside.

"Wanda?" He looked as though he was ready to believe that she was real now.

"Yes. She's stronger, and learning to do new things every day."

He pulled out his radio and called for backup. "This can't go on. People will stop coming to the Village."

I hated to sound smug, but I'd been trying to tell him since the day she'd appeared at our apartment in the Dungeon. "There is nothing we can do until the sorcerer comes to get his bracelet back."

He stared at me. "What?"

I shrugged. "That's what Madame Lucinda says. She told me we can ask him to take her with him. That's all we can do, unless I want to wish her on someone else. It's like she's linked to me."

It got quiet in Polo's Pasta. I saw Wanda fly out and throw me a kiss.

"She's gone now. I suppose it wasn't any fun once everyone else was gone."

"I'm going in to see if Morris is okay. You stay here."

Chase's reinforcements had arrived, and carefully stepped into the restaurant. I could already see the visitors who had been in Polo's spreading the tale via Facebook and Twitter. If Wanda wanted to cause trouble, she was doing a good job.

"What was that?" Merlin asked from behind a privy. "More to the point, is it over?"

I sat on a pretty purple bench in the shade. "It's over for now. Or at least *she's* gone for now. It was Wanda. She's blue, angry, and back for an encore."

He crept to the bench, surveying the spot before he sat down. "How do you know this, Jessie? Can you see her? Can you communicate with her?"

I laughed so hard that tears came to my eyes. I told him all about my last two terrible weeks with Wanda. "She's getting much worse."

"Why didn't you tell *me*?" Chase asked as he came around the corner. "I thought something was wrong with *us*. I don't know. Wedding jitters. Cold feet. Change of heart."

I got up and threw my arms around him. "Never. I would never change my heart about you. I was worried you might change your mind about *me*."

"You said Wanda was hanging around." He kissed me. "You didn't say all those other things were happening that you just told Merlin."

"I was embarrassed." I was glad it was out in the open. "And I didn't think you believed me."

"Yes, yes. Of course he believes you and you two still love each other." Merlin got to his feet, his pointy hat crooked on his head. "Now what can we do about *Wanda*?"

* * *

I told Merlin what Madame Lucinda had told me. He stormed away to speak with her, determined to force her to make Wanda leave the Village.

The security people helped Morris and Lynda clean up the mess. Morris was okay— just a little bruised and battered. He didn't want to go to the hospital. He also demanded that Chase find some way to get Wanda out of the Village.

Wanda had made him a true believer.

Chase and I got large pretzels from a nearby vendor for lunch. We sat on the bench outside Polo's Pasta and ate them with mustard. It was good to be able to *really* talk to him about Wanda's ghost, and my feelings about the wedding.

"I don't know what we can do about the wedding," he admitted. "This is a big deal for the Village. We both love it here and want to stay. If it helps them, it helps us, doesn't it?"

"We could elope first," I suggested. "Then the big wedding would only be another weird event at the Village. I could be Lady Jessie and you could be the Bailiff. I want to start our lives together as Jessie Morton and Chase Manhattan. I hope that makes sense."

"Let me see what I can do." He wiped a smear of mustard from my chin. "I love you. We'll work something out. And we'll find a way to take care of Wanda."

"I love you too." I knew there probably wasn't anything he could do. I knew I was stuck with the big wedding. I was just having a hard time adjusting to it.

The team of security guards, all dressed as peasants, started coming out of Polo's Pasta. They were shaking their heads and complaining about cleaning up the mess. Each of them was covered in tomato sauce. They smelled delicious!

Chase got a call from the castle and frowned. "There are reporters at the gate. Someone took pictures of the stuff flying around in Polo's. They want to walk through the haunted Village with their cameras and see if anything else happens."

"Well, Halloween at the Village is always popular. Maybe real spooks will be good for business too."

"For a while." He put away his radio. "If people get hurt, that will fade very quickly. And if we lose shop owners like Polo's, it will happen even faster."

I walked with him to the Main Gate where he'd have to meet with the reporters. I told him about the bookie that may have been responsible for Dave's death by crossbow.

"I suppose it's possible," he admitted. "After what I just saw, anything is possible. Jessie, have you tried reasoning with Wanda? I know the two of you didn't get along while she was alive, but maybe if you explained things to her, it would help."

"You mean about the Village closing of she keeps it up? I'll try. I don't think she'll listen. Good luck with the reporters." I kissed him quickly and we parted ways.

Merlin was emerging from Madame Lucinda's purple and gold tent. I could tell by the confused and dazed look on his face that she didn't have any better answers for him.

Maybe he'd seen Buttercup!

"There you are!" Merlin pointed at me with his staff. "I want to talk to you."

As he reached me, a group of knights from the Field of Honor thundered by on the cobblestones. Their armor gleamed in the sun, individual colors flashing, swords and lances drawn. Behind them came their squires and lackeys carrying their brightly colored banners, and signs that showed the times of the next joust.

Merlin grasped my arm and held on to his hat. "You know, I've told these riders a dozen times not to ride up so quickly. It scares the bejesus out of me. I'm sure other people are scared too. Not good for business. Not good at all."

But as I looked around, visitors were standing on the grass, to one side or the other of their path. They were applauding and laughing. Children loved the riders. Adults were dazzled by their precision artistry.

"Like Wanda?" I suggested.

"Exactly." He scowled back at the fortune teller's tent. "She was no help at all! I don't think she knows how to get rid of a ghost. I'll have to consult my own sources."

"Chase doesn't know how to get rid of a ghost either, but I'll mention the riders to him," I promised. "I wanted to talk to you about Dave the Madman's murder."

"Yes?" He started up the path back to his apothecary that was so loved by all the visitors. Horace the moldy moose was waiting, along with his colored vials and bugs.

"You know Dave was killed, right?"

"Of course! I know everything that goes on around here."

That might have been an exaggeration, but I wasn't questioning it. "Well, I've been looking into it. I think Dave may have been killed because he owed money to a bookie in Myrtle Beach."

"Really?" He paused and stroked his beard. "Does the bookie have a name?"

"John Healy."

"Never heard of him." He used his staff to quicken his pace past Totally Toad Footstools and the Treasure Trove.

"Apparently, Dave was gambling, and losing heavily."

"Why are you telling me this?" He stopped again. "Why are you so interested? Were you having an affair with Dave?"

"No! Of course not! I'm marrying Chase in two weeks!" I took a deep breath. "I was looking into it because the police are questioning Manny, my assistant. The antique crossbow and bolts Master Simmons donated to the museum are missing too. They may have been the murder weapons."

He'd stopped again near the big fountain on the King's Highway between Our Lady's Gemstones and Sarah's Scarves. "Manny? Oh you mean the young Prince."

"Not you too!"

He chuckled. "You have your sights set on him, don't you?"

"Merlin!"

"Lady Jessie, stay out of police business—for once! Pick some flowers for your wedding bouquet. Deal with that pesky blue ghost. There must be other things you can do!"

I let him walk away that time. There was no use trying to talk to him about it. I could never tell if he really knew much about the Village or he was just crazy anyway. If he did know something useful, it was hard trying to get him to tell anyone else!

It appeared, for all of my belief that I could make things better, nothing was changing.

I caught sight of Detective Almond coming toward me, and would have scurried away, but it was too late. He was already flagging me down.

Now what?

Six

"Jessie Morton," Detective Almond greeted me. "Just the woman I was searching for. I'm looking for a crossbow, and more information about your assistant. The man has no background at all, did you know that?"

"Manny?" I answered cautiously. "Why don't you ask him about his background?"

"Because as soon as we got him to the station, his lawyer took him away, and now we can't find him. Any ideas?"

"Well, I know he had a background check. Adventureland requires it. I couldn't hire him until they'd finished with it." *Manny got a lawyer—smart!* "As far as a crossbow, I can't help you. If you're looking for the one that's missing from the antique weapon museum, you'll have to talk to someone else."

"Have you seen a photo of it or anything? Because right now, I've got zip."

Chase had probably told him about the missing crossbow and bolts. "You know it can't be the murder weapon, right? The crossbow is too old, and the bolts that go with it are warped. I don't think even an expert marksman could hit a person with it."

"Who told you that? It wasn't mentioned in the report on it."

"Uh." *Think fast, Jessie! Master Simmons doesn't want to be involved.* "I saw it. It's valuable because of its age and history, but that's all."

"What about another crossbow?"

"Sure. They sell them all around the Village. Anyone could own one."

"But these bolts were specific to this crossbow, right?"

"I didn't see the bolt that killed Dave. Do you have a picture of that?"

He did, as a matter of fact. He pulled it up on his phone. There was still a spot of Dave's blood on it. "There you go. Recognize it?"

It was definitely one of the antique bolts that went with the crossbow Master Simmons had on his wall for many years. "It looks straighter. I think someone must have fixed it so it could be used to kill Dave."

Detective Almond's eyes narrowed as he gazed at children playing on the swan swing, and throwing rubber frogs against the wall at the frog catapult.

"Why would someone go through so much trouble to use that bolt if they could pick one up with a crossbow anywhere?" he asked.

I thought about it. "To make it look like someone else killed Dave?"

"Someone who owned the antique crossbow?"

"No." I backed away quickly from that position. Whatever trouble Master Simmons had been in, I didn't want to be responsible for bringing it back to haunt him again. "I don't know. Sorry."

"All right." He nodded, and took a deep breath. "This place drives me crazy."

"I know."

"Well, for now, we need to find those records on your assistant, Jessie." He showed me a piece of paper Manny had filled out. "There's no trace of a man named Manawydan Argall. He doesn't exist. I even checked with the Feds. He has no driver's license, no social security number. Nothing. Why do you think that is?"

"Because your computers aren't working right?" I knew Manny was real. "We have that information. I hired him. Adventureland may seem like a crazy place, but they require personal information and they do a thorough background check. Maybe you're not looking in the right place."

"Okay. Show me the information you have on him, and I'll take it from there."

I wasn't sure that was legal. Wasn't he supposed to have a warrant or something?

Maybe Bart would know! I was going to take a chance on it. I didn't want to get Detective Almond even more set against Manny.

"The information is stored at the castle on the computers. I'm sure someone could print up a copy of his employment records for you." *Or Bart could turn down the request.*

"Let's go." His eyes watched mine warily. "I don't know how his lawyer got him out of my hands so quickly, Jessie, but I still want to talk to him. If you know how to arrange a meeting, I suggest you do it right away."

"Like you said, he doesn't have a cell phone. I don't know how to get in touch with him."

"He doesn't have a vehicle registered to him either." His voice was starting to sound impatient. "Does he live here in the Village or off site?"

"I don't know." I shrugged. "I've never noticed."

Detective Almond put his hands on his hips. "Are you holding back on me?"

"No. I'm telling you that I've been too busy to check where my assistant was living. You can alert Chase so he and the security people can look for Manny around the Village. Otherwise, I really don't know what to tell you."

"Okay." He nodded. "Let's start with the castle. I'll call Chase on the way. You better hope Manny's information is in the system."

I started to ask why, but thought better of it. Detective Almond wasn't in a very good mood. Of course, when was he? He always made it clear that he didn't like being called out here.

I wondered what had happened that had made him hate the place so much. After all, he was the original bailiff, way before Chase's, or Roger's time. At some point, he must have liked it. I would have asked him, but that was a conversation for another time.

I took advantage of the twenty minutes it took to walk to the castle to tell Detective Almond about the bookie Dave had owed money to. All the while I was scheming about ways I could help Manny out of his situation.

Clearly the police were short on suspects. Manny not being in the system, admitting that he and Dave had argued, and that he was good with a crossbow, made him an attractive suspect. I hadn't realized how attractive, or I wouldn't have sent him with the police so easily.

"I know John Healy. I'll check your bookie angle," Detective Almond promised as we passed Gus at the castle gate. "How did you find out about that?"

"One of the men working at the museum told me." I didn't think Phil would want me to mention *him* during a police investigation either.

"One of them, huh? Is there something else I should know, Jessie?"

"No. Sometimes I forget things. That's all." I laughed. "You know how it is with the wedding and all."

Gus didn't challenge us as we entered the castle. The police bring out a certain fearful respect from Village residents. No doubt Gus had some past dealings with them too.

We walked past the feasting area where there were dozens of shields and tapestries hanging on the wall. None of them were real or valuable. Anything worth money was kept in the main part of the castle where the king and queen lived.

"Well, well." Bart rolled to his feet. "You're here again, Jessie. And Detective Almond. To what do I owe the honor?"

Detective Almond shook Bart's massive hand. His much smaller one looked like a doll's in comparison.

"Bart. Good to see you. I'm here on official police business. I need the employment records for Jessie's assistant."

"Manawydan Argall," I supplied.

"You know, you should have a warrant for that information," Bart said.

Yes!

"But you're not going to make me get one, are you?" Detective Almond smiled at him, but it was like a sheathed sword. It could come out and cut you at any time.

Bart looked at me. "I suppose it will be all right. Although, if Manny sues the Village, you might be in some trouble."

Oh well.

"The police think Manny doesn't exist," I filled him in.

"Okay." Bart shrugged and sat back down in front of the computer. "I'll look him up."

We waited as Bart searched through the employee records. There were a lot of them. It took a while. Then a tiny screen popped up. "Nope. No Manawydan Argall. Sorry."

"What? I filed his employment application with Adventureland. It has to be in there. Can you look again?"

Bart looked again. He even cross referenced. "No. He's not in here."

By that time, Chase was there—probably alerted by one of his security men that the police were in the Village. "What's going on?"

Detective Almond explained everything about his search for Manny. "Have you seen him around the Village?"

"Not since you took him in," Chase answered. "There has to be personnel information about him in the computer."

"Nope. Sorry. He's just not in there." Bart shook his head.

"I had him fill out an application," I argued. "Adventureland sends me a check for him every two weeks. Doesn't that mean he has to be in the system?"

"Bart, check with corporate," Chase said. "Something is screwed up. In the meantime, we'll look around for Manny. That's about all we can do."

Detective Almond's fleshy face got a tough look on it. I could see something of his younger self in those taut lines.

"I can do a little more than that. I'm issuing an arrest warrant for Mr. Argall. If any of you see him, call me. Chase, detain him when he shows up. I'll talk to you later."

* * *

"I'm sorry, lady," Bart said after Detective Almond had stormed out of the castle. "If you'd given me a few minutes, I might have been able to come up with something for your friend."

"That's okay," I told him. "I didn't expect you to lie about it. I wonder what happened to the information."

"Bart's going to track that down," Chase said. "Aren't you?"

Bart bowed. "I shall endeavor to do the appointed task."

"Thanks." I hugged him. I can't really get my arms all the way around him, but I can hug most of him.

"If you find anything, call me first," Chase told him.

"Okay."

I left the castle with Chase. Gus saluted him as we walked by.

Sir Reginald, who'd served as a knight on the Field of Honor, wished us a good day for our wedding. He was hurrying into the castle as we were leaving. A large group of visitors were accompanying him. They were all dressed in expensive Renaissance garb.

He called attention to the fact that we were the couple getting married in the posters. "Lady Jessie and Bailiff Chase Manhattan are exemplary figures here." Sir Reginald rarely spoke to either of us on a normal day. His stiff collar and snooty nose only allowed him to look at important people in the Village.

There was no doubt the group with him fit in that category, if they were receiving a personal tour of the castle from Sir Reginald.

Chase and I hurried away after smiling, bowing, and curtseying.

"Do you think you might have kept a copy of Manny's application?" Chase asked as we took the cobblestone walkway that led to the other side of the Village, away from the Main Gate.

"I don't think so. I can check in my office—as soon as they let me in the museum again. But I think I'd remember making a copy since they charge for it at the castle. I added Manny's application to the basket of papers that need to be put into the computer, like everybody does. When I got the notice to hire him, I assumed everything was okay."

"I'm sure you're right. It's what I do when I hire a new security person too. This was a bad time for something to get lost."

"I know."

We walked past Polo's Pasta. It was still closed. People were standing outside the door reading the notice that said when it would re-open. It would probably be the most popular place in the Village for a while.

"What happened with the reporters?" I asked him.

"What always happens—they get a free pass to the Village, take pictures, and talk to whoever they want. If it was up to me, they'd have to clear their pictures with security before they post them all over the Internet. But that's not going to happen."

"They're bound to hear some stories about Wanda."

"Let's hope the stories are enough to make the Village sound more interesting, and not so scary that no one wants to come. They call her the Blue Lady now. Have you heard that?"

"That means there are some people who can see her, besides me and Shakespeare. I think a blue ghost is a little out of the ordinary."

Chase was bound for the Field of Honor. "We've had a lot of complaints up there today. Wanda's been busy.

"I wonder if Sir Marcus is still jousting since Wanda's death."

"You mean the young one all the wenches are sighing over?" He laughed. "I think I've seen him up there a few times in the last two weeks. Why?"

"Well, you know he was Wanda's lover right before she died. When I talked to him the day she was killed, she attacked him. But she wasn't as strong as she is now. She could only throw a few leaves around. If he's still jousting, she could make things a lot worse for him."

"Let's check it out."

I wasn't looking forward to searching for Wanda. She'd been quiet. I was grateful not to have her in my face.

But when we reached the Field of Honor, a joust was in progress, and Wanda was doing her best to cause trouble.

The horses were especially vulnerable—which put the knights riding them in a dangerous position.

Wanda was flying up and down the dirt field, scaring the horses into throwing their riders and running away. She laughed as she tossed clods of dirt and horse manure at visitors in the stands. The two young cheerleaders—one for the queen's knight and one for the black knight—were running off the field to get away from the chaos.

Chase saw a young squire, probably sixteen or so, trapped on the field by the frightened movements of the horses. He dashed in and grabbed the boy, tossing him across his shoulder.

The queen's knight fell a second later—heavy with armor and weapons—exactly where the boy had been.

"Thanks." The handsome lad wiped dirt from his face and smiled at Chase, his clear blue eyes sparkling. "I don't know what was wrong in there today. It was like the horses were crazy."

Chase rumpled the boy's red hair. "Just stay out of the arena for now until we can figure it out."

"Not a problem. You're the Bailiff, Chase Manhattan, right? I'm Tim."

Chase shook his hand. "Nice to meet you, Tim."

"Wow! I'd like to have your job someday."

"Maybe you will." Chase grinned. "I started as a squire too."

There was no further time for pleasantries. Wanda was making her way to the second story of the viewing building at the far end of the field. Queen Olivia and her court were watching the joust from there.

"She's going after the queen now," I told Chase. "We have to do something."

"I can't even see her, Jessie. What do you have in mind?"

I saw Sir Marcus leading his horse off the field. "Maybe we can get Wanda's lover to help out."

"Okay. Maybe he can distract her. I'll get the queen and her court out of there."

We split up, and I ran to talk to Sir Marcus. I wasn't sure what I could say to convince him to help me. It could be very dangerous for him.

I was surprised he'd stayed on at the Village after Wanda had attacked him last time. He'd probably convinced himself that it wasn't real, or it was an unusual turn of events. I think that's what most people do when confronted with something they don't understand and can't explain.

"Sir Marcus!" I yelled out. "I must speak with you."

In this case, the young knight had convinced himself that it was my fault that he'd been attacked the day Wanda had died.

"Stay away from me." He held his fingers together to create a cross as though he was fending off a vampire.

Marcus was an exceptionally good-looking and charismatic young knight. He'd only been at the Village a few weeks, but it was long enough to cause havoc with several ladies' hearts.

"Not going to hurt you," I promised, watching Chase herd the queen's large court out of the building beside us. "I need your help."

He pulled out a clove of garlic that was sewn into a knot he wore around his neck. "I'm protected now. Go ahead. Try me."

"It's not me you have to worry about. It's Wanda."

As if on cue, the blue bane of my life showed up beside us.

"Isn't this fun?" she laughed wickedly. "I never knew there was such excitement to be had at the joust."

"Someone is going to get hurt," I told her. "You're getting carried away. I know you're angry because you're dead. I'm sorry about that. I can't change the facts, and you can't make it better by ruining the Village."

"You're not paying attention, dearie." She ruffled Sir Marcus's blond curls, bringing a fearful yipe from him. "The press loves me. They're talking about hiring a medium who can talk to me and take my demands. Doesn't that sound absolutely luscious?"

"Who are you talking to?" Marcus spun around, trying to fend off the unseen hands that caressed him. "Who's there?"

"It's me, my love." Wanda planted a big kiss on his mouth.

He could feel it—bad luck for him.

"Maybe I should take you with me, Marcus, my love. I could use a young lover here. I'm all alone. Wouldn't you like to lie dead with me?"

"Get it away from me!" Marcus was trying to get rid of Wanda like he was shooing a fly. "Get it off of me."

"You can't kill him." I was firm about that. "The fortune teller told me how to get rid of you. If you hurt him, I'll do it."

"I don't believe you." Wanda was lifting Marcus off the ground. "You would've done it already."

"The only thing stopping me from passing you off to someone else is feeling bad for the other person. If you hurt someone, I won't feel like that anymore. Maybe a nice boiler room attendant might be more in your league."

"You wouldn't."

I smiled brilliantly, even though my heart was pounding as Marcus kept moving upward, no matter how hard he tried to squirm away from Wanda's hold.

"No more Village. No more visitors. No more Shakespeare or Polo's Pasta."

Marcus suddenly dropped to the dusty ground at my feet. He appeared to be unhurt, and wasted no time running out of the jousting arena.

"There you go. No need to whine, Jessie." Wanda's smile was awful to behold. "Just having a bit of fun. You should learn to relax."

"Maybe I could if you'd rest in peace somewhere outside the Village."

Wanda surveyed the viewing stand where Queen Olivia had been. It was empty now. "That was a dirty trick. You distracted me until Livy could get away."

"Just remember what I said. I'll pass you off to someone who never sees the light of day, much less the Ren Faire, if you hurt anyone. I'm not kidding, Wanda."

She lifted me slightly into the air. Her face was directly in front of me, blocking out everything. "Don't threaten *me*, Jessie. I could hurt you."

I didn't answer, and she dropped me too. I didn't have as far to fall as Marcus but it still hurt. She laughed and disappeared, no doubt going to make someone else's life miserable.

"Are you okay?" Chase was there a second later and helped me to my feet. "That was something. How can she do that?"

I brushed dirt off of my skirt. I hoped it was *just* dirt. "I don't know. She keeps getting stronger. We need some way to contain her or get rid of her. I'm out of answers."

Chase put his arm around me as the rain that had been threatening all day began to fall. It made little spitting noises on the ground and the wind picked up, blowing the flags and banners around us.

We ran for shelter at the viewing stands as the cold rain became a downpour. The day was probably over for the Village. Some visitors would hang around, waiting to see if the rain let up. Most would just leave, even though that meant forfeiting their day ticket.

"Let's go home." Chase kissed the side of my head. "Maybe Wanda will keep herself busy for a while."

We ran back to the Dungeon where we shared a small apartment above the fake jail cells that were open to visitors. Chase turned off the soundtrack of moaning and wailing from the plastic prisoners who lived in terrible conditions.

"Any sign of Wanda?" He kissed my neck and throat.

"No. Not yet anyway."

"Good." He started unlacing my blouse. "We need to take advantage of this time, my lady."

"What if visitors come in?"

"We'll pretend we're part of the exhibit." He grinned. "At least until I can get you upstairs."

I yelped as he picked me up in his arms and laughed as he handed me the key to the door.

"Hast thou a problem with insufficient hands, Sir Bailiff?"

He playfully slapped my butt. "Not at all, Lady Wench. Open yon portal and grant us egress."

Once we were inside the apartment, we were both laughing and busily removing our clothes, whispering silly things to each other as lovers do.

A knock at the door stopped us.

"Wanda?" Chase mouthed.

"She doesn't knock."

"Lady Jessie," Manny called out. "Are you available? There seems to be a problem."

Seven

Chase and I quickly hopped back into our clothes and opened the door.

"Fred the Red Dragon told me the police were here looking for me today." He stalked into the room and turned around. "He said they want to question me further."

"It's worse than that." Chase pulled up one of the small chairs we had at a tiny table in the corner. "Detective Almond issued an arrest warrant for you. The police get a little testy when you get away without answering their questions."

Manny sat down hard. "I can't believe this. There must be some mistake. I've never done anything wrong. I didn't kill that despicable man. How did I get in this position?"

"It has something to do with not being able to find any records for you." I sat on the bed. "You don't have any ID. How have you gone through life?"

He wrung his hands and looked around the room as though it might provide inspiration. "No one can know who I really am."

"The thing with being a prince, right?" Chase nodded. "Now might be a good time to drop that fantasy."

"It's not a fantasy, Sir Bailiff," Manny protested. "And I must stay hidden—unless I want my father to come and drag me home."

"What about the information you gave me for the employment application?"

"I'm sorry about that." Manny smiled. "I wanted to work here so badly. I gave you false information, Lady Jessie. A friend of mine back home, who is very good with computers, took care of it for me. I hope you can forgive me."

"You don't have to worry about me forgiving you," I pointed out. "The police have to get an understanding of why there's nothing in the database about you."

Manny heaved a sigh. His black eyes were tortured. "If anyone finds out I'm here, I'm doomed."

Chase laughed. "Come on, Manny. I think that might be putting it a little dramatically. What's wrong? Did you leave home with bad feelings? None of that matters in comparison to getting you out of this scrape."

"Yes. I sneaked away from my home." Manny's demeanor changed. He actually looked regal and proud. "My father is the king of Zamboulia. I am his only heir."

"Manny, I think that's the country from the movie *Coming to America*," I said. "Did you recently see that movie?"

"No. Seriously, Lady Jessie. My father is the king of Zamboulia. I am the crown prince. That is why I know so little about your culture. I ran away, hoping to have many adventures before I have to take my father's place on the throne of my country."

"Detective Almond isn't going to buy that story," Chase said. "Not without some heavy proof."

"If I tell him the truth, and he contacts my father, the royal guards will drag me back home. I shall never have this opportunity again."

Chase and I exchanged disbelieving glances.

"How did you get a lawyer?" I asked him.

"Another friend from Zamboulia who I swore to secrecy."

Chase ran his hand around the back of his neck. "Look, I want to help you, Manny. I really do. But I have to call the police. It's part of my job. You can tell them your story about being a crown prince—but it better be true."

"I would rather die!" Manny declared dramatically, but those were real tears in his eyes.

"Okay." Chase got to his feet, towering over Manny. "I think you're gonna have to come clean about—whatever you're into. Call your lawyer, and have him meet you here, and then I'll call the police. I can help you with bail money if the police arrest you."

"I have plenty of gold with me." Manny got to his feet. "I don't need help paying the police to release me, if that is what it takes."

"It's more complicated than that." I tried to explain. "Let us help you. You can hide out here until we see if we can find the bookie that might've killed Dave, or some other lead to his death that will get you off the hook. If the police can't find you, they can't arrest you."

Manny's eyes grew hopeful. "You would do this thing for me?"

"Yes," I solemnly replied.

"No," Chase said at the same time.

"We have to help him," I persuaded. "We're the only friends he has."

Chase grinned at Manny as he grabbed my hand. "Excuse us a minute."

We stepped outside the apartment and stood on the stairs.

"I can't help him," Chase whispered. "I have to call the police. It's my job. I work with Detective Almond. You know that."

"Manny is our friend. We know he's not guilty. We can't just hand him over like yesterday's laundry."

"Funny you didn't feel like that today!"

"That was different."

"He has to come clean with the police, Jessie. You know he's not a crown prince, hiding out at the Village. He might have some problems with his family or something, but who doesn't? Better that than problems with the police."

I didn't know what to say that would change his mind. I thought about what Madame Lucinda had told me about the sorcerer who was supposed to be coming to take back his bracelet.

I leaned against Chase and he held me close. “What if he’s the sorcerer that Madame Lucinda said was coming?” I whispered the words as quietly as I could. I didn’t believe it for a minute, and I didn’t want to give Manny any other crazy ideas.

“What?” Chase said in his normal voice, and I shushed him. In a quieter tone, he said, “Sorcerer? Really, Jessie?”

“You didn’t believe Wanda was a ghost either,” I reminded him.

“I didn’t say that.”

“You didn’t have to. Until we were at Polo’s when Wanda struck, you thought I was just tired and felt guilty about her.”

He frowned. “That wasn’t exactly what I thought. Anyway, I believed that you really thought you saw her.”

“Whatever. It works out the same way.” I started whispering close to his ear again. “What if there really is a sorcerer? We don’t know if he’s good or bad. He obviously wants to keep his identity a secret. Maybe this is him. It would explain the crazy stuff about Manny not having any ID.”

Chase shook his head, his braid moving across his shoulder. “I don’t know. It sounds totally insane. I can’t tell Detective Almond we think Manny is a sorcerer.”

I shrugged. “Don’t tell him anything. Until we know what’s really going on, we could hide him here. If he’s a crown prince—or a sorcerer—we can explain it to the police later.”

His arms tightened around me. I could see by his expression that this wasn't sitting well with him. "All right. For now, anyway. We'll let him stay here."

"Thank you."

He turned his head and kissed me fiercely on the mouth. "But we have to find some way to get around Wanda's ghost and our possible sorcerer for some private time, right?"

"Indeed."

We went back into the apartment. Manny was pacing the floor. He stopped and stared at us like a caged animal.

"Well?"

"We're going to let you stay here with us for now," I told him. "We'll try to figure this out. I can't promise how long Chase can keep this a secret, Manny."

"Thank you." He hugged me first and then Chase. "Thank you both so much. You don't know what this means to me. You will be amply rewarded for your trust. I swear it."

"It's almost six-thirty." Chase looked at the clock on the wall. It had been a gift from the queen for his service three years ago. "If we're going to eat at free or reduced prices, we'd better get a move on."

"There should be plenty since everyone went home early. It's still raining. Let's just eat at the Pleasant Pheasant."

The Pleasant Pheasant was right across the cobblestones from us. Once Manny was settled in, we dashed back out through the rain, and joined dozens of other residents already eating hot stew and spicy chili. One of the violinists from the Stage Caravan was playing, and the mood was festive, despite the rain.

Hephaestus set down two big tankards of ale on the table. “Good evening to you Sir Bailiff, Lady Jessie. We’ve plenty of bread, chili, and stew. There’s a serve-yourself table set. Eat what you like.”

Hephaestus was a tall, broad, heavily-bearded man who’d taken to wearing a hat since his hair had started disappearing. Tonight he wore a red felt cap with a green feather in it.

He was always friendly to residents, and was the head of the Food Guild in the Village. It was a position of great honor since it denoted trust from his fellow foodies. He spoke for them when there was a problem.

There were twelve guilds in the Village. They voted on what their people needed, and negotiated contracts with Adventureland.

There was the Craft Guild, represented by Hans Von Rupp, the blacksmith. They were always feuding with the Artist Guild that Sam DaVinci headed. The Weapons Guild was represented by Master Archer Simmons, and the Magic Creatures Guild was represented by Merlin.

Robin Hood was top man of the Forest Guild, primarily made up of his Merry Men and Women. The Entertainer’s Guild was currently headed by Little Bo Peep—although there was some talk of Mother Goose taking it over. The harp player at the Merry Mynstrel Stage, Susan Halifax, was head of the Musician’s Guild.

Shopkeepers didn't belong to guilds. They were above that kind of things since they paid rent to the Village. Chase and I weren't guild members. We spoke for ourselves, when anyone would listen.

The crowd was a mixed bag, filled with shopkeepers and guild members. Chase and I skirted around some couples who were still wearing their colorful belly-dancer's costumes from Stage Caravan. We filled bowls with the hearty, flavorful stew.

I put a couple of pieces of bread in my skirt pocket. There was no way to take chili or stew back for Manny. There was some yogurt in the mini fridge at the apartment. That would have to do for tonight. Anything else might look suspicious. Tomorrow, we'd have to think of something different.

"So, where do we start looking for our killer?" Chase asked when we were seated again. "There's a rush on this now, Jessie. *You-know-who* can't stay with us forever."

I didn't blame him for not mentioning Manny's name. The pub was crowded. Anyone could hear us talking. The Village was a hotbed of fast moving gossip. If we weren't careful, Detective Almond would be waiting for us when we got back to the Dungeon.

"I think we should work the bookie angle." I sipped my ale. "That's our best lead."

"And what did you say his name was?" Chase pulled out a pencil and paper from his side pouch. "He might've been hired in the last few days. They've been ramping up new hires more than usual for the wedding. Maybe there's some kind of glitch in the computer system that caused

Manny's name to be lost. A glitch like that could let us hire someone like this bookie too."

He looked so cute—kind of like Detective Almond—with his pencil and paper. Only Chase was a million times cuter and sexier. It almost took my breath away thinking that we would be married soon.

"The workman said his name was John Healy. I guess we could have Bart look him up, though he probably wouldn't use his real name."

Chase leaned across the table close to me. "I think it's unlikely a bookie would come and work here to kill a man who owes him money. If he'd kind of randomly stopped in, and killed him, that could make sense. I don't see it the other way. It would be too much work to accomplish the goal."

"You might be right. It's the only thing we have right now."

"The missing crossbow seems to be part of this."

"Except that no one could have used it to kill Dave," I reminded him. "I know it *seems* like that theft is involved, but it might only be to throw the murder off on someone else."

"Someone else like who?" Chase looked up at me. "You have another person in mind?"

"I can't tell you right now. It's another person that works with arrows and bows." I hoped he'd see where I was going with that.

"Oh! I get it. *He* could be part of this?"

"I don't think so, but *he* asked me to keep him out of it."

"That's a little suspicious in itself, isn't it?"

"No. Not coming from *him*." "Jessie—

"

"Not *him*!" He knew how I felt about Master Simmons. I wouldn't give him away for anything, not even Manny. He'd been like a father to me.

"Well, let's hope we can keep *him* out of it."

I told him that I wanted to talk to Roger Trent about Dave's gambling problems. "That could help make a case against John Healy."

He kissed my hand. "You're right. It's best to find out as much as we can about Dave." His radio went off. "What's up?"

"There are lights on at the Lady of the Lake Tavern," one of his security people said. "What do you want us to do?"

Eight

"It's probably only the new owner," Chase returned. "Make sure you see some ID."

After the incident at Polo's Pasta, the security guards were on edge. They weren't happy with the idea of going into the old tavern at night, not knowing who was in there.

Chase sighed. "The two of you wait there. I'll be over in a few minutes."

I could hear the rain still pounding on the roof of the Pleasant Pheasant. It wasn't a nice night to go for a walk.

"At least the Village is closed so you can wear rain gear," I said. "I'd like to go too."

"Okay. Is that to get away from our new roomie, or to be with me?"

I laughed and kissed him. "A little of both."

Chase took my hand, his brown eyes intent on my face. "I happen to know a nice little place over that way that's empty right now. We could stop in for a while after we meet the new owners at the tavern."

I frowned, trying to think of someplace that was empty over there. The only spot I could think of was—"You mean Wanda's cottage? Are you crazy?"

He laughed. "I guess that answers my question about whether or not you want to spend time with me. You don't even want to go into a cottage where a woman was gruesomely murdered."

"That probably wouldn't bother me as much as the appearance of the murdered, blue woman who would be joining us. In the mood for a threesome, are we?" I did my best impression of Wanda's British accent.

"Yeah. Forget that idea. Let's go."

Hephaestus shouted out his farewell as we were leaving. We ran out past Hans Von Rupp, the Village blacksmith. He was with Susan Halifax. They called out quick greetings as the four of us dodged the deluge.

Manny was watching TV when we got back to the apartment. He'd already found the yogurt, and Chase's chocolate power bars. I gave him the bread, and promised we'd try to do better tomorrow.

"Please don't worry about me," he said. "I'll get by. You are kind enough to let me stay here for now. I can take care of myself."

I changed into a pair of shorts and put on my knee-high rubber boots. Chase didn't change. We both got out our plastic rain ponchos and cautioned Manny against opening the door for anyone.

"We'll both be in hot water if Detective Almond finds you here," Chase said. "Jessie and I have keys. Don't answer the door."

Manny bowed respectfully. "I shall obey your commands, Sir Bailiff."

Chase and I went back out into the night. There were only a few street lights in the Village. They were made to look like Victorian gas lights, although those wouldn't have been around during the Renaissance. Most of the light came from the windows of the shops and houses—golden light pouring out into the darkness.

It was a case of trying to provide safety for the residents, without losing the ambiance of the surroundings. Maintaining a Renaissance atmosphere in modern times was always a challenge.

There were several stadium lights that could be turned on to clean up after a late event or do repair work as needed. They were only on a few times a year.

"Did you see what he was watching?" Chase asked as we cut across the cobblestones and walked across the soft, damp grass of the Village Green. "I Love Lucy. The man is either a crown prince, and out of touch with the real world, or he really is a sorcerer."

"I know. I've always known he was odder than the rest of us."

"Yeah." He laughed. "That's a major judgment to make. Odder than Bawdy Betty? Or Bart and Daisy?"

"I think so. Even odder than the Brothers of the Sheaf." I could hear the brothers chanting as they baked bread for the next day at the Monastery Bakery. The scent of the baking bread wafted across the Village, even in the rain.

"I'm afraid I'd still believe the crown prince story over the sorcerer," Chase said. "I've met too many people who said they were sorcerers."

"That's what I was thinking when Madame Lucinda told me in the first place. But now—talking to Wanda—my perspective has changed."

He laughed again, and put his arm around me as we walked through the quiet Village. "You know, this is when I like it best. It's quiet and people are inside for the night. It seems real, doesn't it?"

"Yes." I smiled at the thought. "We would have been excellent Renaissance people."

We could see the lights shining from the tavern long before we reached the front door. The two men Chase had told to meet us there were huddled under the heavy branches of the Hanging Tree. They popped out when they saw us.

"Any movement?" Chase asked.

"No. No vehicles. No furniture." The first man was still in his Renaissance garb. "If someone is moving in tonight, they're mighty quiet about it."

"Well, it's not like they need our permission. We already knew they were coming."

I went with Chase to welcome the new owners of the tavern. I was as interested to see who they were as anyone. You couldn't always trust the gossip even though most of the time, it was correct. Sometimes, it was way off.

The two security men stood behind us as Chase knocked on the solid wood door. It opened slowly, and a slight, older woman answered.

"Yes?"

Chase smiled. “I’m the Village Bailiff, Chase Manhattan. We stopped in to welcome you to Renaissance Faire Village, and to see if you needed help with anything.”

The door opened a little wider. Yellow light from hundreds of candles spilled out into the night. It was amazing that anyone could light that many candles. It must have taken hours.

Everything inside the tavern had changed since that morning. Even the floors had been re-done. The lights fixtures above us were different. It was like walking into a whole other place.

When had there been time to get all that new furniture inside without anyone noticing? How had the floors and lights changed so quickly? The security guards had just seen her moving in.

“Thank you very much. I’m Tilly Morgenstern.”

“Hi.” I offered my hand. “I’m Jessie Morton from the Arts and Crafts Museum. Nice to meet you.”

Tilly daintily shook my hand. Hers was cold as ice. “Nice to meet you, Jessie. I’ve heard your name mentioned.”

Did that mean she was somehow related to Ginny?

Her eyes were like dark diamonds, shiny and hard. Her hair was completely white and hung down past her waist in curls. Though it lacked color, it was thick and shiny like that of a much younger woman. Her face, however, was wrinkled and prune-like.

"And this is Leo, my man servant." She introduced us to a tall, muscled man who looked like a nightclub bouncer. His head was shaved, and his huge arms were covered in dozens of tattoos. The really strange and scary thing about him was that there were no pupils in his eyes. In fact, there was no discernible iris either.

"He's been blind since birth," Tilly explained.

"Hello." I reached to take his outstretched hand after Chase had shaken it.

"He doesn't speak either," she said. "He was raised by African pirates who killed his parents in a raid. They cut out his tongue."

Leo had a lighter grip than Tilly. He stared vacantly forward. It was impossible to tell if he was thinking about anything.

"Nice to meet you," I said.

"I'm sorry to bother you," Chase said to Tilly. "Adventureland requires me ask for your ID the first time I meet you. Just a formality, until we're all familiar with you."

"Of course." With barely a nod, Tilly sent Leo to get a large handbag. "Wouldn't want riffraff moving into my tavern, would I?"

She had a very infectious laugh that sounded like that of a small child. It only took a moment before we were all laughing with her. She showed Chase her ID, and that was that. We were back outside the tavern with an invitation to return when she'd re-opened.

"She was a riot." One of the security men was still laughing, tears rolling down his cheeks. "The tavern should be awesome with her running it."

"Hey look!" The other security man pointed to the tavern sign. "She changed the name a little. What do you think that means?"

We all looked up and read the new sign. There had always been a mermaid with a sword in one hand and a tankard of ale in the other. But now the name Lady of the Lake had been changed to Lady *in* the Lake. It was a subtle difference, but there was nothing subtle about the change in the image.

Now there was an image of a woman in Renaissance garb who was flailing in the water with the pirate ship, Queen's Revenge, behind her. She looked as though she was about to drown.

"Wow. That's some sign," I said. "Does anyone else think the woman in the lake looks like me?"

"I don't think she looks like you." Chase looked away.

"What kind of ID did she have?" I'd been looking as she presented it to him. Now that it was over, I couldn't say if it was a driver's license or what.

"I don't know." He shrugged. "It was valid anyway, and had her name on it. That's all that matters."

He sent the two security guards home for the night. We started back toward the Dungeon.

"I know I was laughing at what Tilly said." I began trying to piece it together in my mind. "But I don't really remember what was so funny."

"Neither do I. We're both just tired. It's been a long day."

But it was about to get longer.

The twins, Rene and Renee, stopped us close to their shop, Our Lady's Gemstones.

I didn't know what it was about them that bothered me, but I felt a little queasy and uncomfortable when they were around. The hairs stood up on the back of my neck, and my skin prickled.

"Good evening, Lady Jessie, Sir Bailiff." Rene made a deep and elegant bow. His long white hair draped down in front of his face like a veil. "We don't wish to bother you, but we were wondering if you could tell us who has moved into the tavern."

"Her name is Tilly Morgenstern," Chase told him. "I hope everyone can make her, and her assistant, Leo, feel at home. It's the best way to heal what happened in the Village two weeks ago."

Rene's sister, Renee, stared into her brother's strange blue eyes for a moment longer. They seemed to share an unspoken conversation.

Was it me, or did they both look unhappy about Tilly moving into the Village?

"Of course, Sir Bailiff. We would be happy to welcome the newcomers." Renee smiled and lowered her head like a cat.

It was difficult to tell Rene from Renee. They were close to the same height and weight. They both had thin, white faces and long white hair. Their eyes were the same shade of blue.

The only way I'd found to tell them apart was that Rene was a little taller, and had a slightly deeper voice. They were as close in looks as two fraternal twins could be, much closer than me and my brother, Tony.

"We are nearly finished crafting your wedding bands," Rene said with a thin-lipped smile. "It would be wonderful if you could come and try them on in a few days. Just to get a feel for them, and make sure that they are exactly what you want."

"Sure," Chase said with a broad smile. "That would be great."

Renee nodded. "Your wedding bands will bind you together *forever.*"

Chase and I both said that we were looking forward to seeing the rings. All of us bowed to each other, and the twins went back to their dark shop.

Another weird thing about them—they never had their lights on.

"You know, the way she said it, I'm not so crazy about marrying you now."

He laughed, and put his arm around me. "It's too late. You're stuck with me."

"Yeah, that's what I'm afraid of. The way she made it sound, it was more a curse than a blessing."

"What is it with you and the two of them?" he asked. "They do awesome work. I never have any trouble from them. I don't understand why they bother you so much."

I shivered, thinking about the twins. "I don't know. They scare me. They have since the first day I met them. It doesn't make sense, but there you have it. I guess I don't always make sense."

We were on the cobblestones by then, headed past the Honey and Herb Shoppe, when I noticed a light in the Arts and Crafts Museum. It wasn't a normal lamp, or overhead light. This was more like a flashlight, moving past the windows.

"What's that?" I asked Chase. "No one should be in there."

"I don't know." His eyes narrowed in the dim light. "Let's go take a look."

Nine

We went quietly up the stairs to the museum. I could smell coffee brewing at Sir Latte's Beanery on the other side of the Village, along with bagels cooking at Bawdy Betty's. There was laughter floating out on the night air, and the sound of someone playing a guitar.

It was what I expected for a Village evening, but whoever had killed Dave—and now sneaked into the museum—had taken away my peace of mind.

The front door was closed and locked, but I saw the small light go by the window again.

"Stay here," Chase whispered close to my ear.

"No way," I whispered back. "There's no one else here to help you."

He sighed. "At least stay behind me. This could be Dave's killer, for all we know."

"Okay. You go first."

We crept to the back door that was on the ground level. It was slightly open. Chase pushed it open a little further and glanced inside before he walked in. I followed right behind him, wishing I had a taser.

The area downstairs was used for storage. There wasn't much here yet since the museum hadn't opened. I planned to eventually have various exhibits kept here that we could pull out in case one of our crafters cancelled.

It was dark and quiet. I saw the flashlight beam again, and pointed it out to Chase.

The intruder tried to brush by us in the dark. Chase moved quickly after him, as he got close to the basement door. I heard a scuffle, and someone cried out. I flipped on the overhead light to see what was going on.

Chase had tackled Pat Snyder, who played William Shakespeare in the Village each day. Pat was sitting on the floor with his head held down, slowly rocking back and forth as Chase held his arm in a taut grip.

Pat was a middle-aged man with a pointed gray beard and thick gray hair. He was dressed in jeans and a T-shirt. He was attractive—especially when he was in his Elizabethan garb. Even the young girls giggled when he spouted a fresh sonnet for them. He struck his thinking pose at his podium, feather quill pen in hand, and women listened.

"What are you doing in here?" I asked him.

"This is the only place I get any peace from Wanda." He wiped tears from his face. "I can't sleep. I can't eat. I can't work. She won't leave me alone. I don't know why, but the few hours I can hide in here are different. Maybe there's some kind of protection spell on the museum that keeps her out."

"Protection spell?" My doubt carried into my voice. "Where would that come from?"

"I'm desperate, Jessie. I don't know what to do."

"Have you tried leaving the Village?" Chase asked. "I've read that some spirits are tied to certain places."

"You've been looking up ghost facts?" I couldn't believe it. I was glad that he was finally interested, but I was surprised.

"We've got a ghost." He shrugged. "I need to know all I can about them."

"I tried spending the night at a hotel," Pat said. "It didn't matter. She followed me. Any other suggestions?"

"That's about the extent of my ghost knowledge right now," Chase admitted. "Sorry."

"We should talk to Madame Lucinda about it," I suggested. "Maybe she knows why Wanda can't get into the museum. I noticed that Wanda can't enter her tent either."

"We should go see her right now then." Pat struggled to get off the floor.

Chase helped him up. "None of us expected to have this problem. We're going to have to figure it out as we go along. I think Madame Lucinda is a good place to start. But breaking and entering isn't necessary."

"I didn't mean to cause any trouble."

"How did you get in?" I asked.

"The back door there was left open. I started hiding in here each night. She's worse at night, you know."

"I don't see any reason why you can't stay here downstairs, until we can control Wanda a little, or get rid of her. I'm waiting right now for someone who's supposed to be able to do that." I smiled at him, knowing how hard it was being around our resident ghost.

She was hardest on her ex-husband.

"Thank you." Pat threw his arms around me and sobbed into my T-shirt. "You don't know what this means to me."

"I'll have a key made for you so you can lock the door when you're not here. We don't have many thefts, but there are a few." I was thinking of the crossbow that had disappeared from next door. Some of our first exhibit about tapestry weaving was old and worth a fortune. I didn't want to go through what Phil was going through.

Chase and I followed Pat outside.

"You know what this means, don't you?" Chase whispered to me. "We gave up the only place we know of that Wanda can't go."

"I know. I'm sorry. Maybe we could sneak in here for an hour or so while Pat is working. We could block off time on a calendar." I smiled and touched his face. "It's not that I don't miss having time alone with you."

"It's okay." He kissed my fingertips. "We'll find a way. She can't be everywhere."

Wanda decided to join us as I struggled to lock the museum door. It had a tendency to stick which was probably why it wasn't locked properly. "How touching. I love lovers, don't you? What is my stupid, ex-husband doing now? Honestly, the man is completely hopeless."

"Why don't you leave him alone?" I said to her.

“Is Wanda here now?” Chase searched the night around us.

I dropped the key and had to find it. “She’s here.”

“Now lover boy believes in me, eh?” Wanda chuckled. “Wonder what happened?”

“Polo’s Pasta,” I told her. “I think you convinced everyone. Of course that encouraged everyone to figure out ways to get rid of you too. You should’ve been a good ghost and you could’ve hung around.”

“You can’t get rid of me.” Wanda laughed in that evil maniacal manner reminiscent of cartoon characters. She floated up into the night air, getting larger and even scarier, if that was possible. Her eyes glowed with phosphorescent brilliance. She spread her arms and the stadium lights came on for a moment. Then they crackled, and exploded into sparks.

“I can’t see you, Wanda, but if I find you, I’m going to wring your neck!” Chase took out his radio to call his security team. “Meet me on the Village Green for damage control in ten minutes.”

“Hide me! Hide me!” Pat wailed as he tried to run back inside the museum.

I’d finally locked the door. I wasn’t going through it again that night. “You’ll be fine. Stay with me until we get to Madame Lucinda’s tent.”

We walked around to the front together, Shakespeare clinging to my arm.

Madame Lucinda limped out of her tent, belting her robe closed. “What’s going on out here? Oh. It’s you again. Be gone. I’m trying to get some sleep.”

Wanda disappeared in the middle of a loud cackle that echoed around the Village, and brought several residents out on the cobblestones to see what was going on.

“That’s better.” Madame Lucinda sighed and started back to her tent.

“Wait!” I ran after her. “You have to help us. This is Wanda’s ex. She won’t leave him alone.”

“Lady Jessie.” She inclined her head. “Wanda’s ex.”

“Shakespeare, Madame.” He struck a pose. “William Shakespeare.”

“Interesting.” She shook her head. “As we’ve discussed, there are only two lasting ways to get rid of Wanda Le Fey. The first, you have refused. The second has not come to pass.”

“What are you talking about?” Pat kept his eyes on the sky around us. “What is she talking about, Jessie?”

I briefly explained. “I’m not wishing Wanda off on some poor, unsuspecting person. We’ll have to see about the sorcerer.”

“There’s a sorcerer? My goodness!” Mrs. Potts, in a pink mob cap and matching robe, had wandered out of her apartment in the Herb and Honey Shoppe. “I hope he’s handsome. He is a man, right?”

“He is, according to Wanda,” I said. “I haven’t met him. At least I don’t think I have.”

"Are you saying all of this that's been happening in the Village is a result of dark magic?" Brother Carl had left the Monastery Bakery without his sandals.

"I'm not saying anything one way or another." This was getting out of hand.

Madame Lucinda was leaving. Dozens of residents were discussing magic and ghosts. There were many more people than I'd realized who'd seen Wanda in the last two weeks.

I didn't want to get involved in creating more gossip. Instead I followed Madame Lucinda into her tent. Out of the corner of my eye, I saw Pat grab Mrs. Potts and hold on tight.

When the tent flaps parted, I saw something I thought I would never see.

Madame Lucinda was a human woman from the waist up. Her legs, which she had so much trouble getting around on, were something else. Only one word came to mind.

Dragon.

Her legs were squat and thick, covered in scaly, green skin—just like Buttercup who was perched on the shelf over the table. There were claws on her large, non-human feet. She had a large green tail too, also covered with scales. No wonder she had such a hard time sitting in a chair.

She quickly pulled her robe around her and growled at me. "How dare you? Leave at once."

Remembering when she'd gotten rid of Wanda the first time I'd come in, I expected to be snatched out of the tent by unseen hands, and thrown into the street. I felt a tug, but I resisted. Nothing else happened.

"That's surprising." Her voice was more modulated now. She pulled her robe back on, and secured it around her waist. "There's more to you than meets the eye, Jessie Morton. We'll have to explore that in the future. Of course, I knew something was different. You can see Buttercup. Not everyone can."

I struggled for words. What do you say to a woman who is part dragon?

"We need your help." I cleared my throat as the words barely squeaked out of me. "We need your help, please."

"You know what I know about your ghost. Have you changed your mind about giving her to someone else?"

"No. I can't do that."

"What are you asking of me then?"

"You can get rid of her, like you just did outside. I've seen you do that in here, too."

"I would have to spend every moment of every day concentrating my power on keeping her out of the Village. I'm afraid that's not going to happen. You'll have to cope until the sorcerer gets here."

"Why can't she go into the museum?"

"Your guess is as good as mine." She shrugged. "It could be a bad memory that keeps her out. It could be something about the way the place is built. It would take extensive research, and knowledge of the place, that I don't have."

"Could it be because Wanda's bracelet was put in there to frame me for her murder?" It was a shot in the dark.

"Probably not—unless she's no longer bothering you and the Bailiff at home. You said you have her bracelet now?"

"Yes." My heart sank. I'd hoped I was on to something.

Pat ran into the tent. "Does she know anything?"

"I know a great deal, if you're speaking about me." Madame Lucinda's voice was huffy. "But if you're looking for a permanent cure for your ghost, you must seek it elsewhere."

"Okay." Pat looked around the tent and swallowed hard. "What about protection? If we can't get rid of her, is there a magic charm or something I can use to protect myself?"

I hadn't thought of that.

Madame Lucinda brought out a piece of quartz and gave it to Shakespeare. "You must keep it on you always. Never put it aside."

He pocketed the rock and thanked her. "You've made my life so much better, Madame. I shall compose a sonnet to you."

I followed him out of the tent. There was nothing more to say to Madame Lucinda. I knew the answers to the problem. I hoped the sorcerer got there soon.

"That was weird in there," Pat said. "Did you see all that stuff? How did she get all that in there?"

"Yes. Did you see the dragon, the *real* dragon?" I went on to describe it, but I could tell from the look on his face that he didn't know what I was talking about.

"What now?" he asked with an exhausted sigh.

"We'll figure out why she can't get into the museum. In the meantime, you stay there."

"Are the police done looking around or were they finished for the night?"

"I'm not sure. I'll call Detective Almond in the morning. Our tapestry exhibit opens tomorrow. I hope that's it."

Pat got caught up in the large group of people still out in the cold, fall night. No doubt he was telling and re-telling his harrowing account of what had happened. There was some lightning off in the distance, probably the storm heading out to the Atlantic Ocean. It added to the strange mood of the night.

I went to find Chase. He was busy with the cleanup of the stadium lights. The security guards were with him, and a truck from the electric company was rolling into the Village.

I didn't want to bother him. He had enough on his hands. I felt shell-shocked, and wished I had answers.

Had I really seen a woman who was part dragon?

It could be a costume. There are weirder things here.

Surely she didn't walk around wearing part of a dragon costume at night while she slept?

Seeing her lower extremities made me understand why she walked with a limp, and seemed to be in pain most of the time. It couldn't be easy being part dragon.

Go to bed! You're not making any sense. How can someone be part dragon?

I ended up with a large group of other residents at the Pleasant Pheasant. Hephaestus lived above the pub. He was awake, like the rest of us, after Wanda's crazy escapades. I guess he'd decided to open again. He was charging a quarter for a beer or ale.

"What was that awful racket?" Sam DaVinci, the artist, asked. He was working on his second pint of ale.

"Something smashed into the stadium lights. Probably birds, confused by the storm." Lord Maximus yawned. He was the master of ceremonies of the Birds of Prey show at the Hawk Stage. "I think they were struck by lightning."

"It's just the storm," Mother Goose said like it was gospel. She'd been at the Village longer than almost everyone else. She had her goose, Phineas, with her. She rarely went anywhere without him.

"Guess we better batten down the hatches." Fred the Red Dragon was still in the bottom half of his costume as he swallowed the last of his beer.

Seeing Fred in that partial dragon costume made me shiver. It was too much like what I'd seen for real in Madame Lucinda's tent.

It wasn't for real!

On the other hand, seeing him that way made me realize that she wasn't *necessarily* part dragon-part woman. Sometimes things were unbelievable here in the Village. On a crazy night like that, anything seemed possible. In the clear light of day, it wouldn't seem the same.

"More ale, Lady Jessie?"

I looked up. It was the young man from the Field of Honor that Chase had saved. He didn't look old enough to serve alcohol, but I knew Hephaestus would have checked him out thoroughly before he let him work there. We had to abide by the same laws as businesses outside the Village.

Like many others here, the young man probably had to moonlight at another job to make a living.

"Sure. Why not?" I flipped him a quarter—my last one. "How are you doing after all the excitement?"

He smiled as he poured the ale. "I'm fine. A little excitement is good for the soul, don't you think?"

"Maybe. A little." I marveled again at his smooth good looks. He was so young. I knew he had to be twenty-one, but he didn't look more than twelve. "I'm sorry. I forgot your name."

"Tim." He sat down opposite from me. "Did you see the lightning hit the stadium lights?"

"No." I mulled over how much to tell him. He'd been at the jousting field. He had to know something was up. "It was the same ghost again. She's determined to do whatever damage she can. She's dead before her time, you know. I don't really blame her. It wasn't her fault that she was murdered."

His clear, sky-blue eyes stared into mine. He didn't seem surprised by what I'd said. "You mean Wanda Le Fey."

"Yes. Do you believe in ghosts?"

"I guess I'd be foolish not to, wouldn't I? It would mean doubting the evidence I'd seen with my own eyes."

"That's very mature of you." I sipped my ale. "I wish I could be more mature about it."

"Wanda annoys you?"

"She's annoying the whole Village. With me, it's more than that. I think she's taking it out on me because she has to go through eternity painted blue."

He laughed. "Is that what happened? I was wondering."

I lowered my head and whispered, "You can see her?"

"Yes. Can't everyone?"

"No. They can't. And if you're smart, you won't let on that you can see her either. She'll ruin your life. Her ex-husband, Shakespeare, is hiding in the only place we know of that she can't go in for some reason—except for Madame Lucinda's tent."

"You mean the fortune teller." He nodded. "I haven't been to see her yet. They keep the squires busy during the day."

"I know. I was a squire for a while." I sipped more ale. "I'm going to have to do some research. There has to be some reason why Wanda can't go into the museum."

"I know why." My brother, Tony, joined us. "Adventureland probably buried bodies at all four corners of the foundation as eternal sentinels to prevent evil from getting inside."

My brother and I were fraternal twins—and there the likeness ended. He thought responsibility was a dirty word. He had a hard time committing to anything. He went through money like there was no tomorrow—a problem I'd had to bail him out of many times.

Tony got my father's brown eyes, and I got my mother's blue ones. We were both almost exactly the same height—six feet—and we both wore size twelve shoes.

"That was a common practice many years ago," Tim agreed with him.

"Come on. Nobody buried any bodies in the Village to prevent evil," I scoffed. "Yes, they did it centuries ago, but the Village isn't that old. There's something else."

Tony swallowed the last of his beer. "I'm out of quarters."

"Me too. Sorry," I said before he asked me for change.

"I wanted to talk to you about the wedding, Jessie." Tony sat down. "I'd like to give you away. I don't know if you have anything planned like that. I just thought, since Dad is gone, I'd be the one to do it."

I was surprised, and happy, that Tony had thought about it. I hadn't wanted to ask him. I was afraid he might think it was stupid.

"I'd like that. We'll work it in." I hugged him. "Thanks for offering."

"Sure. While we're talking about it, I might need some help getting something decent to wear. You think Chase could lend me a few bucks?"

My heart sank. He seemed as though he'd been changing the last few months. I'd hoped he was growing up.

I sighed. I loved him, despite everything. Maybe he *was* changing. Renaissance wedding finery didn't come cheap. "I've got some money. Get something, and put it on my account at Stylish Frocks."

"Thanks, Jessie." Tony hugged me again. "You'll be proud of me. I promise."

"I'm going to call it a night." I smiled at Tim. He jumped to his feet as I got to mine. "Thank you, Sir Squire, for your very fine service this evening."

"I was most happy to spend time with you, Lady Jessie. Sleep well."

"I'm hanging out here for a while longer," Tony said. "Will you go with me to see Beth tomorrow? She's always hated me."

"I have a fitting tomorrow anyway. I'll meet you at Stylish Frocks at nine."

"Thanks, Sis."

I walked outside. The rain was gone but it had left a dense mist over the Village that seemed to permeate everything. I was about to cross the cobblestones, when three police cars drove slowly through the mist. The cars had their lights on, but no sirens.

"Manny!"

Ten

I ran into the dungeon, and shut the downstairs door behind me. There was a man in a pizza delivery outfit walking down the stairs from the apartment.

He tugged at his cap. “Evening, ma’am. Sorry if I startled you. I couldn’t drive through the gate so I had to walk in. Have a good one.”

I smiled, thanked him, and darted into the apartment. I closed and locked the door behind me, and turned off the lights. “Manny, what have you done?”

He removed a slice of pizza from his mouth. “What? What’s wrong, Jessie?”

“You ordered pizza.”

“The name and number were on the board.” He pointed to it. “Naturally, I assumed it was correct to order from that location.”

“It should’ve been—in normal circumstances. Did you use your name?”

He thought about it. “Of course I did. Who else’s name would I have used?”

There was pounding on the apartment door. “Open up,” Detective Almond said. “I know you’re there, Mr. Argall.”

Manny froze and stared at me. “What should I do?”

"We don't have any choice now. You'll have to go with them."

"I may be able to jump out of the window."

"Seriously, you'll have to go with them. We'll figure something out later."

I opened the door.

Detective Almond had a smug expression on his face. "Well, well. What do we have here? How long have you been hiding him, Jessie?"

Before I could speak, Manny said, "I have only been here for a few minutes. Lady Jessie was informing me that you wanted to speak with me, sir."

Detective Almond looked skeptical. "Yeah, right. Get over here. We're gonna have a talk at the station. Where's your lawyer?"

Manny nodded. "I'll call him, of course." None of the fear I'd seen in his face a moment before showed. He was as cool about being taken in by the police as he might have been about being asked what he wanted to eat for lunch.

"Don't panic," I told him. "It will be all right."

"Certainly, Lady Jessie. I hope to return in time to help with the tapestry exhibit tomorrow."

"I hope so too."

Detective Almond glanced around the apartment. "Where's Chase?"

"He's helping with the storm damage." It was just as well that Chase wasn't here with Manny.

"I'll be in touch."

One of the officers that had come with Detective Almond walked with Manny down the stairs. I saw Chase come in through the downstairs door to the Dungeon. He stopped and spoke with Detective Almond for a moment and then came up to the apartment.

"I was afraid something like this would happen." He closed the door with a grim expression on his handsome face. "Now Detective Almond thinks I'm involved with hiding Manny, and withholding information. We didn't gain anything."

"I'm so sorry. I didn't think about him ordering pizza. I suppose the police told them to call if Manny's name came up."

He sank down on the bed, soaking wet and exhausted. "That's okay. You couldn't have known. He's your friend. You wanted to protect him."

"Detective Almond will get over it. He doesn't have much choice since no one else wants to be Bailiff here."

"That's true." He smiled. "I have a job no one else would have in a crazy place haunted by a mean ghost. I guess this means Manny probably isn't a sorcerer."

"Probably not." I sat on the bed beside him. "You know you're getting everything wet, right?"

"I suppose." He frowned, prepared to get up.

"You should at least get out of these clothes." I pulled on his soaking shirt until it came out of his pants.

"Yeah?" I saw hope in his blue eyes. "Wanda isn't here?"

"Not right now. Quick before that changes."

* * *

It was raining again the next day, and even cooler. Fall weather seemed to be settling in.

That meant traffic on the cobblestones would be limited today. It also meant nothing much was going on. Chase and I had both slept through the night without his radio going off—or Wanda rearing her ugly head. It was wonderful.

"I guess Wanda left us alone last night." Chase put his arm around me and I snuggled closer.

"I haven't seen her since Madame Lucinda banished her. Maybe she's gone for good."

He kissed me. "I hope so. It's not easy competing with a ghost for your time."

"Do you have to see Detective Almond today?"

"Yeah. He's not too happy with me." He rubbed the dark stubble on his chin. "That means I have to put on civilian clothes."

"You look good either way," I assured him with a big smile.

"You too." He rubbed his nose on mine and then kissed me.

I kissed his chin. “Thanks. “

“Just think, in less than two weeks, we’ll be married. I’m excited. Are you?”

“Except for the ridiculously large wedding, the dress fittings, and going to see Renee and Rene about the ring, I’m delirious.”

“What about just being with me for the rest of your life?” He stared into my eyes. “Are you good with that?”

I wrapped my arms around him. “That part, Sir Bailiff, goes without saying.”

Chase got up, showered, and put on jeans and a Ren Faire T-shirt before he went to see Detective Almond. He promised to find out what was going on with Manny while he was there.

I kissed him goodbye, thinking how handsome and sexy he looked even in his street clothes. I was a lucky woman to have Chase, and be able to share my Renaissance passion with him.

I promised myself that I’d try not to complain about the wedding anymore. It was just one day. We’d have the rest of our lives together. Who cared if that one day would be on the Internet forever? Somehow, we’d still find a way to make it our own.

That thought was good, but likely to change several times during the day.

The fitting for my wedding gown went fine. The dress was mostly finished. Beth Daniels, the owner of Stylish

Frocks, had taken personal charge of all of the clothes for our wedding. The shop provided costumes for all the residents of the Village as well as visitors.

Beth had me try on the gown once more with the veil and train. The gown was beautiful—pink and white velvet with gold trim. The veil was handmade lace shot through with gold threads. The train was as long as I was tall. It was made of white and gold tulle that glistened when I moved.

This was actually the second gown Beth had made for me. The first gown had been in shades of purple, red, and blue. It had been the same as the one Queen Olivia had planned to wear. Something had to change.

“I don’t know about that neckline,” Beth complained, pulling at it a little. “I’m not happy with it. I still have time to work on it.”

I looked at the heart-shaped neckline that was trimmed in gold. “What’s wrong with it?”

“I don’t know. Ask me again in a few days.”

Beth and two of her assistants helped me remove the heavy dress. I watched them replace it on the headless mannequin. It was so stiff, it could almost stand up by itself.

Tony showed up with two of my bridesmaids. Beth worked on their outfits, assuring my brother that he’d be wearing black velvet with gold trim. Chase’s groomsmen were wearing light blue with gold trim, just like my ladies.

Master Armorer Daisy Reynolds was my maid of honor. She argued with Beth about wearing her breastplate over her gown. Beth was insistent that the breastplate wouldn’t fit. Daisy, a large woman with badly dyed blond hair, appealed to me.

"I don't care if you wear it if it fits over the gown," I told her. "I'm not sure if I'd know you without it anyway."

Her bright blue eyes twinkled. "Hear that, dressmaker? The breastplate better fit over the gown. I'm wearing my sword, sheathed, of course. I'm making a gold girdle for you, Jessie, so you can wear your sword too."

The girdle sounded nice. It would be worn on the outside of my gown, around my hips. I wasn't sure about the sword. I knew Daisy felt naked without a weapon. I was a little less militant.

My other bridesmaid was Adora. She owned Cupid's Arrow, a shop that stocked love potions, lingerie, and incense. The two women were my best friends in the Village, but couldn't have been more different if they'd tried.

Chase's groomsmen were Bart, and Phil Ferguson from the Sword Spotte.

Bart wasn't there since he was performing his duties as the Queen's Guard at the castle. Beth grumbled about his absence because he was hard to fit.

Phil had taught Chase, and me, to use a sword. Beth said his fittings were over days before. He was very punctual about getting things done.

"I have to go." I glanced at the sundial-shaped clock on Beth's wall. "The Main Gate opens soon, and I haven't met my weaver yet. This is my first exhibit at the museum. Everything is screwed up about it. Wish me luck."

"I wish you a lack of dead bodies. That would be nice for a day," Portia, Beth's assistant, said in her usual droll way. "I don't think that would make for a good tapestry exhibit."

"Good luck," Daisy said, and then yelled at one of the women working with her gown. "*Oww!* Don't stick pins in me if you know what's good for you!"

I was very excited about the grand opening of my museum. A few select visitors had been in the Arts and Crafts Museum earlier, before it had been closed by the police. It was like a soft opening until my weaver could get there. They seemed to enjoy it. I hoped that a thousand or so other visitors would feel the same way about it today.

That was my number. Everything else was gravy. But for an exhibit to stay open in the Village, a thousand people a day had to pass through its doors. I had my fingers crossed.

Despite the rain that morning, Village workers had put up the large canvas banner over the front door of the red brick building. It proclaimed the museum to be open, and advertised the tapestry exhibit. We were lucky the crime scene people had finished their work on the front entrance before the museum was scheduled to open.

I realized as I ran up the steps that I didn't have a key. I'd given it to Shakespeare the night before. I had a brief moment of panic until Shakespeare opened the back door, and we went inside.

He was dressed in his usual costume, stiffened and stuffed, as all Elizabethan garb was. His doublet was laced in front, the sleeves laced to the armholes, and the bright gold doublet laced to the hose. His pointed beard was carefully trimmed.

He put the key into my hand. "I hope that you don't mind that I made a duplicate key from yours. Best night's sleep ever. Not a whiff of Wanda. Maybe she's gone for good."

"I hope so. It was the same with me."

I invited him to stay for the opening festivities. He declined, saying that he'd neglected his podium in recent days and needed to get back, even if it was raining. "I'm hopeful that the magic stone Madame Lucinda gave me will prove useful in keeping Wanda away."

I wished him luck with that, eager to get upstairs.

"It's amazing what a good night's sleep can do for you." He bowed deeply. "Thank you, Lady Jessie. I am going to write an ode for your wedding. I shall read it myself at the event."

I curtsied and thanked him. I hoped there was time for everything everyone in the Village wanted to do for the wedding. In my new spirit of thought, I realized what a great event it was going to be. And if that benefited Adventureland, I was glad.

I missed Manny as I walked through the museum one last time before our big moment. We'd both worked so hard for this day. I hated that he wasn't going to be here. He deserved some praise, and to see the project through to the end.

The old tapestry loom was set in the center of the main room upstairs. It had been difficult—and expensive—to find a loom which was very similar to what would have been used during the Renaissance.

But it was much harder to find a weaver who could use it. I'd finally located a man in Pennsylvania who was knowledgeable about weaving, and was comfortable talking on the subject in front of a crowd. He also had three days he could dedicate to my opening. The price was right, and the deal was set.

The front door opened and my master weaver, Oliver Northman, came in, shaking the rain off of his great coat. "It's a rather gloomy day. I hope you are Jessie Morton." He introduced himself.

I shook his hand as two monks from the Monastery Bakery brought in fragrant trays of bread and cinnamon rolls along with clay pots filled with coffee. They would be there for the first few hours of the exhibit to help me welcome our guests. They spread a white linen cloth over the wood table at the back of the room, and set up their food.

There were antique tapestries on the walls that held beautiful ladies, unicorns subdued by maidens, and colorful flowers.

Harpist Susan Halifax came in out of the rain with two flute players. We talked for a few minutes and then they set up in another corner of the room.

The king and queen, with some members of the royal court, were due to grace us with their presence—also some Adventureland board members.

The Arts and Crafts Museum, along with the antique weapon museum next door, were the first of their kind for the Village. They weren't games or rides, basically only learning exhibits. Everyone was interested to see how attendance would be. That's why there was such a big send-off.

Two news crews from local TV stations were supposed to come for the event. Only one had agreed to come at first. The other came because of the murder—and the ghost stories.

I didn't care why they'd agreed to come. I wanted my museum to be popular. I wanted thousands of people to walk through what I'd created and appreciate it.

I knew if they didn't, the museum would close, and the red brick manor houses that had sat empty for so many years, would be empty again. That would be a terrible waste of space, as I'd convinced the board in my proposal for the museum.

There was a ruckus coming from the front door. I knew the king and queen must be there. Because their group of courtiers, nannies, knaves, and fools was always so large, it also made a lot of noise.

I had dressed to impress that day, wearing a colorfully beaded over-shirt on my white blouse, and full-length brown skirt. I also wore a small veil and head piece on my hair, and some faux antique jewelry that wasn't expensive, but looked wonderful with my outfit. It was never good to outshine the king and queen.

I didn't have to worry about it.

Queen Olivia was resplendent in a red gown, with white fur trim around the neck and shoulders. She wore a gold girdle about her hips, and her hair was bound back by the same gold filigree.

King Harold matched her, as they always did when they went out. His shirt was red and gold. He wore a short cape with it. His sword hilt was gold filigree, like the queen's girdle and head piece.

Even the baby, Princess Pea, was dressed for success, and to match her royal sires. Two royal nannies attended to her every whim. She was bound to be the most spoiled child in the world as she grew up.

The rest of the courtiers were dressed nicely, but a step down from the royal couple. They wore lighter colors and less jewelry. Their clothes were still very posh and regal.

"Lady Jessie." The queen addressed me, and I dropped into a deep curtsey, head down. "We are pleased to see your success here at the new Renaissance Arts and Craft Museum."

Photographers snapped her picture while video cameras caught everything.

Queen Olivia was always at her best in the spotlight. She loved every moment of it. She was petulant, spoiled, and demanding, but she was our queen and we loved her.

"Thank you, your majesty," I responded with a smile. "You are most welcome to our humble museum. I hope you find something that pleases you here."

King Harold said a few words on behalf of the Village, but they were more to invite people to come out and join us than about the museum.

The royal couple passed the entry way, and began strolling through the exhibit. The press followed them, but only until Merlin, in his modern day suit and tie, made his remarks about Adventureland, and Renaissance Faire Village and Marketplace.

Again, it was promo, and included a mention of the great wedding day.

"More than two hundred and fifty couples will be married right here at the Village," he said to the reporters. "Another possible two thousand couples will be married with a live feed which is going to Renaissance Faires and Festivals throughout the world. Guinness believes this may be the largest wedding day in history."

"It's weird seeing him that way." Chase surprised me, coming up from behind.

I looked at Merlin in his pinstripe, three-piece blue suit—one hand casually in his pocket. His crazy hair was smoothed back on his head. He'd even shaved for the occasion. He was every inch a successful CEO.

"I'll say." I took Chase's hand and smiled at him. "I'm glad you could make it."

"I wouldn't miss this moment. You've worked really hard for it, Jessie. I know the museum is going to do well."

"Thanks. I wish Manny was here to enjoy this too."

"He has only himself to blame," Chase reminded me.

"Maybe."

Merlin finished his speech to a round of applause from the other board members, and high ranking officials from Adventureland and the Village.

All of the guild masters were also present, and dressed in their finest—except for the Knaves, Varlets, and

Madmen's Guild. They looked as they always did in torn dresses, shirts, and britches. Most were barefoot. They carried their trademark pots and pans with them as though they were scepters.

Madman Bob, who spent most of his time banging his pans together at the Village Green, was dressed as he always was in torn shirt and britches. He had thrown on an old brown hat that lent him an air of sophistication.

He bowed low and gracefully to me as we met. "My Lady Jessie. May I have words with you?"

"So good to see you, Madman Bob. I am a trifle busy at the moment. Could it wait?"

He lowered his voice. "Perhaps not, my lady. It involves the night a murder happened right here at this museum."

Eleven

I glanced at Chase. "Perhaps you could speak to the Bailiff, sir. He is directly involved in the matter."

"I shall only speak with you, lady. None other will do."

With Madman Bob insistent that he had to speak with me, I had no choice but to lead him into one of the secondary rooms.

Chase was equally insistent that he was going to be there. Bob wasn't happy about it, but he finally gave in.

A dozen beautiful tapestries were hanging here, but the crowd was still enjoying food and music in the main area. Oliver Northman was setting up his loom.

"What's so important that you have to bother Jessie today?" Chase took a slightly belligerent tone with Bob. He stood, glaring down at him, his arms folded across his chest.

"I will speak to Lady Jessie, Sir Bailiff, if you don't mind."

I didn't have time for a staring match. "What is it, Bob?"

"You have been asking around the Village for anyone to come forward who had knowledge of the night Dave was killed. I was afraid to say anything, but decided I must gird my loins and tell you what I know."

"What did you see?" Chase asked.

I put my hand on his arm. "What was it, Bob?"

"I think I saw the silhouette of the killer. It was tall, though not as tall as the bailiff. There was a cloak, but I also saw a quiver of arrows on the back, and the outline of a tall bow. The person walked up the stairs to the museum. The shadow lingered for a minute. I'm not sure if it was a man or a woman."

Chase got out his pencil and paper. "What time was that?"

Madman Bob gave up the demand to speak only to me. "It was near midnight."

"What were you doing out here at that hour?" Chase asked.

"I was going to see Madame Lucinda." Bob smiled. "She is helping me with an affair of the heart."

"Why didn't you say something sooner?" I wondered.

"I was afraid, my lady. In my former life, I did some things I'm not proud of. These things could still have outstanding warrants. I don't want to talk to the police."

"There's nothing I can do about that," Chase said.

"Unless we can find a way around it." I gave Chase a hard look. We obviously needed Bob's information. We didn't want him to run away.

"Unless we can find a way around it," Chase agreed with a sigh. "But I need you to write this down and sign it with your real name. I won't use it unless I have to."

Bob seemed okay with that. “Thank you, my lady. I knew you would protect me.”

“You are quite welcome, Bob. Thank you for coming forward.”

People from the party in the big room began drifting our way. Bob took his leave of us.

“What is that supposed to mean?” Chase demanded. “Why did he think *you* could protect him, Jessie?”

“I don’t know—except sometimes you come on a little mean and grumpy.”

“Mean? I’m the Bailiff. I’m supposed to be tough . . . and grumpy . . . when it calls for it.” He grimaced. “Whatever. I have to go. It looks like your opening event is turning out okay. I love you. I’ll see you later.”

The next hour or so was spent with Oliver Northman’s talented hands on the big loom. He was not only an expert at creating beautiful tapestries as they had hundreds of years before—he was also entertaining. He told jokes about the history of weaving, and his great-great grandfather who’d built the loom where he worked.

The Main Gate opened at ten, and visitors began to pile into the already crowded room. It didn’t take long before the coffee and cinnamon rolls were gone. They had only been planned for the opening ceremonies, so it was okay. I thanked the two brothers who’d brought the coffee from the bakery. They bowed and left.

Susan Halifax and the flute players left with the Adventureland board members and the guild masters. Queen

Olivia and King Harold departed the museum after allowing photos from the first visitors to arrive.

Oliver took a break after the first hour. The king had given him a park pass for the day so he could wander at will between his times working on the loom.

"That was quite a crowd," he said with a smile. "I've never used the loom in front of royalty before. That's something to write home about. I hope there were pictures."

"I saw the Adventureland publicist here taking pictures. I'm sure she'll send you some. Otherwise, you should be all over Facebook and other social media already."

"Odds bodkins! I'm famous! I think I'll see if that will buy me a cup of ale at the local pub."

Obviously, he was enjoying his time at the museum. I'd hoped he would be a good sport about being at the Village for the day. You never knew about people. Some just didn't understand, or like it.

"I missed everything, didn't I?"

I heard Manny's voice behind me and ran to hug him. "You're not in jail! I'm so glad to see you."

He adjusted his vest and jacket, smoothed his hair and checked his watch fob. "No, I'm not in jail. My lawyer proved who I was to the satisfaction of the police. I will pay for it later, no doubt. But for now I'm a free man."

"I'm sorry it didn't happen in time for the opening, but everything went beautifully."

"Where's our loom master?" He glanced at the old loom with the start of a new tapestry on it.

"He's taking a break. He'll be back soon."

"And what of the person who killed Dave the Madman? Has the Bailiff had any luck locating that person?"

"No." I told him what Madman Bob had said, as well as recounting what I'd gleaned from Master Simmons. "I don't know if that will matter, especially since he may be a criminal himself."

Manny had a look of complete shock on his face. "I thought there were background checks here. How could such a man come to work outside our door?"

I laughed at him. "The same way *you* did, I guess. Adventureland's background checks must not be worth much."

"Are you comparing me to a killer archer?" He looked at his shiny shoes and perfectly creased Victorian clothes.

"No. Not at all. Come on. Let me show you the work Oliver did this morning."

* * *

When Oliver came back from his break, I left Manny in charge at the museum.

I believed Madman Bob. He probably saw something important the night Dave was killed. Whether it would be helpful or not, was another story. It was a piece of the whole puzzle. I needed to find what went with it.

I walked down to see Roger Trent at the Glass Gryphon. He was working on a large flying horse he was creating from iridescent glass. It was an incredible piece. I couldn't wait until it was his turn at the museum to show off.

"I don't need to ask why you're here." Roger put the piece aside. "You want to know about Dave, right? I've been waiting for Chase, or the police, to realize that I had valuable information. I should've known it would be you!"

We sat down together with his wife, Gullah basket weaver, Mary Shift. Both of their shops were slow for the moment.

I'd apprenticed with both of them. Everyone was always so busy, it was hard to find time just to sit and catch up. I enjoyed seeing them.

But Roger wasn't interested in a tea party where we could gossip and talk about what we'd been doing.

"He's in one of his moods," Mary told me as she worked on a sweet grass basket.

"They don't appreciate me, Mary," he complained. "They send Jessie to ask me questions. Here I am—an experienced, retired police officer. They ignore me."

"I'm sure it's nothing personal." She looped the grass together with her fingers, barely looking at it.

Mary was a slight, black woman with an interesting face and hands that were never still. She was dressed in a long purple cotton skirt and matching blouse that was tied in the front.

"You know I'm naturally nosy," I told him. "Tell me about Dave. I know that you had problems with him gambling."

He nodded, apparently willing to overlook my menial status in order to talk about what he knew best. “I had to roust him several times. The man didn’t know how to win, but he was obsessed with trying. A bookie once paid someone in the Village to break his legs because he owed so much money.”

“Did that happen? Did you catch who was responsible?”

He grinned. “Ever hear of Zachary the Giant in the Village?”

“No. Is that who broke Dave’s legs?”

“That’s right. I was an excellent Bailiff in my day.”

“Was the bookie named John Healy?”

“I don’t think that was him. But this was a few years back. There’s probably someone new in town now.”

“Have you heard anything that could tie into this?” I told him what Bob had said about seeing the figure at the museum the night Dave was killed.

“The only thing we hear about every day is the ghost, the Blue Lady.” Mary crossed herself. “I haven’t seen her yet—they say it’s Wanda Le Fey.”

“Yes. It’s Wanda. I’ve seen a lot of her lately.”

Roger got up and went back to his glass work.

“He doesn’t believe,” Mary said. “If he can’t touch it, he doesn’t think it’s real. Why did I fall in love with a man like him, Jessie?”

I laughed. "It seemed to me at the time that you couldn't help yourself!"

"That's true enough." She smiled, and never lost track of the grass she was weaving. "How is it with you and Chase?"

"It's good. It's a little weird right now with the wedding, and the ghost. But we're okay."

"Good. I can't wait until the wedding, you know. I love a good wedding."

We talked for a while longer about her family, and Tony. I finally had to say goodbye, and took my nugget of information with me. So this had happened before, when Roger was the Bailiff. A bookie didn't come into the Village—he hired someone already here.

What if that was what had happened to Dave?

It was still drizzling a little outside. The cloud layer above me looked heavy and ready to pour down again at any moment. I went back to the museum and checked in with Manny. After the initial visitor rush, things were quiet. He and Oliver were heading out for lunch. I sighed as we closed the museum, adding the *Gone to Lunch* sign at the door.

There were going to be bad days, I reminded myself. When it rained, people didn't come to the Village. It didn't mean my museum was going to fail. I had a great line up of craftsmen and artisans coming for the Thanksgiving and Christmas seasons, which were always busy. It would be all right.

As I hit the cobblestones, I saw something I'd hoped never to see again—Morgan Stanley Manhattan, Chase's brother.

I knew Chase's family was coming for the wedding. Morgan was as handsome as Chase, but devious and underhanded. He'd brought Chase's former fiancée to try and lure him away from me on a previous visit. The results had been catastrophic.

Long story short: Chase and I had survived and Morgan had gone away.

I supposed the handsome older gentleman with Morgan was their father. I hadn't met him yet. He'd been in prison for a short while for insider trading. Not surprising with children named for financial institutions.

The older woman, blond and blue eyed with the best tan ever, was probably Chase's mother. I hadn't met her yet either. According to Morgan, she thought I wasn't good enough for Chase. That was why she'd sent Morgan to get rid of me.

They were walking along in that manner that people have when they don't know where they're going.

"Are you sure Chase said he lives in a Dungeon?" Mrs. Manhattan questioned.

"I've been here before, Mother. Chase and Jessie live over there." Morgan seemed already bored with the whole ordeal. "They call it the Dungeon."

"If the boy wants to live in the Dungeon, who are we to interfere?" Mr. Manhattan declared.

"That's why our brilliant son lives in this place," Mrs. Manhattan accused. She got her six-inch heel caught between the cobblestones, and had to be extricated by her son and husband.

I quickly and carefully moved away from them before Morgan noticed me. I was in no mood to deal with Chase's family. I knew I wouldn't have any choice at some point, but not now.

"Want me to do something particularly nasty to them?" Wanda watched them with me. "I could throw something at them, or put them on top of the castle. I'm getting quite good at wreaking havoc."

I knew it was too good to last. Wanda wasn't completely gone yet.

"That's okay. Not that you listen to me."

"I want us to be friends since we're going to be together for the whole rest of your life." She laughed.

"I'm not kidding about giving you to someone else," I threatened. "I'll do it."

"You're far too squeamish, sweetie. You can't stand the thought of hurting someone's feelings. You wouldn't banish me that way."

She was probably right, though I didn't want to admit it. Otherwise I would have already done it. How could I give the plague that was Wanda to someone else? It wouldn't be fair. At least I kind of deserved it.

After they were gone, I sneaked back to the Dungeon and changed clothes. It had occurred to me that I was leaving one stone unturned—I hadn't been to Sherwood Forest yet. Someone there might be able to identify the late night archer Bob had seen at the museum.

I had a man's ragged shirt and britches that I wore when I helped Chase with Vegetable Justice—that wild throwing of squishy vegetables and fruit at wrong doers. I slipped those on and put on my boots. I didn't want to run into the Manhattan clan again without some kind of disguise. Besides, the forest was bound to be muddy after the rain.

I looked at my dresser. My cell phone stared back at me.

Technically, employees weren't supposed to have cell phones on them while the Village was open. Of course, many violated this rule. Getting caught could mean a stint in the castle kitchen washing dishes, unless you were willing to be terminated.

I didn't plan to get caught. I shoved my cell phone into a small cloth bag that I could tie to my belt. Normally, I abided by the rules, but there had been some occasions that I'd wished I had some way to get in touch with Chase, or the police.

I wasn't going looking for a killer without my cell phone.

I also picked up my quiver of arrows that I'd made myself. I slung that over my shoulder with my bow—also handmade under Master Simmons tutelage.

There were two boys in the dungeon when I went back out. They looked like they were nine or ten. They were closely investigating the fake prisoners who called out to them. They jumped, startled, when they saw me as I was locking the door to the apartment.

"It's all right," I said. "Just watch out for that one in the last cell. He *bites*."

They looked uncertain at that, and I laughed as I was walking out the door. That was one of the things I loved most about the Renaissance Faire. There was always surprise and uncertainty about the things people saw. Not just kids either. I'd seen adults so involved in a joust that they fell off of the bench where they'd been sitting.

I ducked behind The Jolly Pipemaker's shop to make sure the coast was clear. I called Chase while I was back there to let him know that his family had arrived.

"Are you out in the Village on your cell phone?" he asked, no doubt hearing the music from the Dutchman's Stage next door.

"Of course not. Love you. Gotta go." I turned off my phone and put it back in the bag.

I stayed off the cobblestones until I got to Sherwood Forest. The forest practically empties out in front of the museum. If the archer wasn't one of Robin's men, or women, it was likely that someone saw him or her. There was usually a guard from the forest at the gate all night.

Sometimes this was to facilitate a pretty visitor who needed to be escorted out of the Village some secret way after her time there. Other times, it was for keeping watch to protect themselves from other guilds whose members might be about to invade. It happened.

The forest was five acres of trees, rocks, and dirt. On a sunny day, the trees blocked out most of the light. On a cloudy day like this one, it was gloomy and damp. The Merry Men lived in treehouses built in the largest oaks and pines.

These weren't treehouses that could've been built by kids either. These were elaborate, multi-storied, several room edifices, created by architects when the Village was first built. Each treehouse had water and electricity, but that was as far as amenities went.

Several Merry Men and Women stayed in each treehouse and frequently shared them with visitors who stayed the night, even though it was against Village rules.

They had some bad habits—like stealing toaster ovens from other residents. If you didn't have a toaster oven in the Village, you were lost since housing was usually small, an there were few kitchens. It was the best way to cook a meal.

Robin and his men had been known to trade toaster ovens for other items they needed, even though many times the ovens didn't belong to them.

I started down the path to the heart of the forest, stepping around a few obvious traps that would have caught me in a snare or a net.

Capturing visitors, and the occasional resident, was another bad habit of Robin and his followers. Visitors loved it, so it continued. Most residents didn't venture in here.

I knew what to look for because I'd lived here for a while—years ago. The Merry Men hadn't changed their habits. What they did was popular—why bother? It made them predictable.

Before I'd reached the encampment, one of the Merry Men jumped out in front of me. He was new. I recognized his face under the little green hat, but I didn't know his name.

"Welcome to Sherwood Forest, my lady. You must know the password to get any further, and you must pay the toll."

"I want to see Robin. The password is—take me there now. You'll pay the toll if you don't."

He laughed. It was that over the top, stage laugh that Robin encourages. His head was thrown back, and the laugh went on for several minutes. "You don't scare me." He laughed again, but not as long.

By that time, I'd slipped an arrow out of my quiver. It was aimed at him.

"My lady." His voice was a little squeaky, and there was real fear in his eyes.

When you're new to the Village, you don't know what to expect next.

"Take me to Robin *now*."

"I knew I should've been a Templar Knight," he muttered as he walked in front of me down the path to the camp.

"You're not tough enough," I told him. "Maybe you should consider being a squire."

The twelve treehouses overlooked the central park area where a huge fire burned most of the time. The Merry Men frequently cooked their daily meals on the fire and hung out here. Whittling, and practicing their archery, were their most popular amusements as they waited for new groups of visitors.

Several men and women dressed in forest green dropped down and took out their bows when they saw me. I put my bow away and they calmed down. The new man ran for the woods when he had the chance.

"What's going on?" My brother, Tony, yelled down from the treehouse where he lived. Tony did PR work, mostly online, for Robin Hood. "Jessie!"

He dropped down gracefully with one hand on a rope.

"Nice move!" I gave him a hug.

"Thanks! What brings you here? You hate Sherwood Forest."

"I don't hate it. It's more a been-there, done-that kind of thing. Where's Robin?"

"He's still sleeping. He had a late night."

The rest of the Merry Men had joined us by then. They stood around listening and watching, their swords sheathed and peace-tied, bows on their backs.

"Fine. I'll talk to you then." I explained about the unidentified archer I was seeking. "Madman Bob saw him, or her, the night Dave was killed at the museum. Any ideas?"

They kind of muttered between themselves, but no one was forthcoming with information.

"You think one of us killed Madman Dave?" Alex joined us. He was Robin's second in command. "Why us?"

I knew Alex really well. He'd been my boyfriend when I'd spent time in Sherwood Forest. Now he was married to a woman named Sally, who was an English professor at Auburn. I knew what that life was like, and how hard it was to live apart, so I had some sympathy for him.

Alex was also a handsome, charming rogue who could be Robin Hood if Toby Gates, who played the master of the forest, ever left.

"It's obvious, isn't it? You have most of the archers in the Village. Sherwood Forest is right across the cobblestones from the museum. I need to know if one of you was there so I can cross you off the suspect list."

"Just go ahead and cross us off now, my lady." Robin Hood himself jumped down from his treehouse and did an elaborate bow. "Welcome to Sherwood, Lady Jessie. How may I serve you?"

"I think you already heard my story." I returned a deep bow since I was dressed like a man. "I need some names and confessions. Did any of your Merry Men come to the museum after it was closed?"

A tall, large woman stepped forward. She was dressed in forest green, and had long, strawberry blond hair. She was older for a Merry Man, or Woman, and very pretty. She pinned her green eyes on me. "I was there. I didn't kill anyone."

Robin and Alex looked at her. She was taller than both of them, and had broader shoulders.

"Why were you at the museum, Sofie?" Robin asked her.

"I was there on a personal matter." Her voice was hard and tough, but the faint blush in her cheeks told its own story.

"You were there to meet Shakespeare, weren't you?" I guessed.

"What if I was? We're consenting adults. He said we couldn't meet at his place anymore because of that witch of a ghost he used to be married to. We sure couldn't meet here. The museum was safe, and he had a way in."

Lady Marion, Robin's girlfriend, supported Sofie's position. "I knew she was going. I don't blame her. Trying to find any private time out here, living with all of *you*, is impossible. I was thinking about borrowing the museum myself."

Reminder to self: Have locks changed at the museum and be sure backdoor is locked. Otherwise you risk becoming the Village make-out spot.

"I'm sorry one of mine caused trouble," Robin apologized.

"No problem. I was hoping Sofie, or one of your people, had seen something that night that could help find Dave's killer."

"I might know something," Sofie muttered. "I was there in the basement with Shakespeare. There were some voices outside. I heard two men arguing. They kept their voices low, so I didn't recognize them."

"That's what I was looking for. Anything else that might be helpful?"

"Shakespeare said he could tell one of the men was Master Archer Simmons. You should talk to him."

Twelve

"Thanks," I said to Sofie. "I'll talk to him again."

Why was Shakespeare keeping things from me? Was he afraid he might implicate Master Simmons, as I was? He'd been there as long as the master archer. He probably knew more about that part in his life that he wanted to keep hidden.

I thanked Alex and Robin for their hospitality. Robin did his famous laugh with his hands on his hips, and his head thrown back. I knew it wasn't for my benefit—there had to be visitors behind me.

I turned around. They were obviously ardent fans of Sherwood. Each of them wore green outfits and carried a bow.

"I'll walk you out, shall I?" Marion offered, slipping her arm in mine.

"We have guests in the forest, Lady Marion," Robin reminded her.

"You can handle them," she called back. "I need to talk to Jessie about the wedding."

Marion was more excited than I was about the wedding. She also had more questions than I had answers.

"Jessie, you need a wedding planner. How else are we all going to know what's going on? What if the Queen's gown is going to clash with your wedding gown? What if Chase looks better than the king?"

We both laughed at that. Of course Chase was going to look better than King Harold.

"You know what I mean," she said when we'd stopped laughing. "Everyone is buzzing about it. There are even pictures of your dress on the Internet."

That was news to me. I'd been too busy doing other things to spend much time online. "Who could've done that?"

"I'm sorry. You didn't know? I think it was Portia. You know how she likes to rattle your cage."

"I don't care." I did, but it was too late. "Beth has already changed my gown once for the queen."

"But would she tell you if there was any other problem? You need somebody in your court."

I thought she was offering for a moment, but that wasn't her agenda. "I certainly hope your wedding isn't overshadowed by this murder. That would be terrible, wouldn't it?"

Apparently, she wanted to rattle my cage too. "I don't think I have to worry about that. The murder of a madman at the Village isn't going to get that much press. Wanda's ghost might."

"Speaking of the ghost, have you thought that she might have killed Dave? After all, she seems vicious enough. It was a cruel thing to do, wasn't it? Why else would someone want to kill poor Dave?"

"I'm not sure yet why anyone would want to kill Dave, but I don't think Wanda did it." The rumors were getting more elaborate. "Although I'd rather it be her than someone else we all know."

"I suppose," she sighed. "Well, I'm off to do some shopping. I'm embarking on a new career, you know. I'm going to be a world famous actress!"

"Congratulations," I muttered as she squeezed my arm and then headed toward Stylish Frocks. I wondered if Robin knew her plans.

The museum was busier when I stopped by again. It might have been because the rain was driving everyone indoors. The cobblestones and the soggy Village Green were mostly empty. I could see visitors hanging out in the Honey and Herb Shoppe too. Everyone was hoping the rain would pass before the whole day was lost.

I stood off to the side and listened as Oliver explained about weaving as he worked the loom. He told the crowd about how tapestries were first used to hang on walls to help keep drafty huts and castles warmer in the winter.

"These rich hangings were full of color and life," he continued as his sure hands worked the loom to create his own tapestry. "We have to imagine that they brought a much needed relief to the drab world of the Dark Ages."

Oliver's tapestry, which he gladly showed visitors, was of a country scene with a colorful cottage. There was great detail of swans on the lake and birds in the air. Clouds hung in the blue sky. It was an idyllic world.

Manny saw me listening, and made a quick march over to where I was. “Is this the way the director of the museum dresses? I think not. No wonder you’re hiding over here in the corner. What are you doing?”

“I’m looking for a killer so you don’t have to go to jail.”

“You don’t have to worry. With my father, the king behind me, there is no problem.”

“Does he know you’re in the Village now?”

“Yes, unfortunately. There will no doubt be hell to pay.” He grinned. “I love that expression, don’t you?”

I laughed. “Have you seen him yet?”

He lifted his chin. “No. But it is only a matter of time.”

“No matter what, whether your father is a king or not, we still need to find out who killed Dave.”

“I don’t understand why.”

“Because it’s important. We can’t go around letting people kill other people here. That would be worse than getting a reputation as a haunted Renaissance Faire.”

He assimilated the explanation. “I understand. What can I do to help?”

“I’m not sure right now. Just keep the museum running, and I’ll let you know.”

Chase came in the door and looked around until he saw me. He inclined his head to a few ladies as he passed, headed in my direction.

"I've been looking for you. Brother Carl said he saw you enter Sherwood Forest. What was that about?"

I started to explain, but it seemed we were short on time.

"Tell me as we go. We have to go see the twins. I know you don't want to, but it's necessary. We want the rings to be right."

I left Manny in charge again, and walked back out with him.

We couldn't use ponchos, or real rain gear, in the Village. Plastic and rubber didn't exist in our time period. It meant getting wet in the cold rain with little chance of drying off during the day. Not a pleasant feeling.

There were pretty cloth parasols. They were better than nothing. I always kept one handy. Chase never used one, of course. It didn't go well with that tough guy image.

"I talked to King Harold," Chase told me as we went down the steps to the cobblestones. "My parents and Morgan are going to stay at the castle until the wedding."

"At the castle?" I'd been hoping they were going to stay at a hotel. "Until the wedding?" *Almost two weeks?*

"Yes. And the king and queen have invited all of us to a special dinner held in our honor."

"When?" I felt like I was asking about a disaster.

"Tonight. Think you can make it?"

"Of course." I smiled at him. "I can't wait."

The twins were waiting at Our Lady's Gemstones. I felt not only churlish, but surly as well. Rene and Renee were trying so hard to be accommodating. They had us sit in beautiful black brocade chairs and brought out tiny glasses of wine with cheese and sweet almond cookies. They presented the rings in grand fashion on blood-red satin pillows.

The cynical part of me believed this was due to the huge amount of money Chase had spent with them for my engagement ring and our wedding bands. But I had never heard anything bad about the twins. It was only my personal dislike of them that kept me from enjoying their company.

I reached for the ring on the pillow. Rene lightly slapped my hand. "No one but the jeweler who made the ring should slip it on your finger before your wedding day, Lady Jessie."

"It's terribly bad luck," Renee confirmed. She put the broad, white gold band on Chase's finger. "How does that feel, Sir Bailiff?"

Chase flexed his fingers, and gazed at the handsome piece. "It feels fine. Thank you."

Rene slid the wedding band on my finger. His icy hands made me shiver. "There now. How is that, Lady Jessie?"

"Fine. It's wonderful." I tried to work up some enthusiasm.

The ring *was* beautiful. The band was set with tiny diamonds that were in the shape of the constellation Gemini. One of the first things Chase and I had done together was visiting Galileo in the Village. He'd shown us the constellation that was prominent on that day. Our rings reflected that memory.

"There's something written inside." I took the ring off and started to look at the inscription.

"I wish you'd wait," Chase said. "I'll wait to look at your inscription too. Okay?"

My inscription? Was I supposed to have something *inscribed* on the ring?

With less than two weeks to go until the wedding, my heart was filled with terror. I didn't know what to say inside Chase's ring. Was there even enough time to do that?

"A wise choice." Rene gave me a knowing look. "This way you two can share your messages together for the first time as man and wife."

Renee put her hands together and smiled. "What a wonderful plan."

Chase put his ring back on the satin pillow. Thank God he hadn't looked inside. He would've been so disappointed.

But what was I going to say? Maybe I could sneak a peek inside my ring to get some idea about what he'd had inscribed.

I put my ring on the pillow, trying to see what was written in it. It was no use. It was too small, and I didn't have time before Rene put them away. I'd have to come back and look at it later.

"Thank you so much for your craftsmanship, and everything you've done for us." Chase clasped hands with Rene first and then his sister.

He gave me a nod, and I thanked the twins too. Maybe not as elegantly, but I thanked them anyway.

Lucky for me, Chase's radio called out another problem that required his attention— there were two naked women in the Good Luck Fountain—it happened at least once every month. He excused himself to the twins, gave me a kiss, and was gone.

Rene and Renee stood staring at me with knowing eyes.

"You have to tell me what he had inscribed."

Renee shook her head, her long white hair following the movement. "We cannot. We swore an oath to our customer, the Bailiff. We would dishonor him, and ourselves, if we did not uphold it."

"Okay." I felt a little desperate. "Was it more than one line? Was it a famous quote? Give me something to work with here. Is there still time for me to inscribe something on his ring?"

"There is plenty of time remaining," Rene confirmed. "But we cannot divulge what he said."

"Please," I begged. "I don't know what to say inside a ring. I never even thought about it."

The twins did their intent staring session, as they had many times before. I felt sure they were communicating with their minds, though I had no proof of that.

Finally, Renee agreed. "The words on the ring are not a quote, nor are they words that ever belonged to anyone else. The words belong to the Bailiff."

"Okay." *Thanks for nothing!* So I have to come up with some clever saying that you can inscribe on the ring. How long?"

"Three days." Rene nodded.

"Three days. Thanks. I'll get back with you."

Anything else? My poor tired brain was screaming. Find Dave's killer. Get ready for the wedding. Have dinner with Chase's parents who hated me. Run the museum. Wait for a sorcerer to come who would deal with Wanda's ghost.

I was on the verge of a meltdown.

I saw Master Archer Simmons with his team of archers practicing for the wedding, despite the rain. It would be quite a show—if I lived to see it. For the moment, it looked like something familiar, a sanctuary from my crazy world.

"Lady Jessie!" Master Archer Simmons greeted me. "I'm so glad you're here. You can give us your opinion of our performance. We've been working very hard on this."

"Gladly." Anything for a distraction. What would it look like if I inscribed *You shot an arrow into my heart* inside Chase's ring?

No. That was too plain. Anyone could say that. I was pretty sure the little heart-shaped candies that were out at Valentine's Day said something similar.

The archers lit their arrows—difficult because of the rain and mist. They took aim, and fired into the dull, gray sky. The arrows flew true, some extinguishing from the moisture, others returning to the earth, still on fire.

The archers ran to retrieve their arrows.

“Wonderful.” I applauded. “That was really exciting.”

Could I have *Your love is my aim?* inscribed in Chase’s ring?

No. I had to think of something better than that.

“Do you think we should aim at a different trajectory?” Master Simmons asked.

“I think that was fine.” I was only half paying attention.

“If you don’t mind the royal court going up in flames.” Wanda’s mocking voice interrupted my thoughts. “Why do you think they used to shoot flaming arrows at their enemies? Use your head, Jessie. *I* want to be the one to spoil your wedding, with no help from you.”

“I suppose you should position the archers so the arrows drop into the lake,” I suggested.

Master Simmons looked surprised. “That’s probably a good idea. I’m not sure yet where everyone will be sitting. The king told me that the plans aren’t finalized. I’ll be sure to tell him of your suggestion.”

What about: *You’re the king of my heart?*

No! That was awful.

In the meantime, the archers continued lighting their arrows and shooting them off until the whole area was smoky.

It was a good time to ask Master Simmons about why he was at the museum the night Dave was killed. "I've heard you were outside the museum that night? Is that true?"

He sighed and hung his head. "I was afraid you might hear of that."

"Better me than the police. Why didn't you tell me?"

"I wasn't there with Dave. Phil and I had a few drinks and we were talking about my missing crossbow. One thing led to another, and we were arguing about it. I felt that he could have paid more attention, you know? Done a better job protecting it. The crossbow was valuable, and only on loan. I was supposed to get it back a few weeks after the museum opened."

"Did you see Dave when you were there?"

"No. Although, as usual, there were several people out and about. I saw Shakespeare, and his new paramour, sneaking into the museum. There was an archer out too, dressed in black."

"That was Shakespeare's new girlfriend, Sofie."

He frowned. "No. This was someone else. I tried to see the face, but he or she wore a hood. Shakespeare had already gone inside with Sofie."

"Can you describe the archer?"

"It was dark, but I'd say tall and thin. He or she carried a long bow, not a crossbow, so it couldn't have been Dave's killer. That's about it. I'm sorry."

"That's okay." I took it all in. "Thanks for your help. I'll try to keep you out of this, but there are other lives involved too."

"I understand. Do what you have to."

I started back toward the museum, thoroughly soaked by then. The pretty umbrella wasn't much good against real rain.

The crowds had thinned out even further as people began to realize that the weather wasn't going to clear. That was the only trouble with paying so much to get into the Village for the day with no pass for rainy weather. I felt sorry for those families that had paid for a few adults and several children. I hoped they'd return on a nice day.

"I know who you are now," a soft voice said near my ear.

I turned, and saw the Village's newest resident, Tilly Morgenstern, beside me. She kind of just appeared. *Where did she come from?*

Beside her was her assistant, Leo. He stood there like a huge statue, unblinking. It was hard to tell if he was even breathing.

"Yes," I agreed. "We sort of met the other night when you were moving in. I was with the Bailiff. Jessie Morton."

"Of course." She drew a gray shawl closely around her thin shoulders. It looked as though it had been woven with cobwebs. Her curly white hair held rain droplets in it. "You're the woman who made the ghost blue."

"You can see her?"

"Yes. You were fortunate that you didn't go to prison for her murder, as my sister did."

"I know. It was a terrible thing. I'm sorry for you and your family."

She smiled in a way that sent tingles of alarm down my spine. "Those are just words. Come now. We are both women of the world. You could have walked away. You chose not to. You put my sister in that terrible place with your actions, and your testimony. That makes you responsible."

I wasn't sure what to say. I hadn't looked at it from that perspective. I thought I was doing what needed to be done.

"I'm sorry you feel that way," I finally said. "I wish it hadn't come to that end. I really had no choice. She would have killed me."

Tilly looked away, her gaze following the trails of smoke left behind by the flaming arrows. Her nod toward Leo was almost imperceptible.

He slowly turned his head and faced me. There were horrific scars on his pale face. His blank, white eyes made me shudder. He took one step toward me. His large hands became fists that he ground together.

"It happened." Tilly laughed in her strange little girl way. "I won't forget it. I won't let *you* forget it either. Sometime. Somewhere. There *will* be retribution."

I truly hoped she was talking about a bad prank, but I didn't think so. I gulped. She scared me. I wanted to run away fast, but my feet wouldn't move.

You know how people say they were paralyzed with fear? I'm not kidding. I couldn't move at all. Leo could have knocked me down. I would have fallen like a bowling pin.

Instead, Tilly gazed at me malevolently, and Leo went back to his normal, zombie-like blankness. They walked away through the smoke and mist toward the tavern.

"I don't think she likes you very much, Jessie." Wanda watched the two leave. "In fact, I think she might hate you. What do you think?"

Thirteen

Feeling a little vulnerable, even though Tilly was gone, I ran into Eve's Garden to try to wait out the new downpour—and to think about an inscription for Chase's ring.

It smelled wonderful in the garden shop. Flowers of all colors and sizes were growing there. I was ashamed to admit that I had no idea what most of them were.

Eve, a quiet woman with long brown hair, tended this garden. She had the most gentle, sweetest manner about her. She knew everything about plants and herbs used during the Renaissance. She gave tours here each day, and shared her knowledge with visitors.

"Lady Jessie. Come to choose your bouquet at last?"

I hadn't thought about that either. "Bouquet? Of course. What would you suggest?"

"Lilac would be lovely." She showed me the purple bloom with tiny flowers. It smelled wonderful. "It means love's first emotions. A nice sentiment."

"Very nice."

"Or perhaps stephanotis. Very popular for wedding bouquets. It means marital happiness."

I looked at the trumpet-shaped flowers. "Those are nice too."

She kept telling me about all the flowers that would be good for the bouquet. It made me remember how I'd first decided to write my dissertation on my favorite subject—Renaissance arts and crafts. It also made me remember when I fell in love with Chase.

I'd been working at the castle at the time. He was the queen's favorite knight. All the ladies loved him.

I was a castle drudge, one of many. I'd seen Chase from a distance, but had never met him. He was too busy with the royal court, and Princess Isabel, to notice much of anything else.

I dropped one of the huge serving trays during the King's Feast, an event that takes place every Sunday night. Hundreds of visitors pay premium prices to sit in an arena and eat Cornish hens and baked potatoes while swilling ale and watching knights and jugglers perform.

I cursed without the fluency I learned later while I was on the pirate ship. There was nothing else to do but pick up all of the lost food and go back for more. Rita Martinez threw a few blistering words my way. That was way before we were friends.

"Here, let me help you with that," a warm, male voice said.

Chase was dressed regally in blue brocade. The lights from the candles and lanterns in the Great Hall danced in his eyes. I thought I'd never seen anyone as handsome. I felt like Cinderella, and wished he was my Prince Charming.

He got down on one knee, despite his finery, and began helping me pick up the mess.

"You're Jessie, aren't you?" He smiled as he tossed dirty Cornish hens back on my platter.

"Yes, my lord."

"I'm not a lord. Just a knight. I've seen you here before. You're new to the Village, aren't you?"

"Yes. This is my first summer." Nothing like a conversation with the most fantastic man in the world over a pile of spilled vegetables and chicken.

"Are you having a good time?"

"Absolutely." I smiled and tossed my hair, which was long at the time. I knew I didn't stand a chance with him, but what the heck? "I'm going to write my dissertation about Renaissance crafts."

Our eyes made direct contact, and my heart jumped right out of my chest.

"Sounds great," he said.

Our hands met as he gave me the rest of the coarse bread to pile back on the tray. I wanted to rip off his clothes right then.

Rita called out a sharp warning to get going. Princess Isabel personally came to take Chase away. The moment was over, but I never forgot it.

It was years later that Chase and I finally got together. We were friends after that moment at the castle, but he had his lovers, and I had mine. Still, I always noticed when he walked by places where I was working. He never failed to call out a greeting to me when I watched him joust at the Field of Honor.

"My lady?" Eve called. "I fear you are daydreaming about your wedding."

"Yes," I agreed with a smile. "I suppose I was."

As a matter of fact, I'd come up with something to inscribe into Chase's ring. Maybe it wasn't much, but it was from the heart.

I ordered some stephanotis for happiness, and red roses for passion for my bouquet. She smiled, and I was happy when I left the garden. I went right over to see Rene and Renee to tell them what I wanted inscribed in Chase's ring.

Maybe the wedding was going to be okay after all. If I was there with Chase, how bad could it be?

The rain continued throughout the evening, at times torrential. I loved the scent of the sea that accompanied those storms, a reminder that just outside the Village was the Atlantic Ocean, and the party city of Myrtle Beach.

The Main Gate stayed open until six p.m. as it was supposed to, even though there were very few visitors on the cobblestones by that time. Still there was music and laughter from the Tornado Twins, and the Green Man shook hands with visitors who were leaving. A few colorful fairies flitted around, their wings a little bedraggled by the weather.

Night settled in early. Chase and I showered and put on our dress Renaissance clothes. Chase was handsome in midnight blue velvet. I wore a paler blue silk gown with a sapphire studded girdle about my hips. They were fake sapphires, but they looked pretty.

There wasn't much I could do with my hair. I added a short veil that was attached to a pretty blue comb. I put on a little light lipstick, and that was it. I probably should have worn my sandals, but I opted for my boots instead. No one could see them under my gown anyway. I didn't want to ruin my good sandals in the rain since I'd planned to wear them for the wedding.

"You look beautiful," Chase said when I was ready. "You should've been a princess instead of just a Bailiff's lady."

"Not unless you were the prince." I kissed him. "I'd rather be a madman's lady, if you were the madman."

He smiled a little sadly. "My mother was making the point today that I'm a madman."

That evil woman! "She probably wishes she could live here all the time too."

"Yeah. I'm sure that's it." He laughed and picked me up, spinning me around in the confined space of the apartment. "I love you. I hope I tell you that often enough."

"You must," I replied with a smile. "I want to spend the rest of my life with you."

"I guess we should get going. I've arranged transportation, my lady." He swept me a gallant bow. "The carriage waits."

I looked out of the foggy window. One of the Cinderella carriages was indeed waiting. My old friend, D'Amos Torres, was driving.

"I suppose that means we should go." I sighed. "No matter how much I'd rather stay here and eat a frozen burrito."

Chase offered me his arm, and we went down the stairs together.

D'Amos jumped down from the driver's seat, and took off his feathered hat before opening the carriage door for us. "Good evening, Sir Bailiff. You are looking lovely as always, Lady Jessie."

I dropped the Renaissance act long enough to hug my friend. D'Amos had once worked at the Columbia Zoo, which is where we'd met. He loved animals. Now he took care of all the animals in the Village.

"I can't believe you didn't send a minion or a lackey to pick us up," I told him with a smile. "This is not a fit night for man or beast. Yet here you are."

"I chose not to send minion, lackey, squire, or varlet because the night is bad. I told Chase I would take care of this for him. You know I'm not one to back out of a promise."

"I'm glad to see you anyway. There's something I should tell you about the problems you've been having with the animals."

He nodded at Chase. "If you're talking about Wanda's ghost, Chase already filled me in. My grandmother was a great believer in spooks and such. I've heard those stories all my life. I never gave them much thought, until yesterday when I found a goat riding on one of the elephants. Now I'm looking for ghost repellant."

"If you find any, please let me know." I glanced around us at the dark night. "She likes to shower with me. I could use all the help I could get."

D'Amos laughed. "I'm looking into some herbs my grandmother said would work for our problem. I'll let you know."

We finally got into the carriage, and he drove us sedately toward the castle.

"It's still impressive, even after all these years," I told Chase as I looked out the window at the lighted structure above the lake.

"I know what you mean. I can't imagine wanting to live anywhere else. I heard today that Mike Manchester at Sir Latte's is retiring next month. That surprised me. He's not that old."

"What's he going to do?"

"He inherited a schooner, and he plans to sail around the world."

"A worthy endeavor." I thought about Lady Marion. "Have you heard anything about Robin and Marion breaking up?"

"No. Why? Is she leaving the Village too?"

"I don't know." I explained about her new career.

"You know that kind of stuff goes on all the time, right?" Chase took my hand and kissed it. "People come and go here. They fall in and out of love, like they do everywhere."

"You know Wanda told me she purposely had women try to lure you from me while I was in Columbia."

"Really? I guess I didn't notice."

"Liar." I kissed him.

"Never, my lady."

We reached the castle. D'Amos opened the carriage door and bowed as we got out.

"Come in for dinner with us," I invited.

His older, dark face was comical in its terror. "I had the privilege of meeting the Bailiff's parents already today, lady. I think I shall eat leftovers in front of my TV. Dancing with the Stars is on tonight."

"I don't blame you," I whispered. "Thank you, good sir."

Gus was at attention inside the doorway to the castle. He was dressed in his best armor, and saluted us as we approached. "Welcome Sir Bailiff and Lady Jessie. The king and queen wait within."

Chase and I were led into the castle by Sir Marcus Fleck who was once the Black Dwarf. He'd also played the Town Crier for a while. He seemed to like the castle where he was a royal herald and major domo.

He inquired after our health as we walked into the castle. "Your wedding will be a joyous event! We're all looking forward to it. I hope there's plenty of champagne."

King Harold and Queen Olivia were waiting for us in the sitting room. Chase's family was with them. It made me wish I'd thought to invite Tony since he was my only living relative. It was probably just as well, though it made me feel a little alone. Tony can be crazy sometimes. It was hard enough coping with Chase's family.

"Good evening, Sir Bailiff and Lady Jessie." King Harold—Harry to those of us who knew him well—greeted us. "We are so glad to have you with us during this joyous time in your lives."

Queen Olivia, Livy—when we were talking about her behind her back—agreed with him. "Yes! We are very excited about your wedding, and looking forward to spending the evening with you and your lovely family."

Chase's parents, and Morgan, sat like statues on the antique furniture that filled the sitting room. There were beautiful tapestries on the walls that had more life in them than Chase's family did. Cold eyes regarded me as I was introduced to Chase's parents, shook hands and prepared to spend some fun-filled time together.

The royal nanny brought Princess Pea into the sitting room for the king and queen to say their goodnights. She was a precious little thing who was partially named after me. I'd helped deliver her, after saving the queen's life, but that was another story.

"Goodnight, darling Pea." The king lifted his daughter and kissed her. "Sleep well."

Pea was almost one year old. She struggled in her father's arms, and said a few words that I couldn't understand, but her proud parents didn't care.

Queen Olivia laughed, looking younger and so much happier since the princess was born. "She wants a story, Harry," she told her husband. "We can carry on without you for a few minutes. We don't want to disappoint Pea."

Harry also seemed much happier and, as far as I knew, had stayed faithful to his wife for the last year. It was a royal feat in itself.

"Storytelling is one of my favorite times of day." Kind Harold grinned as he got up from his chair to accompany the nanny and his daughter back to her room. "I shall return."

When he was gone, Mrs. Manhattan cleared her throat. "May I ask why you call your daughter Princess Pea? I mean, I get the princess part, but why Pea?"

Livy smiled graciously. "She has such a long name—Henrietta Olivia Jane Jessica—we just decided to call her Pea for short. It's much easier to say than all of that, don't you think?"

Mrs. Manhattan shrugged and looked bored.

"Let me ask why you decided to name your son, Chase, after a bank." Livy returned the favor.

Mr. Manhattan glanced at his wife. "It seemed appropriate. I was a financial advisor for many years."

Queen Olivia nodded. "And your son, Morgan, is also named for a financial institution. How quaint."

I hoped this wasn't going to get ugly. I knew from Chase's tales of his family that they had always thought themselves a step or two above everyone else. It seemed as though his father going to prison for insider trading hadn't changed that.

They'd always felt Chase was too good to live in the Village also, and was definitely too good to be with me. I'd hoped their attitude would change over time, but time had passed, and they'd remained the same.

Mrs. Manhattan's smile was barely a slight upturn of her lips. "At least we don't fool ourselves into thinking we're actually a king and queen living in a real castle instead of one constructed from an old Air Force control tower."

Livy's right eye twitched a little. "For all intents and purposes, we *are* a king and queen. Our daughter is a princess. Your son is our respected Bailiff, whom we love dearly."

"Our son," Mr. Manhattan said, "is a highly trained, well educated, attorney who should be out making some real money instead of dressing up in weird clothes, and hanging out here researching patents in his spare time."

I felt a headache coming on. For the first time since Wanda died, I wished she'd come and interrupt everything.

Fourteen

"Why don't we all have a drink," Morgan suggested with a smile. "I know I could use a drink or ten."

"Good idea." Chase got to his feet and rang for castle help.

"We have champagne for an appropriate toast, Sir Bailiff," the annoyed queen said.

"I think we might need something now, your majesty." Chase bowed elegantly to her.

Livy giggled. Chase had always been one of her favorites. "I could never deny you anything. Order what you will."

"This is ridiculous." Mr. Manhattan shot to his feet.

Chase ordered a bottle of good whiskey when the castle servant appeared.

"Make that two." Morgan clapped his brother on the shoulder. "Do I say forsooth now?"

"No," Chase said. "Thank you, and a tip, works."

Mrs. Manhattan got to her feet too. Before she could say anything, King Harold rejoined us. He approved the whiskey, and asked for a third bottle.

Good idea. We needed a roomful of drunken snobs to make the evening perfect.

"Why don't we go into dinner," King Harold suggested. "I am looking to change up my portfolio. I was thinking you Manhattans might have some suggestions."

That seemed to mollify Chase's family a little. We went into the elaborate dining room that could hold twenty people.

"I'm thinking about an emergency coming up in time to save us from this mess," Chase whispered as we walked together.

"It's going to be fine." I squeezed his hand.

He didn't deserve to be stressed by this—not if I could help it.

The first course was wonderful—a light pumpkin soup. The whiskey was poured, and everything seemed to go better.

King Harold, Morgan, and Mr. Manhattan were deep into stocks and bonds, divestitures, and upgrading portfolios.

That was good for them, but left Queen Olivia, me, Chase, and Mrs. Manhattan with nothing in common.

"We're so glad you had the extra time to be here for Chase and Jessie's wedding." Queen Olivia managed to say it in a polite, non-snarky voice.

"Our family is so busy," Mrs. Manhattan returned. "It's difficult for us to get away."

"I can appreciate that," the queen responded pleasantly. "There is so much to be overseen for the wedding. Catering for more than a thousand people is difficult."

“Do you have the menu yet?” Chase’s mother asked.

“It’s not complete,” Queen Olivia admitted. “There was some hold up bringing in enough fruit, if you can believe it.”

The first course was removed by quiet waiters dressed in castle finery. The second course, a shrimp salad, was served.

This night is never going to be over. I sat still and held Chase’s hand under the white linen table cloth. Where was Wanda when I needed her? Why hadn’t any elephants or camels escaped?

“Shrimp!” Mrs. Manhattan leapt to her feet, knocking over her crystal water glass, and sending the shrimp salad flying into the air.

Chase was quick on his feet, catching the plate before it hit anything. He couldn’t stop the shrimp salad from flying all over me. I took several tiny shrimp out of my hair and off of my gown.

“Oh no, Lady Jessie, what bad luck!” Livy called the waiters and one of her ladies in waiting. “Lady Leticia, would you help get Lady Jessie cleaned up?”

I stared at Mrs. Manhattan. She couldn’t have done it on purpose, right? It would take perfect timing and responses. It was just an accident.

“Excuse me,” I muttered and managed to continue smiling. “I’ll be right back.”

A little shrimp salad wasn’t going to stop me from being at Chase’s side. I couldn’t tell if it was deliberate or not. I told myself it didn't matter. Once the wedding was over, I wouldn't have to see Chase's family again for a year. Chase flew home to Arizona once a year in the winter, when the Village was slow.

I figured this visit, and the wedding, was his visit for the year.

Lady Leticia was very nice and efficient in helping me get cleaned up. There was nothing I could do about the stain on my bodice. She loaned me a beautiful lace shawl that would cover it.

"Thank you so much for your help," I said to her before I went back.

She curtsied, and her nineteen-year-old face went pink. "It was a pleasure to be of service, Lady Jessie."

I didn't need her help finding my way back to the royal dining room. But before I reached that spot, the door opened, and Mr. and Mrs. Manhattan stalked out.

They didn't see me. I was behind one of the ornate pillars that pretended to hold up the roof of the castle.

"This is a farce," Mrs. Manhattan said loudly. "I won't allow my son to get caught up with this gold-digger. We have to find a way to stop the wedding."

Mr. Manhattan shrugged in his thousand dollar suit. "That's why we're here early, right? I don't think we're off to a good start."

"He has to be made to see the truth behind all this," she hissed. "Chase's heart has always been too soft."

They were too busy hurrying out of the castle to say anything more. I didn't want to hear anything else they had to say. That was plenty.

Chase and Morgan came out of the dining room.

"I don't know what you expected," Morgan drawled. "You knew they weren't happy about this wedding."

"Why did they come?" Chase asked. "Why are you here?"

"My only brother is marrying the girl of his dreams." Morgan slapped him on the back. "Probably in tights. Why wouldn't I be here?"

It occurred to me at that moment that Morgan and Wanda would have been a perfect match. They were both hateful people.

"Go home and take them with you," Chase said. "I invited you because I thought you'd be happy for me. I can see that's not possible."

"They aren't going anywhere. They want to stop the wedding. Watch out for them. They usually get what they want."

Morgan smiled, and left Chase standing there. I wasn't sure if I should act as though I hadn't heard what was said or tell him how crazy his family was.

I decided to show my support.

"Jessie. I was hoping you were still getting cleaned up. I guess dinner is over."

I put my arms around him. “What happened?”

“They started talking about the wedding.” He shrugged. “That was it for my parents.”

“I heard what they said—and what Morgan said. They can’t stop us now. We’re not little kids they can tell what to do.”

“No,” he agreed. “But they can make us miserable.”

We went back into the dining room, and made our apologies to the king and queen. They were surprisingly unaffected by Chase’s parents.

“You know, the queen’s parents didn’t want us to marry either.” King Harold sipped his whiskey. “They thought I wasn’t good enough.”

Queen Olivia smiled. “They didn’t know you like I did, Harry.”

“Exactly my point,” the king said. “Chase, you and Jessie are going to make a great couple. Don’t let anyone stop you.”

We smiled and agreed. As we were leaving the castle, Chase grinned. “Do you think he’s taking such an interest because we’re the stars of his wedding plans?”

“Your guess is as good as mine.”

We walked out into the dark Village. Looking at it from the height of the castle, it was picturesque. Hundreds of tiny cottages and shops gleaming with yellow light that spilled onto the cobblestones.

"I love the Village," I sighed, resting my head against his shoulder.

"Me too. Especially when it's quiet like this. I'm glad we live here."

As he kissed me, there was a heart pounding scream from somewhere in the night.

"I suppose you have to go down there and see what's wrong," I said.

"It's my job."

"I'm coming with you."

He bowed. "After you, my lady."

It was easy to figure out where the scream had come from. Shakespeare was crying and ranting outside the museum. He hadn't quite made it to safety when Wanda had attacked him. He was covered with sheep dung and hay. It was smelly and messy, but he wasn't hurt.

"When is this madness going to stop?" He called out in his best oratorical voice. He turned full circle and faced the crowd that had gathered around him. "I beseech you, good neighbors—let us find a way to rid ourselves of this ghostly nuisance. We must take up pitchforks and clubs to beat her out of our lives."

Bart was there, still in his queen's guard uniform. "I don't think clubs and pitchforks will have much of an effect on a ghost."

"Maybe swords then," Shakespeare recanted.

"Not swords either." Daisy, the sword maker, shook her head.

"You have to fight ghosts with fire," Fred the Red Dragon told them. "We need torches."

As everyone was agreeing with him, Chase stepped into the middle of the group. "No one is carrying around torches in the Village. Most of the shops and houses are made of wood. We'd go up in a big bonfire. I don't think anyone wants that."

All of the residents hesitantly agreed.

"But what should we do, Chase?" one of the elephant handlers asked. "Things are crazy with the ghost around here. We have to get rid of her."

They agreed enthusiastically with that.

What they didn't know was that Wanda was flying around between them, cackling at their anger. I guess I was the only one who could see her—and stupid enough to stand around. Anyone else was probably home cowering in their beds.

"I can get rid of her." Tilly Morgenstern from the tavern was suddenly there with Leo beside her.

They made a scary couple in the dim light. A cool wind was blowing up from the ocean after the rain had passed. It blew her hair around, and made her look even more frightening.

"What can you do?" Peter Greenwalt from Peter's Pub asked.

“I can banish her from this place,” Tilly promised. “For a price.”

The shopkeepers, craftsmen, and other residents, exchanged glances. If there was money involved with it, they were less likely to look at it favorably.

“How much?” Roger Trent asked. The light from above gleamed on his shaved head.

“Not much.” Tilly’s face was sly. “One percent of all your profits for the next year. One percent. Wanda Le Fey will never bother you again.”

“We don’t work that way here,” Chase said. “You’d have to clear that with Adventureland. I don’t think they’d appreciate a fee for ghost removal.”

“She can’t do that.” Wanda appeared next to me. “No one can stop me from being here. This is my home.”

I glanced around. No one was near me, so I whispered, “They don’t *know* that. You’ve made their lives miserable. They just want to get rid of you.”

She looked a little afraid. “Tell them, Jessie. Madame Lucinda said only you could get rid of me.”

“You heard that did you?”

“I couldn’t hear her say it, but I’ve heard you tell Chase.”

I folded my arms across my chest. “I’m not speaking up for you. I don’t care if she banishes you forever.”

"But she can't, right?" Wanda put her blue face right in front of mine.

It was weird looking through her to sce the people I knew on the other side. "I don't know. Maybe Madame Lucinda is wrong. I think Tilly may be a witch. In that case, maybe she knows a spell or incantation that can disperse you."

She wrapped her arms around me. "No! You can't let her do that. This is all I have to keep me in one piece. Without it, I'd be gone for good."

People were beginning to look at me oddly. I didn't attempt to reassure Wanda.

"I don't think you want to get between me and what I want, Bailiff." Tilly's tone was threatening. "I'm not a nice person. Don't cross me."

Chase looked down at her with a mixture of sympathy and courage in his face. "We aren't taking you up on this offer. If you continue trying to disrupt the Village, I'll have you removed. That's the way it works around here."

I saw Leo's hands become fists. Big, hammy, hurtful fists. His dead-looking face was turned toward Chase.

Tilly slowly put her hand on her assistant's arm, and his fists relaxed until his arms were hanging slack at his sides again.

"I can see why they have you here to keep the peace." She slowly smiled at Chase. "I won't oppose you on this—not now anyway. Let Wanda keep disrupting your lives. You'll come to me in time."

I felt like I blinked, and she was gone. The big man was gone with her. I knew it wasn't possible. It was a trick like other things in the Village.

Madame Lucinda limped out of her gold and purple tent. It reminded me of Glinda, the good witch, showing up after the bad witch was dead.

"Good people of Renaissance Faire Village," she addressed the crowd. "Do not believe for one minute that the woman who was here can save you from this apparition. There is only one among us who can do that."

Please don't say it's me.

"Lady Jessie Morton."

Rats.

Fifteen

I kind of backed up. There were images of pitchforks and torches from Frankenstein movies in my head. It's not a good thing to tell angry people that you have the answer to their problem when you don't want to use it.

"Hey, look. You all know how Wanda and I felt about each other when she was alive. She wasn't my biggest fan, and I sure wouldn't keep her around if I could do something about it."

"She was the worst nurse in the world," the blacksmith, Hans Von Rupp said, spitting on the ground.

This led to everyone else agreeing by spitting. It was a common way to let people know what you were thinking at the Village. Not exactly hygienic, but it happened.

"We all know that." I laughed nervously. "Madame Lucinda says a sorcerer is coming who can take Wanda away. Anyone know a sorcerer?"

One of the new King's Tarts, a pretty girl who always wore red, stuck her hand up. "My boyfriend is a sorcerer of the First Kingdom. Maybe he could take care of it."

Chase was at my side, probably more for moral support than because he was afraid someone would hurt me. But I was glad he was there anyway.

"That's what I was talking about," he whispered. "I'm fairly sure there are no real sorcerers."

"I don't know anymore," I admitted. "Probably not her boyfriend, but maybe someone else."

It seemed everyone knew a sorcerer. I collected their names and emails before the crowd dispersed. Peter Greenwalt invited everyone over to his pub for a free drink.

I wanted to go home and forget this night. Chase agreed, and we hurried back to the Dungeon.

Wanda was sitting in the middle of our bed when we got back. She was sobbing, and holding her head in her hands. *Literally*. I guess it was a new trick.

"What's wrong?" Chase asked. "Wanda?"

"I'm afraid so."

He frowned, and went to change out of his dinner finery in the bathroom.

"For someone who doesn't want to be sent away, you have a strange way of showing it." I removed my veil and headpiece. "What do you want, Wanda?"

"What everyone wants," she snapped back. "Life, liberty, and the pursuit of happiness."

"You're dead. We can't change that, but quit messing around with the people who can see you—and the animals—and you could stay."

A voice from the bathroom added, "And stay out of our apartment."

"Chase is right. You know you shouldn't be here."

Wanda sobbed harder. “In other words, give up everything I enjoy about death, and I can stay. Well, where’s the fun in that? Maybe it would be better to be sent away.”

“If that’s the way you feel.” I sat on the bed, and took off my boots.

“Of course, you’ll have to find a sorcerer—a real sorcerer—first.” She stopped crying, put her head where it belonged, and rubbed her hands together.

“Not just any sorcerer,” I reminded her. “The one who gave you the bracelet.”

She was in the air the next moment. “I didn’t realize that. He would never do such a thing. He loved me. I guess all of you are quite screwed.”

Wanda vanished. I hoped it was for the remainder of the night.

“Is she gone?” Chase glanced around as he came out of the bathroom.

“Right now.”

He laughed as he came toward me. “Quick then, lady. Out of those clothes.”

* * *

It was a long, wonderful night without Wanda. The sun came out the next morning and got rid of all the creepy fog. It looked like it was going to be a nice day. For the first time in a long while, I was looking forward to it.

Chase and I parted company after coffee and cinnamon rolls. He was off to find out what had caused a water line break that was keeping the Good Luck Fountain closed for the day.

I was wearing my lucky pink blouse and matching long skirt with a tied black vest that made my waist look really small. My first stop was going to be the museum. I hoped it would be a busy day for us.

Brother Carl stopped me before I could leave the Monastery Bakery. "Lady Jessie, with the ruckus outside last night, did you notice Madman Bob in the crowd?"

"No. I didn't notice him. But there were a lot of people out there. He could've been there, and I didn't see him. Why?"

He took two cast iron pans from behind the serving counter. "I found these outside on my morning constitutional. I've never seen Bob leave his pans behind. I hope nothing is wrong."

I wasn't sure what to say. Madman Bob may have dropped his pans and run away after all the craziness last night.

"You should probably tell Chase if you think something has happened to Bob. I'll keep a lookout for him. He's probably around somewhere. You know how those madmen are."

Brother Carl held up one more piece of evidence. "Would he leave *this* behind?"

It was Bob's change cup. It was filled with change and dollar bills. There was a bright red stain on one side. It flared out at me from the burnished metal.

"I'll call Chase," I told him. "It's probably nothing, but let's check it out anyway."

I hung around and waited until Chase arrived. Lucky he wasn't really busy and it didn't take long for him to get there.

"Bob might've left his pans because he was scared or whatever," I told Chase. "But he wouldn't have left his money behind."

Chase held up the money cup. We'd already placed it in a plastic bag for safekeeping.

"I hope that isn't blood on it," I said. "Where does Bob live?"

Chase had a map that showed where everyone in the Village lived. He looked up Bob's house. He lived with a group of madmen on the other side of the Village, near Wicked Weaves.

"I'll check it out." He called it in to the rest of the security team. "I heard from Detective Almond this morning. He's on his way out here. He has another suspect for Dave's murder."

"I'll keep an eye on things here if you want to go with the Bailiff," Manny said. "Though I'm happy the madman is gone from the front of the museum, I wouldn't wish anything bad on him."

I stared hard at him. "Manny, are you the sorcerer that gave Wanda Le Fey her enchanted bracelet?"

His dark face was affronted as he straightened his red vest. "Most assuredly not! How could you even ask me such a thing?"

I glanced at Chase and shrugged. "It was worth a shot. Let's go."

We took the back way from the museum on Squire's Lane and walked through the damp grass through the Village Green to the King's Highway.

Shakespeare was not at his podium, even though the Main Gate was open.

"Adventureland isn't going to keep Pat on if he keeps hiding out," Chase remarked. "I know he's scared, but the Village needs William Shakespeare."

"Maybe this whole thing with Wanda will be over soon. Pat created the role. I'd hate to see him lose it."

We passed Fabulous Funnels, where the aroma of cooking funnel cakes was enough to make my stomach gurgle. The Lovely Laundry Ladies called out to Chase and begged him to walk their way—as always—as they carried their clothes to the well. They'd gossip loudly and call out taunts to visitors all day as they pretended to wash clothes.

The Three Chocolatiers were dashing about, waving their swords as they practiced inviting visitors in to sample their wares. Their new, plumed hats were so large that I could barely make out their faces. Their chocolate was to die for—really. One of them had died in a vat of it last year.

We walked past the Lady Fountain where some artist had thought it would be amusing to have a fountain gushing up under the poor woman's dress. I never liked that fountain.

Phil Ferguson at the Sword Spotte waved and shouted at us.

"I need to go over and get my wedding sword," Chase remarked. "I'm sure it looks great."

"You get to wear a sword?" I asked. "I need a new sword too."

He snickered. "Girls don't get to wear swords with their wedding dresses."

I bumped him with my hip and laughed as he stumbled. "I think I can wear a sword when we get married if I want to, Sir Bailiff. I may need to defend myself against Tilly and Leo."

I'd told him about Tilly's threat. Between that, and last night, he'd be keeping a close eye on them. They hadn't actually done anything wrong so he couldn't do something official.

He frowned. "Better make it a broad sword if you're gonna fight that guy. He's huge."

"Let's hope it doesn't come to that, and we can all be friends."

"I hope so, but I'm not eating at the tavern for a while."

I linked my arm through his. "My thoughts exactly, good sir. They are too expensive anyway."

We laughed together, and waved to Mary Shift. "Good morning," she called out. "I have something for the two of you."

We veered off course from the madmen's house and went to visit her shop. Hundreds of sweet grass baskets lined the walls. They were created for all types of purposes from gathering eggs to holding fruit and flowers. Some of them were so small that they could only hold a ring. A few of them were so large—a small child could've slept in them.

"I hope you don't mind." She had a broad smile on her dark face. "I want to give you your wedding present early. There is no way to wrap it, and I don't want to hide it."

She disappeared into a backroom for a moment, and came out with a small cradle made from pink-tinged sweet grass. "I know you probably aren't ready for this yet, but I wanted you to have it. Don't mind the pink—it used to be for boys too."

Tears started to my eyes. "This is beautiful. Thank you so much."

Chase and I hugged her. We both traced the lines of the sweet grass where it formed the basket, sides, and hood of the cradle.

"And it comes with my best wish of happiness for both of you." She held our hands in her callused ones. "Have a *good* life together."

We all hugged again. Tears were streaming down my face by the time we left her.

"Where are we going to put all the wedding presents?" Chase nodded at the cradle. "This probably isn't the only big one, and I don't know where it's going."

"We might have to get a storage room. It can be like Aladdin's treasure cave. We can visit it once in a while."

He shook his head. “We’re gonna have to think about a bigger place to live, Jessie, even if I have to give up being the Bailiff.”

“Give up being Bailiff?” I couldn’t believe he’d even consider it.

“Roger was the Bailiff, and he opened his own glass shop. Maybe we have a craft that we can do. I could see myself as a craftsman.”

He squared his shoulders and puffed out his chest. His brown braid had swung across one shoulder. He raised his left eyebrow and peered down at me.

I laughed out loud at him. “Let’s just stay with what we know for now, huh? We can deal with that later—if we make it through the wedding.”

He agreed, and knocked at the house next door. “Let’s hope Bob is hanging out here. I think we’ve got enough on our plates without looking for him too.”

But none of the twenty or so madmen had seen Bob since yesterday. He’d left the house in the morning, as usual, to head over to his spot at the Village Green. There was nothing else they could tell us about his disappearance.

We stepped back out into the sunshine—away from the smell of dirty gym socks that seemed to pervade their dwelling. It reminded me too much of a frat house.

“Great,” Chase said. “Now Bob is missing. Anything else?”

"Bailiff! Bailiff!" Lord Maximus called out imperiously. "I believe there's a dead madman on the Hawk Stage. Would you please remove it? I have a show to put on in less than twenty minutes."

Sixteen

Now Bob the Madman was dead too. This was crazy.

It didn't look like an accident either. Bob was splayed out on the Hawk Stage with an bolt dead center in his chest. There was blood everywhere. Lord Maximus wasn't putting on any show that day.

It was terrible, but I had to admire the amazing accuracy of the shot. It wasn't easy hitting a target that small, especially since it was probably moving. From the trajectory, I could tell it wasn't like the killer was standing near him. This had come from up and over.

Detective Almond was there a few minutes later with appropriate ambulance and police support. At least he didn't have to make an extra stop since he was already on his way here.

"Anyone recognize this bolt?" He held it up, protected in plastic, after the assistant medical examiner had removed it.

"I recognize it, sad to say." Grigg had gone AWOL from the *Queen's Revenge* and joined us. "It's one of Master Simmons's bolts from the antique crossbow that used to hang on his wall at The Feathered Shaft. I've looked at it many a'time."

My heart felt like it was breaking. I recognized the bolt too. It had been straightened again, as had the first one that had killed Dave. The markings from the crossbow on it were the same too.

Master Simmons couldn't be the killer. I wouldn't believe it. He was a good man. He wouldn't have killed Bob or Dave. He just wasn't made that way. I'd never known a kinder, more generous person.

"Jessie, I would've thought you'd be the first one to speak up with your background in archery." Detective Almond razzed me. "Not that it matters, someone else in the Village knows their stuff and didn't mind sharing." He took out his cell phone, and there was a picture of the missing crossbow and bolts. "I received this yesterday."

I defended Master Simmons. "Why would he kill Bob, or Dave? There's no motive there."

"We've done a little checking on your Master Archer friend. He has a record for assault and battery with a lethal weapon. Want to guess what kind?" Detective Almond smiled.

"You have the wrong person." I wrapped my arms across my chest.

"Let me see." He read from a report. "Edward Simmons. He used to live at 2060 Shell Court in Myrtle Beach. He shot an arrow at a man he was having a disagreement with. The man was wounded and pressed charges. Mr. Simmons paid a fine and did community service."

"He was fooling around with my wife!" Master Simmons had stalked up while Detective Almond was reading. "He wouldn't give her up. He deserved worse."

"Did David Olson deserve worse?" Detective Almond's usual voice had an edge to it. "I understand there was an altercation between you because you thought he stole your antique crossbow from the weapon museum."

"We had words. But when I left, he was alive and healthy." Master Simmons sounded defensive. His voice wavered a little.

I went to stand beside him. "He didn't kill Bob either."

"Are you sure about that, Jessie?" Detective Almond put away his notebook. "Because my helpful source from the Village was Robert Maxwell, our new corpse. He sent us the photo which was taken in Mr. Simmons's apartment here at the Village."

"I found the crossbow," Master Simmons admitted. "I was hiding it because I didn't want it at the museum again. It belongs to me."

"Where did you find it?" Chase asked.

"I found it at the entrance to Sherwood Forest, where the note said I would."

"What note?" Detective Almond demanded.

Master Simmons shrugged. "It was just a note I found at the shop. The thief said he was returning it."

"Do you still have the note?"

"No. I threw it away."

Chase looked grim. "What about the bolts?"

"They weren't with it. I didn't say anything because I knew Dave had been killed with one."

It struck me that Sofie might have been able to make this shot with a crossbow. There was no motive, as far as I could see, but there was no motive for Master Simmons either.

Sofie, Master Simmons, Phil, and Shakespeare were all out around the museum the night Dave was killed. It didn't make sense why any of them would kill him. What was going on?

Someone was definitely trying to set up Master Simmons. We knew the antique crossbow wouldn't have worked to kill Dave or Bob. It had to be a new crossbow shooting the repaired bolts. The chances were good that the police wouldn't know that. The killer seemed to be betting on that fact.

"Betting!" I said it out loud without really meaning to. Everyone stared at me.

"Jessie?" Chase smiled.

"What if the bookie, John Healy, set this whole thing up? What if he hired someone in the Village to kill Dave because he owed him money?"

"Okay." Detective Almond shrugged. "Mostly bookies don't kill people. They just hurt them so they pay the next time."

"But what if this had gone too far and Healy wanted Dave dead?"

"I don't know where you're going with this, Jessie," Detective Almond said. "Unless you're saying Mr. Simmons is working for the bookie."

"Sofie. Master Simmons, Shakespeare, Phil Ferguson, and Dave were all around the museum the night Dave was killed."

"Are you saying one of them is working for Healy?" Chase asked.

"Bob told me about seeing the archer at the museum the night Dave was killed. I found out it was Sofie. She and Shakespeare are having an affair. I didn't think she killed Dave, but maybe I was wrong."

"At the museum? Why would anyone have an affair at a museum?" Detective Almond glanced at me. "Help me out here."

"Go ahead," Wanda prompted. "Tell him that my ex-husband is afraid to leave the museum because he's afraid of me. I dare you."

"Shakespeare is having some . . . issues with his own place. Sofie lives in the forest with the Merry Men. You could see why she wouldn't want to bring him there."

"Of course. If I lived in the forest with the *Merry Men*, I wouldn't want to bring Shakespeare home either." Detective Almond threw up his hands. "This place is a loony bin. I've said it for years. Walters, Macintyre—round up Sofie, the forest lady, and bring her and Mr. Shakespeare with us. Mr. Simmons, I'd like to continue this conversation with you at the station."

Master Simmons hugged me. There were tears in his eyes. "Don't worry, Jessie, everything will be fine."

The police took him, leaving me sobbing into Chase's shoulder. "Robin's going to hate me."

He put his arm around me. "You told him what you knew. He'll sort it out."

* * *

Chase stayed to help with the crime scene work at the Hawk Stage—and to deal with Lord Maximus. The police went to Master Simmons's apartment at The Feathered Shaft and found the antique crossbow. I saw them take it out of the Village as they went.

I took our beautiful cradle back to the Dungeon. There was a place for it if I took everything off of a shelf—which I did. I hated to think it would have to be stored somewhere away from us, but what choice did we have?

I went on to the museum, thinking about everything that had happened the last few days. I didn't believe the three people the police were questioning had killed Dave.

And what about Bob? Had he mentioned seeing an archer with a long bow to the wrong person and been killed for it?

The antique crossbow wouldn't have worked, even with the bolts straightened. *What was I missing?*

The museum was crowded with visitors. Oliver Northman had a good crowd watching him as he spoke about the history of tapestries, and his hands moved quickly on the loom. He was a natural entertainer. The visitors seemed mesmerized by him.

"Tapestries have been used since at least Hellenistic times. Samples of Greek tapestry have been found preserved dating from the third century BC. Europe was slow to catch on." He laughed. "It wasn't until the fourteenth century that tapestries were made in Germany and Switzerland.

"These tapestries are beautiful," one of the women in the group said.

"Thank you, dear lady." Oliver grinned. "And they are for sale. I hope I mentioned that?"

Everyone smiled or laughed discreetly.

"By the Middle Ages and Renaissance, these portable coats of arms were all the rage. Weavers could scarcely keep up. They were woven with symbolic emblems and mottoes, called a baldachin. These were hung behind thrones as a symbol of authority."

"What's going on now?" Manny whispered. "You were late again today."

I told him about Bob's death. "The police took Master Simmons and Shakespeare to the police station, and picked up Sofie from Sherwood Forest."

Manny nodded. "Bad news all around then. Back home, we are required to know how to use a bow, as well as a crossbow. I am quite proficient with both, actually."

"Yeah, well, keep that to yourself unless you want to be back on the suspect list. Simmons wasn't the only one who liked to argue with Dave."

"It wouldn't matter." He smiled at me as though I was a silly child. "The police can't keep me in custody. That's the only good thing about being part of the royal family."

I didn't know whether to laugh or slap him. With everything going on, I was a little tired of people making things up. He wasn't delusional—definitely not a sorcerer—even a pretend one.

"Let's not go there. Why don't you go across the street and get us some coffee."

His dark eyes looked hurt. "But it is true that I was ranked at the top of my countrymen with a bow. It's important at home because it's a life skill, not unlike using the cell phone and computer are here."

I got up in his face. "Please drop it. I don't want to hear anymore fantasy about royal families, dragons, ghosts, or witches right now. Okay?"

He nodded and quickly departed for the Monastery Bakery.

I listened as Oliver Northman described the early uses of tapestries to decorate, even poor homes. "They were one of the first forms of artwork even peasants could own. They were affordable, and relatively easy to make."

Had that been me that just said I didn't want to hear any more fantasy? What was wrong with me? I *lived* for fantasy. My life was a fantasy.

Obviously the strain had been too great, and I had lost my mind. Detective Almond would have laughed to hear me say it.

I apologized to Manny when he returned. "The wedding, and Chase's parents, and everything else—it's been too much. I shouldn't have taken it out on you."

He nodded and pushed his glasses back on his intelligent face. "I understand, Lady Jessie. I wish there was something I could do to help."

"You could speed up the wedding. Or zap Chase's brother and his parents into an alternate dimension. That would help."

"For someone who doesn't wish to indulge in fantasy, your thoughts are a bit shy of reality."

"Finer words were never spoken, sir. I bow to your superior knowledge."

I curtsied politely just as Oliver Northman was finishing his program. The visitors that had been watching him turned to us. There was no photography allowed in the museum. Instead of taking pictures, they waited with eager faces to see what we were going to do and say next.

Manny was at a loss for something to say—possibly the only time since I'd met him. He stared at me in panic.

Piece of cake. "Life is good here in the Village, don't you think, Sir Manawydan?"

He cleared his throat and nervously replied, "Why yes, Lady Jessie. I am quite enjoying my time here."

"Aren't you the woman on the posters who's getting married?" one visitor eagerly asked. "Is this your fiancée?"

I smiled. "Oh no. My fiancée is the Bailiff of this place, Chase Manhattan. He is currently occupied with another event."

Manny wiped the sweat from his brow with a clean white handkerchief as they left us. “That was extremely difficult. I don’t know how you costumed people do it every day.”

Oliver had finished covering his loom, as he did between programs. “I’ve spent time at many historical towns and villages. You have to learn that the people watching you are interested in what you have to say. Talk to them as you would anyone else.”

“I don’t know if that will ever become commonplace for me,” Manny admitted. “But thank you.”

“I’m not saying I’ve ever been in a historical village quite like this one.” Oliver rocked back on his heels, a grin on his face. “I was out for a stroll yesterday and the Big Bad Wolf ran by chasing Little Red Riding Hood. I assume he doesn’t really eat her?”

I laughed. “Don’t be silly. It would be too hard to recast Little Red Riding Hood every day.”

Oliver and Manny laughed too. Oliver went out for an early lunch.

Manny told me he was going to meet with his father over lunch. “I’m concerned, but I am finished hiding. I am master of my own fate, so to speak.”

“Good for you!”

“Lady Jessie, if I might offer a word of advice.”

“Of course.”

"Long bows can be modified to fire bolts from crossbows." He shrugged. "I've done it myself at home. Perhaps that is what you seek."

Seventeen

Lady Marion was on her way back from Stylish Frocks. One of her minions from the forest carried her green (of course) gown and matching suede boots. She told me it was her outfit for my wedding.

"I am really looking forward to this," she said with a bright smile. "I don't know if I told you, but I hired an agent from Hollywood. I'm hoping your wedding is going to be my key to the big time."

Big time? "I didn't know you had those kinds of ambitions."

She giggled. "Doesn't everyone have some ambition? Did you think I planned on spending the rest of my life in Sherwood Forest?"

I really hadn't thought about it, and quickly changed the subject. "Did the police come for Sofie?"

"I don't know." She shrugged. "On another topic, Beth is working on a whole new wardrobe for me. Not just Ren Faire issue either."

I knew Robin Hood wasn't going to be thrilled about that. How could he afford her? Tony's Internet promotion work must have been bringing in a lot more money.

Lady Marion chattered on about her future plans. "It cost me three thousand dollars just for a portfolio. Who knew a bunch of pictures could be so expensive?"

I hoped Robin was planning on filing bankruptcy. Did he realize Marion was burning up his credit card?

We skirted around the traps that lay in waiting for the unwary traveler. Several visitors hung from nets above us. They weren't calling out for help. They were excited to be part of the drama.

A handful of visitors were in the treehouse encampment area too. Robin had put them to work tending the fire and making lunch. The smell of roasted meat on the spit filtered through the forest.

"Lady Marion, my love." Robin Hood swept the little green hat from his head. "You abuse my generous heart and meager resources. How many gowns do you need for one wedding?"

I could tell from his tone that he was really upset. He was making a show of it for the visitors.

"Lady Jessie." He nodded politely to me. "Welcome. What brings you to Sherwood?"

"I have come with ill news and wish to inquire about Sofie. Is she here?"

He gave me a hard look. "I believe you know that she is not. The police were *very* specific when they picked her up."

Two teenagers dressed in green T-shirts and jeans looked up at the word.

"Police?" one of them asked. "That's not cool."

Robin Hood gave them one of his crazy laughs, and assured them that everything was fine. "We routed the blackguards. They won't be back again. Keep your eyes on that chicken so it doesn't burn, eh?"

The boys shrugged, and went back to turning the spit over the fire.

"Come with me, Lady Jessie," Robin invited. "My Lady Marion, we shall discuss this later."

Marion shrugged. "Get a life, Toby."

She went quickly up the stairs to the treehouse that they shared. Robin led me to their storage area at the side of the encampment.

"You gave Sofie up to the police. Really? For killing Dave and Bob? What were you *thinking*?"

"It was the circumstance. You had to be there. The police were accusing Master Simmons of killing Bob because he saw an archer the night Dave was killed."

"So?"

"Sofie was the archer that Bob saw at the museum. I don't think she killed either of them. But I don't think Master Simmons did either."

"You could've waited to check that out." He shook his head. "I understand you were in a bad place. I wish you would've given us a heads up so we could've gotten Sofie out of here."

"Sorry. I did the best I could with what I had."

He looked up at the deep blue sky that showed through the trees above us. "I know you did. The word is that the bolts that killed Dave and Bob were one of the Master Archer's old toys."

"He said his crossbow was returned when he found a note at his shop that led him to Sherwood."

"Anyone could've written that."

"Yes." I told him about the photo that Bob had sent to the police. "Someone wants to frame Master Simmons for Dave's murder."

"Why would Bob do such a thing?"

"I don't know, because now he's dead too."

Robin put his hand on mine. "You know you have our full backing looking into this, Jessie. If you need anything, let me know."

I smiled. "As long as it doesn't require any money, right? I think you must be broke by now with Marion's ambitions."

"You don't know the half of it. She used up my credit card the first day. Since then she's been using her own money. Don't ask me where she got it, but Tony said she has twenty thousand dollars in the bank."

"That's a lot of money considering what she makes out here. Did she have a relative that died or something?"

"Not that I know of." He sighed. "But she and I have been drifting further and further apart since she decided she was the Renaissance answer to Marilyn Monroe. I don't know what's gotten into her."

"I'm sure she'll be fine. Everyone goes through these things."

He lifted my hand to his lips and kissed it. "You have always been so understanding. Chase is a lucky man. If you ever change your mind about him, let me know."

"Have you ever heard of modifying a long bow to shoot bolts?"

He frowned. "I have, but I've never done it. I'm not crazy about a crossbow."

A thought occurred to me. "Would you mind if I look through Sofie's things since she's not here?"

"Looking for a modified long bow?"

"Maybe."

He shrugged his broad shoulders. "I'll take you to her room. She's staying in my spare room."

"Marion allows that?"

"I don't think she cares anymore."

We climbed up into the highest branches of the giant oak. Robin had the biggest of the twelve treehouses (of course). The treehouse was nice. It had two bedrooms on two floors, a bathroom, a tiny kitchen, and a large living room.

The furniture was what you'd expect to find in a log cabin—kind of early American rustic. Everything was made of wood, some of it hand carved. It was nice, in a rough kind of way. I'd always thought it was relaxing.

"Here's Sofie's room." He showed me the smaller of the two bedrooms. "She doesn't have much space to hide anything. I'll check under the bed."

I looked in the tiny, makeshift closet. There were boots and cloaks and two long bows, but neither had been modified. Two quivers of arrows were full.

"I don't see anything in here."

"Not here either." He rolled over from checking under the bed. "I don't see Sofie as a killer anyway, Jessie. Do you?"

"No. But I don't see Shakespeare or Master Simmons as killers either." I told him about the bookie that might be involved in the murder. "Any ideas?"

"What's going on in here?" Lady Marion stopped to check on us.

"Nothing to trouble yourself with, my love." Robin smiled at her. "Just conjecturing on who killed the Village madmen. That's all. Looking for a long bow modified to use as a crossbow. Seen any around recently?"

Really?" She stared at both of us as like a trapped animal stares at her captor. "I'll choose what I worry about, my love."

The beautiful Lady Marion pulled a small gun from her boot and pointed it at us.

Eighteen

"Oh *no*." Robin fell back on the floor as though he'd been wounded. "I can't believe it. Marion—why would you do such a thing?"

"For money, lover." She kept a steady eye on us as she dialed her cell phone. "Johnny? I have a problem in the forest. I need help." She finished her call and put the phone in her pocket.

"Let me understand this," Robin elaborated. "Not only have you killed two men, you've been *seeing* this bookie?"

"You shouldn't be surprised." She advanced into the room and took a seat on the bed, crossing her legs. "Or maybe you should since you have no idea what I'm all about anymore."

"Marion," he appealed.

"Shut up!" She threw a pair of pantyhose at him. "Tie her up, Robin."

"Marion." It was my turn to reason with her. "We're in the middle of Sherwood Forest. People come in and out of here all the time. Chase will come and look for me when he can't find me."

"Thanks for reminding me. Gag her too, Robin." She tossed him a scarf. "And then we'll tell your precious Merry Men to close the forest off for the day and leave."

That sounded like a plan I wasn't going to like. Robin had already bound my feet and hands together. He tied the scarf around my mouth, and whispered in my ear. "Don't worry, Jessie. I'll take care of this outside."

"A little love talk?" Marion laughed. "Seriously, Jessie? You have Chase. Why do you want Robin too?"

It was too late for me to answer. I was on the floor in Sofie's bedroom, tied and helpless. I couldn't even scream for Tony, who was somewhere right below us.

Robin and Marion left me there. I could hear Robin yelling for the men to close off Sherwood.

The awful part about it was that no one was going to question it. Visitors might complain, but that would take a while to filter down to Chase. Sherwood Forest closed once in a while for repairs, or when a tree fell on the path. Unless they asked for help with a situation, Chase left them alone. That was going to be a bad precedent for me this time.

"Having a bit of fun, are we?" Wanda was sitting on the bed beside me. "Who knew you did this sort of thing? I'm sure Chase would be surprised. You're very tame with him. You might want to break out this wild side occasionally. It might help you keep him."

I mumbled through my gag. Was there some way I could provoke her to help me? Could she remove the gag or the pantyhose if she tried?

It seemed as though most of her ghostly powers were directed toward scaring people, although she somehow put the goat on the elephant's back, and levitated objects and people at the Field of Honor—including me.

But either she didn't want to help or she was ignoring me.

Marion returned with Robin at her side, her gun shoved into his back. "Good work, lover. Now get down there with Jessie. Johnny will know what to do when he gets here."

"Oh! A threesome!" Wanda laughed. "I'm staying ringside for this!"

Robin winked at me. I knew he had something in mind. Maybe when Marion got close to tie him—he planned to take her out.

Marion may have anticipated that move. She only got close enough to him to use the butt end of the gun on his head. He slumped on the floor beside me. She got another pair of pantyhose to tie him up, and a wool hat that she shoved into his mouth.

Wanda watched. "It looks like I was wrong. Goldilocks has other plans for you and Robin Hood, doesn't she? How fascinating! I wonder if the Bailiff will come to your rescue in time."

"Now you two stay right here." Marion smiled and patted Robin's head. "I'm sorry this had to happen, Jessie. I was so looking forward to your wedding. I probably can't return my new dress for that either. What a waste!"

I glared at her, but there was only so much you can do without speaking or moving.

"Of course, poor Chase will be in dire straits, won't he? Maybe I can console him. We'll see. I'll be back in a little while."

What could I do? Robin was no help. He'd already ordered Sherwood Forest to be closed. The chances of Chase coming to see what was wrong were so miniscule. Marion's bookie boyfriend, who'd obviously paid her well to kill Dave, was on his way.

I figured Bob was probably a freebie. Marion was afraid he'd recognized her after he'd seen her silhouette. She was willing to let someone else take the fall for being that archer too. How desperate to be famous could someone be?

"I always knew snooping around that way was going to get you into trouble, Jessie." Wanda's words of wisdom were uttered with a sigh. "And here you are, right before your wedding, about to meet your maker. Perhaps you and I can be chums, eh? I'd like that, I suppose."

I stared at her, hoping she might be telepathic and she'd get what I was thinking.

No such luck.

"What am I saying?" She floated off the bed. "We didn't like each other when I was alive! The only reason I can stand you now is that you've become a source of amusement for me. I suppose it wouldn't be that way at all if you were dead too."

Untie me. You don't want me to die.

I guess we'll see how things unfold, won't we, dearie?"

She was gone. I was alone with Robin. Both of us were helpless.

I hoped Tony would think something strange was going on when I didn't come down from the treehouse. Even if he was just snoopy enough to find out if I was doing something with Robin that he could shame me for—I'd be happy with that.

Usually, I liked being right. I wasn't so crazy about it then.

I searched the room with desperate eyes. There had to be some way to get free. I'd seen spies get out of worse situations in movies. If I didn't panic, maybe there was a way out of this.

It was going to take John Healy a few minutes to get here, and get through the gate. I might have twenty minutes or so.

I saw a sword near Sofie's bed. If I could push myself over to it, I might be able to get close enough to the blade to cut the pantyhose. It was a long shot, but I didn't have anything else to do anyway.

It took me five minutes to maneuver myself into position near the sword. If the floor hadn't been carpeted, it would have been easier. There was no sliding at all. When I got up against the blade, the sword fell, knocking over the lamp on the bedside table. I couldn't get my arms or feet near the sharp part at all.

I lay on my back with a sigh, and tried to think of another plan.

I thought about my cell phone in the bag at my waist. There was no way to get at it. I tried breaking the lamp so I could use a shard of it to cut the pantyhose. I kicked at it, and brought my feet down hard on it. The lamp wasn't breaking either.

Come on, Jessie. You've been in worse situations! Think!

Had I been in worse situations? Possibly. Wanda was right about my snooping. Any bad situation I'd ever been in at the Village was caused by being nosy about people and events I probably had no business looking into.

I swore, if I got out of this mess, that I would never snoop again.

I should have been talking to people about my wedding. I should have been enjoying my time at the Village. This was the life I'd always wanted. And I was about to lose it all.

Robin groaned. I rolled toward him as quick as I could. If he woke up, we'd have a better chance of finding a way to get free.

I rolled so far that I was almost on top of him. He groaned again, and his face scrunched up.

"*Mmhhmmgmm*." I rubbed my face on his as I tried to make noises that might wake him up. "*Rommbmm, wmmhmm umm*!"

Finally, he came around and stared into my face with startled eyes. "*MmhhmmJmm*," he said.

That's right, I encouraged him silently. *You can do it!*

I rolled off of him so we could plot our strategy. "*Rmmhmm. Wmm hvmm tgmm oumm hmm.*"

"*Domm yumm thmm uh thmm*?" He shot back at me.

I nodded toward the sword. He shook his head. His hands were bound behind him, which made doing anything helpful even harder.

Or not! I suddenly recalled that horror movie where the woman had chewed off the other captured person's rope. Maybe I could do that.

I pushed myself against him and nudged him on his side. Like an inch worm, I got my face close to the pantyhose that held him. My face was up against his butt as I tried to gnaw the fiber away.

The gag prevented me from using my teeth at all.

Robin got the idea though as he nudged me over on my back and rolled over on me. His head was deeply pushed into my chest as he lay across me, trying to rip the pantyhose off of my hands.

The gag kept him from doing that too.

"*Mmhhmmermm*," he mumbled, his eyes apologetic.

"Whoa! Wait! This is *so* wrong!" Tony's voice came from the doorway. "Jessie! What are you doing?"

Nineteen

"I am so glad to see you!" I hugged Tony when he cut me loose.

"Good job, Tony!" Robin rubbed his wrists.

"You know I almost turned around and went back out," Tony said. "I couldn't believe you were . . . *you know*. If Jessie wouldn't have made that squealing pig noise, I probably would've left you alone."

"I'm glad you didn't. Where's Marion?"

Tony shrugged. "I think she left the forest after she had Hank close it down. Why? Did she do this?"

"She's the one who killed Dave and Bob," I explained.

"For money." Robin spat the words as he untied his feet. "Like an assassin."

"Wow!" Tony grinned. "That's kind of hot, huh?"

"Not at all," Robin assured him. "Who of my men are still in the forest besides you?"

"Hank is down there. I'm not sure who else. Marion made it sound like we should take the rest of the day off. I think most of them left when she did."

"We can call the police." I took out my cell phone. "No bars? Why would it be on International Roaming out here?"

"I don't know," Robin said. "But I suggest we get out of Sherwood before the bookie gets here. We have no weapons but swords and arrows. They aren't much good against guns."

We heard voices coming into the encampment and rushed to the window to see who it was.

"Great!" Robin moved back quickly. "I think that may be the bookie."

I peeked out. "And Marion is with him."

"What now?" Tony asked. "I'm only good with computers. I don't think that's going to help in this situation."

Marion had returned with a group of ten men. They were all big and tough-looking. I had a feeling they were all armed too. Security guards at the Main Gate were looking for bows and swords, maybe a few knives. They didn't search people for guns, and visitors didn't go through a metal detector.

"Where are they?" The big man in the middle of the group, beside Marion, searched the trees with his eyes. "I hope they're not up there."

No doubt that was John Healy. He looked as big and tough as the other men, but he was well-dressed in an expensive black suit. His shiny Italian loafers looked out of place as he stood on the dirt track. His black hair was thinning, swept off to one side to make it look like he had more up there.

The other men scanned the trees too. They were dressed more casually in pants and shirts.

"I left them up there." Marion nodded at the treehouse.

"You two," Healy pointed to two men nearest him, "go up and bring them down."

The men nodded, and headed for the stairs to the treehouse.

"There's a back way out," Robin said. "I suggest we take it."

Tony and I followed him to the back stairs, which was really just an escape ladder. We climbed down quickly.

"We won't have long before they know we aren't up there." I wiped spider webs from my face and hands. The ladder hadn't been used in a while.

"We can't walk out around them," Tony whispered. "We could scatter in the woods, but that's about it."

Hank, the new Merry Man, rustled through the leaves to reach us. "I thought I saw you back here. What's up? Who are those dudes?"

"Bad guys," I replied. "Is anyone else in camp?"

"Nope. I was about to leave too, when I saw them come up."

"So what's the plan?" Tony asked with an eagerness born of fear.

"I think we have no choice but to follow your excellent suggestion and scatter into the woods," Robin said. "We don't have guns."

"I have my knife." Hank held it up so we could see it.

"Any other suggestions?" Robin asked.

"I'm good with scattering. We can call the police from the other side of the forest." I held up my cell phone again. *No service? My next phone will get service out here!*

We heard the two big men trudging through the treehouse above us. One of them leaned out the front window where we'd seen them first come up. "They ain't here, boss. What do you want us to do?"

"Come back down." John glanced around himself at the treehouses and the rest of the camp. "I think the thing to do in this situation is to light the place up."

"Burn the forest?" Even Marion sounded concerned.

"Sure. If they're out there, they'll run back, right?" John smiled. "If they don't make it, too bad. They weren't long for this world anyway."

"But the rest of the Village." Marion smiled at him. "Instead, we could get out of town for a while. It would be okay, right?"

"Nope. I don't like loose ends. Let's torch it. Better safe than sorry."

"What *now*?" Tony muttered.

"We can't just leave and let them set the place on fire," I replied. "It could take half the Village with it."

Robin's eyes narrowed. "Thanks for your concern for my personal well-being! There is no Robin Hood without Sherwood Forest!"

"I didn't mean it that way," I recanted.

While we were discussing our options, the men in front were stoking the fire where the Merry Men did their cooking.

"Throw whatever you can find on it," John instructed. "Any gasoline out here, Marion?"

"No." She looked around. "We don't usually need it."

"Okay. No gas. Let's get those shovels over there and walk some fire into the trees." John pointed to the shovels by the storage shed.

"Johnny, please—" Marion tried to appeal to him.

"What? You called me for help. I came. Just like those knights of old, right?" John grinned. "Maybe you should get out of here. You might get hurt."

Marion didn't move. I could see this wasn't what she'd had in mind—though what she had in mind had been much worse for me and Robin. Apparently, she didn't mind killing people as much as she disliked burning the forest.

"We have to confront them," I said. "We have to stall for time while one of us runs for help. They don't know Tony and Hank are here. If we go out and surrender, Robin, it would stop them from burning the forest."

"I like being Robin Hood, Jessie. But I don't want to die for it."

"I hope we won't have to." I looked at Hank. "Are the nets set in the trees?"

He shrugged. “Sure. We always keep them set.”

“Okay. This is what I think we should do.”

* * *

Robin and I walked out from behind the treehouse with our arms in the air. The first shovel of hot embers was about to leave the safety of the fire pit.

“Well, well!” John grinned when he saw us. “I thought the idea of being roasted might bring you out.”

Three guns were immediately trained on us.

Marion looked relieved to see us. “Call them off now, Johnny. There’s no need to burn the trees, right?”

He put his arm around her and kissed the side of her head. “She’s such a softie.” He told his men to put their shovels down. “You’re right. We can shoot them with a lot less fuss. Give them those shovels, and let’s do some grave digging.”

“You mean dig our own graves?” I asked him. “You’ve got to be kidding. You’re going to shoot us anyway. Why would I do that?”

“Because we could shoot you in the foot and then make you dig,” one of John’s men said with a laugh. He handed me the shovel. “Dig.”

“Besides, this takes more time,” Robin quietly reminded me, picking up his own shovel. “We need time, remember?”

“I know, but this is *so* corny!”

“Shut up and dig,” John said.

Five of his men were standing together to the right of us. None of them were holding their guns. Robin nodded at them.

Tony was using the other asset he had besides working on computers—his long legs. He'd been a track star in high school. That had been a long time ago, but he also knew the back forest better than I did. He had my cell phone and could call for help as soon as he could find signal.

Hank was waiting to do his part. At Robin's nod, he pulled the net that was under five of the men. They flew up into the trees, yelling and pulling at the net that held them. But there was no way out of the net until someone released them.

Robin looked at me. "Run!"

I didn't wait for another invitation.

We ran toward the entrance to Sherwood Forest. It had never seemed so far away from the camp. John, and his other five thugs, came after us. I could still hear the men in the nets yelling.

"They didn't take the time to let them down," Robin said as he ran. "I hope Hank has time to get to the curve in the path."

"Me too!"

I had really thought John and Marion would help the other men down first before they came after us. Marion knew how. Of course, John may have left her behind to accomplish that, and just come after us without her. Maybe that's why they always showed large numbers of bad guys traveling together on TV.

"They aren't shooting," Robin huffed beside me.

"Maybe they don't want to draw attention," I replied.

"Almost there."

We hit the curve in the path where the Merry Men snagged their largest group of visitors each day. The net was well-hidden under leaves and dried grass. I hoped Hank had time to make it here. We weren't far from the entrance.

"Speed up!" Robin yelled.

"I'm ahead of you!" I reminded him.

"I was talking to myself."

There was a *whooshing* sound behind us as the net went up. It was immediately followed by yelling and cursing as it took at least some of John's men with it.

I wasn't willing to wait and see how many were captured. I sprinted for the entrance, not looking back. My lungs felt like they were going to burst.

The first thing I saw when we reached the cobblestones was the Tornado Twins, Diego and Lorenzo. They were offering to sell their fat, pink piglet to a visitor. The visitor and her companions were laughing as she said no and tried to keep walking.

The twins weren't that easy to escape. "Yeah, we can't afford to feed her." Diego mimed crying, and Lorenzo used a large handkerchief to wipe away his tears. "If she stays with us much longer, I'm afraid she'll become bacon."

John and two of his men were still behind us. I didn't see Marion.

Robin and I kept running.

"Get out of my way, freak!" I heard John yell.

That was all Diego needed. It fit right in with his act. He threw himself at his feet and wouldn't get up. "Please! Please! Take me with you. Don't leave me here. I'm not really a freak like the rest of them."

"Get off!" John tried to kick at him.

Lorenzo threw himself into the act. He managed to wrap himself around one of the other men and kept asking for his support. "I know there must be a wallet in here somewhere."

Instead, his eager hands dislocated a small knife that clattered to the cobblestones as he dropped it. The thug held up his gun and fired three times. Visitors and residents began screaming and running toward the Main Gate.

"Shoot *them*!" John yelled at his men behind him as he pointed at me and Robin.

The Green Man was ambling by. He wrapped his huge, leafy tree branches around the man. His gun fell to the ground too. The Green Man held him tightly in his embrace.

People had stopped running to take pictures. I was completely amazed.

A dozen fools, with bells jingling on their heads, pushed the second of John's men into a goat cart. A nearby pickle vendor grabbed the top from his pickle barrel and trapped him in the cart.

I could see some of Chase's security men running toward us. I knew John was still behind us with a gun. There was no way to let them know.

But I couldn't run anymore. I couldn't draw a breath. I dropped to my knees as a severe cramp in my mid-section stopped me. Robin stumbled over me, and we rolled off the walkway and into the grass.

"He . . . can't kill us . . . right here in front . . . of everyone." Robin panted and groaned at the same time.

Or maybe he could.

John hadn't backed away. His deeply lined face frowned down at us. He pulled out a very large hand gun, and everyone started screaming and running again. They tripped over each other, and across fairies, knocking the pickle vendor over. Bo Peep's sheep tried to get out of their path, and a goatherd ran into a privy.

"Think they'll know, in all this confusion, who killed who?" John grinned and aimed his gun at us.

I squeezed my eyes closed tightly as I painfully gasped for breath.

There was a dull thud above me. I *knew* that sound. It was an arrow hitting its target.

John slumped down on the cobblestones next to me. "My arm! He shot my arm!"

I looked across the street and there was Manny in front of the museum—a long bow in his hand—and a smile on his dark face.

A large arrow protruded from John's shoulder. Robin jumped up and grabbed his gun. He threw back his head to laugh, but didn't have enough air to do it. He slid down to his knees.

"Welcome to Renaissance Faire Village and Marketplace, Mr. Healy," I managed to get out. "I hope you enjoy yourself while you're here."

Twenty

The Village was closed for the rest of the day. Police were everywhere. Several ambulances had come and gone with the injured. None of the visitors were hurt—that was a good thing.

Tony had made it to a spot where there was signal, and had called the police. It was after we'd nearly caused a stampede on the cobblestones. He returned to the Village, triumphant, and came to see me right away.

Chase had propped me up against the side of the Honey and Herb Shoppe where Mrs. Potts was bringing me tea and honey cookies. I couldn't move a muscle to get inside, and I wanted to see everything that was going on.

"I'm glad you're okay." Tony gave me a brief brotherly hug. "Where's Robin?"

"He wasn't hurt, as far as I know. He may be in Sherwood, nursing his wounded ego. He never saw this coming with Marion."

Tony grinned. "I'll go help him. I could give him some tips with women, you know? When they start using your credit card, it's over."

"You don't have a credit card." I laughed and then regretted it as the pain in my side returned.

"Exactly! See you around."

The police were questioning everyone in the Village about what they'd seen and heard. Most residents hadn't seen anything since they were on the other side of the Village. Only a small group had taken part in the melee. I would be sure to personally thank the valiant pickle vendor, the jingling fools, and the Green Man.

Diego and Lorenzo?—not so much. They didn't even know what they were doing.

Manny found me. He was grinning from ear to ear. An older man and woman were with him. They were dressed in elaborate, colorful robes and wearing heavy gold chains. The diamonds in the woman's ears were the size of marbles.

"Lady Jessie Morton," Manny began with pride in his voice. "May I present King Aengus, my father. And Queen Brarn, my mother."

The king took my hand and smiled. "We understand that you have been a good friend to our son. We thank you."

Queen Brarn also smiled. "My thanks to you also, Lady Jessie. Though we had hoped Manawydan was hiding out here because he was in love with you, it is good to know he has such a friend in this country."

"They are going to let me stay!" Manny was so excited that he could barely keep his glasses on. "I don't have to hide out any longer."

I held his hand. "You saved my life, Manny. I'll never forget it."

Chase came up and bowed to the king and queen. "I have arranged for you to stay with Queen Olivia and King Harold at the castle until the wedding, if you like. Please accept this as an official invitation."

King Aengus inclined his regal head. “We would love to attend your wedding, Sir Bailiff. Thank you for your kindness.”

“Manny, maybe you could see them up there and get them settled in,” Chase said. “They are expecting you.”

Manny’s face was serious as he bowed to Chase. “We thank you, sir.”

Chase dropped down beside me in the grass as they started toward the castle. I hadn’t even noticed that they had *real* courtiers and servants walking behind them.

“That should be interesting. Two kings and two queens, plus your parents at the castle until the wedding. I hope the castle is still standing.”

“Come on.” He helped me to my feet. “It will be fine. Let’s get you home. I believe you are in need of some rest, my lady.”

I thought he was being extremely optimistic about the kings and queens getting along, but I was done with worrying about anything—at least for that day. “Why sir, you wax poetic. Mayhap you should take a turn on the Romeo and Juliet Stage.”

“You are too kind.” He smiled and bowed. “Perhaps we could share a repast at Peasant’s Pub later today.”

There were no visitors around. We were just playing, but it was fun.

Chase got a wicked smile on his handsome face as he took me in his arms and dipped me close to the cobblestones. “Keep this on thy lips, my lady.”

As he kissed me, the crowd of knaves, fools, varlets, lords and ladies around us went wild. There were no photos, but there were dozens of good wishes.

I fanned my face with my hand, and the ladies around me smiled and nodded.

We walked back to the Dungeon, though Chase had offered to carry me. I was sore, and still a little winded, but I was capable of getting there on my own two feet.

“Did they find Marion?” I asked him.

“Yes. She was trying to leave the Village. I don’t think she’s going any further than the police station.”

“That’s so sad. Why in the world did she suddenly think she was going to be a famous actress?”

“Who knows?” He shrugged. “Why do people want to take off their clothes and get in one of the fountains? Why do visitors rush into the Field of Honor while the knights are jousting? People do crazy things sometimes.”

“I get that.”

“You’re lucky you weren’t killed today.” He kissed my hand. “Is there any way I can get you to stay at the museum all day and not get involved with crazy people who want to kill you?”

I thought about it. “I don’t think so. Maybe someday when I’m too old to walk or ask questions.”

"That's what I thought."

His radio went off, as always. He ignored it.

"You know I'd give all of this up for you, right?" he asked with the sweetest sincerity in his brown eyes.

"I know. You'd get a job as a lawyer somewhere that your family feels is appropriate, and play golf every week. I could join a garden club, and drink martinis with women I don't like—and sleep with their husbands while you're working."

"Wait a minute!" he protested. "I didn't say anything about all of that!"

I laughed and kissed him, feeling lighter than cotton candy. "I love you, Chase. I'd live wherever you wanted, but I'm glad we live here."

His radio went off again, this time somehow more demanding.

"It's Detective Almond. I have to go. Sorry." He kissed me again with a fierce hunger that weakened my knees. "But I'll be back."

"I'll be waiting!"

The wedding was sounding better and better. I was eager to start our new life together—wherever it led us.

I shut off the moaning of the prisoners in the dungeon, and dragged myself up the stairs. We hadn't talked about a honeymoon. I wasn't even sure Chase could get the time off. But if we did have a honeymoon, I wanted to stay somewhere with a tub. The shower was fine, most of the time. I just really wanted a few days with a hot bath—maybe one big enough for two.

I unlocked the door and couldn't believe my eyes. Tim, the young squire from the Field of Honor that Chase had rescued, was sitting in the middle of our bed.

"Hello?" I looked at the door that had certainly been locked. "What are you doing in here?"

"I wanted to have a private word with you, Lady Jessie." He smiled as he scanned the apartment. "This seemed appropriate."

"You're lucky it wasn't Chase that found you here." I sat on the edge of the bed. "He would have booted you out of the Village."

He smiled shyly. "It would not have been the Bailiff who found me here. I cannot be found when I don't wish to be."

I had been in such a good mood. Now I was suddenly tired and cranky. I wanted to be alone for a few minutes. Was that too much to ask?

"You should go."

"I am leaving very soon."

"No. I mean you should go now."

"I haven't completed my business here, lady, or I would oblige you."

"What do you want?" I admit that I was whining.

The lid on the box that held Wanda's personal belongings opened, and the beautiful bracelet with the blue stones that I'd always admired, floated across the room to him.

"Oh my God! You've got to be kidding me." I watched with disbelieving eyes. "*You're* the sorcerer?"

He bowed his head, his hand on his heart. "Yes. I came for this. I rarely give gifts, and when I do, I retrieve them when something happens to the people I give them to."

"Like Wanda?"

"Yes."

"So you and Wanda . . .?" He was just a kid.

"I am not always in this form, lady."

The smile he gave me almost melted every bone in my body. There was a wealth of knowledge in his eyes that I knew I would never have.

"Okay." I put my hand to my head, wishing I could pace. But I was too sore and tired to do it. "Okay. So you're the sorcerer who can take Wanda away with you, right?"

"I shall gladly grant you a boon for retrieving this gift for me. It saved me from having to search for it elsewhere."

"Yes! Please take Wanda away. I don't care what you do with her. Just take her away from here. Please."

He nodded. "Wanda Le Fey: come to me."

As if his low voice had called her, she was suddenly there with us.

She looked around herself. "Jessie? How did you do that?"

"Wanda."

She finally stared at the boy beside me. "You! Who are—?"

"*Know me*," he murmured.

"Oh my God! I thought I'd never see you again!" She hugged him and then stood back. "But why have you come in this form?"

"I am never the same to look upon." He got to his feet, her bracelet in his hand. "Come. It's time to go."

"Go?" She stared at me. "What did she tell you? I haven't done anything that bad. Please don't take me away from here."

I was confused. "Don't you want to go with him?"

"You don't know where he spends most of his time. There's nothing there. It's like living in a vacuum." She was crying. "Please don't take me there. I'll die of boredom."

He nodded to me. "Lady Jessie requested a boon of me. It was to remove you from this place."

"How could you?" She turned on me. "All I've done is have a little fun. Can you blame me? I was murdered, cut down. I want to live here. I've always wanted to live here. Please don't send me away."

She threw herself on my feet. *Seriously*. It was cold and felt kind of slimy touching her.

"Please, Jessie? Please don't send me away. You of all people understand how I feel about the Village. I want to stay here. Don't let him take me."

I glanced at the sorcerer. He shrugged. It meant nothing to him either way.

I thought about it, moved by her plea, despite myself. She was right about me. I knew what she meant about staying here. If I died, I'd want to be a ghost here too.

But there had to be some guidelines.

"Is it possible to keep her out of my apartment?" I asked the sorcerer. I couldn't think of him as Tim anymore.

He nodded. "Surely. If she gives her word on that today, I shall enforce it."

I faced Wanda's pathetic ghost face. "Okay. This is it. You can't *ever* come in here again, no matter what."

"Done," she agreed. "It wasn't all that much anyway."

"And you can't do anything to hurt animals or people in the Village."

"Define hurt?" she quizzed.

"I think you know what I mean."

"Oh, all right." She stared at the sorcerer. "Does this mean I can stay?"

"If Lady Jessie wills it."

She turned to me. "Jessie?"

"All right."

Wanda was gone with a loud cackle.

"I hope I don't regret that," I said with a sigh.

"You have a good heart." He smiled. "And I wish to give you and Chase a wedding gift."

"Thanks, but we don't have enough room for what we have right now. Just getting Wanda out of our bedroom is a huge wedding gift."

"Allow me to honor you and your union."

He barely blinked, and everything changed. Our tiny, one-room apartment was suddenly large and spacious. There were three bedrooms, two baths—one with a tub, and a nice living room and den.

"My gift to you."

I ran through the rooms like one of the crazy people Chase and I had been talking about earlier. Suddenly, I wasn't tired or sore at all.

There was no furniture, but it had become a house. There was even a kitchen where we could microwave our meals. It was amazing, and impossible.

"You can't do this here." I calmed down by taking deep breaths. "We can't take this from you." It suddenly struck me what it must look like outside.

"There is no change to the outside of the Dungeon, or to the downstairs jail." He said as though he'd read my mind. "Only you and Chase will see this inner space. It will be your secret for as long as you live here."

Was that even possible?

"Just a minute." I ran outside and looked around. The old building that was the Dungeon looked exactly the same. It wasn't any larger at all.

I ran back inside. "How is that possible?"

"Magic." He smiled. "And now I must leave. I wish I could stay for your wedding, but I must be elsewhere."

"I don't know how to thank you. It's incredible."

"There is only one thing I must ask of you, Jessie."

"Okay."

"Someday, I may need to take sanctuary here. I have enemies. This would be a place they would never search for me."

I thought about it, but it was very brief. "Sure. That's fine. Our house is your house."

Before I could finish speaking, he was gone.

I ran through our house again, laughing and singing. We had a real place to live!

* * *

Chase got back about an hour later. I had already put some things into the other rooms. I picked out one room for the baby basket that Mary had made for us.

"Jessie!" he called out in strangled-sounding voice. "What the—?"

I ran into the room that had once been our only room. "You aren't gonna believe what happened!"

Twenty-one

The day of the wedding dawned bright and clear. It had turned cold, and there was frost on the ground. It had created a white sheen that sparkled in the sunlight on roofs, cobblestones, and grass.

Needless to say, Chase and I had gone on a monumental shopping spree. If anyone wondered where we were putting all that furniture, no one asked. Maybe that was part of the spell.

The house was shaping up. There was a wonderful red velvet sofa in the living room, and a huge, overstuffed chair that matched it. We bought a super-size new refrigerator, and our own washer and dryer.

The bedroom was to-die-for. We'd made the whole thing deep blue (Chase's favorite color), and purple (my favorite color). I'd woken up in a king-sized bed that morning and padded to the new bathroom across some wonderful rugs we'd found. Chase had put in a few nice Tiffany-style lamps on the dressers and bedside tables.

"Hey," he called sleepily. "Where are you going so early? I thought we were sleeping in today?"

"I have to take a bath."

"You just took a bath last night!"

"You can't have too many! Come on!"

We fooled around in the tub for an hour and then went to find breakfast. Yes, we could have cooked, but old habits die hard.

It was good that we didn't stay home, because the Monastery Bakery had a special wedding feast for us for breakfast that morning. We'd wondered why there was a young monk waiting outside the Dungeon door who'd scuttled off as soon as he saw us.

Half the Village was there, and we had a champagne toast. I cried and laughed at the same time. I had never been so happy. There were hugs all around from all the people I knew so well who had shared so much of my life.

Chase's parents and brother weren't present. They would be at the wedding, but their feelings about our marriage hadn't changed. We'd had dinner again with them, but it had been a cold, angry affair.

"This is the way my family is," Chase joked. "We only have to see them once a year."

I could see the hurt in his eyes, but there was nothing I could do about it. There was no magic spell for making his parents different. And I didn't want *us* to be different.

Manny's parents, on the other hand, had been delightful. They might be royalty, but they weren't a bit pompous or overbearing. I didn't understand why Manny had felt the need to run away, but it must have made sense to him at the time.

There had been dozens of rehearsals for the actual wedding. Not only did it have to be good for us, it had to be right for the cameras. Our movements were choreographed, and hairstyles approved.

One of the producers from Adventureland had wanted me to wear a corset. I flatly told him it wasn't happening. He'd talked to Merlin, and I'd told Merlin the same thing."

"But just think how—" he held his rounded hands out in front of his chest—"*great* you'd look."

Merlin even went so far as to send me a new corset from Adora's shop, Cupid's Arrow.

I tried it on for Chase and he gasped. "I don't think you should wear that for the wedding either, but you could wear it around here *any* time!"

"Thanks." I kissed him. My breasts felt like they were in my face. He didn't seem to mind.

The wedding gown was finished, and approved. It didn't clash at all with Livy's dress. Our rings were ready. Eve had my bouquet set. We'd been consulted about the food, but I'd approved it without really looking at it.

What did it matter what we ate? Chase and I were finally going to be married.

There were huge screens that would show all the couples getting married at once from different angles. It was going to be like going to a concert.

A huge round dais was set up where Chase and I would stand. We'd practiced that too. It made me feel like the figure on a wedding cake. It kind of looked ridiculous and cheesy.

But that didn't matter either, right? Because Chase and I were going to be together.

It hit me when I saw the two-hundred-and fifty couples coming into the Village with their families, clothes, and wedding gear. We were going through with this. It wasn't what I wanted. It had been created by people I didn't even know to please an audience of strangers.

I panicked.

At noon, I slipped out of the Village. I caught a bus a few blocks down. I joined other people on their way to work, school, and entertainment. They didn't know me. I wasn't wearing Ren Faire garb. I was just another person.

I stayed on the bus until it reached the north end of Myrtle Beach. It was Friday, and a good crowd was gathered for the weekend. I'd seen dozens of posters put up for the wedding at the Village. Not that it mattered by then—the event was sold out.

My cell phone rang over and over again. I ignored it. I knew it was Chase, and I didn't want him to worry, but I couldn't talk to him. I needed some space.

I finally got off at a public access spot to reach the ocean. I wandered over the stairs, sand dunes, and plants surrounding them. Every spare inch along the road that faced the ocean was taken up with hotels, except for these places. Here, anyone could spend time at the beach on a sunny day. Anyone could get lost in the cry of the seagulls and the roar of the Atlantic.

I sat on the sand and watched the children at play. It was too cold for most people to actually go into the water, but there were a few swimmers and surfers who weren't too timid. I heard languages from all over the world being spoken around me.

A little crab was trying to burrow into the sand to get away from the noise and the people. I helped him by getting out of his way. I picked up a few shells and put them in my pocket.

The wind whipped at my hair, and the sun burned my eyes. I didn't care. I needed that moment of peace and quiet.

It didn't really matter about the wedding. I would have been happy living with Chase in the Dungeon without a ring—or an enchanted house. I just wanted us to be happy, and love each other. I didn't care about anything else.

I had to remember that today while I was standing on top of the 'cake' and trying to pay attention to all the people shouting orders at me. This day was for Adventureland and Renaissance Faire Village. After today, was for us.

That's where Chase found me a half hour later. He sat down beside me and looked out at the ocean. "Runaway bride syndrome?"

"I don't think so." I glanced at him. "How did you find me?"

"Have you looked around?" He nodded to a crowd of people with cameras surrounding us. "The radio station that's broadcasting our wedding has been getting calls. There is a 'Jessie Watch' out. People are probably gambling on whether or not you're going to be there for the wedding."

I laughed. People took pictures. I was used to it.

"Are you?" He took my hand. "Because if *you're* not going to be there, I'm sure not going."

"Yeah. I'm going to be there."

He helped me to my feet. "Let's go then. We're going to be late for our own wedding."

* * *

At two p.m. the trumpets sounded from the castle. That was our cue.

King Harold and Queen Olivia were escorted from the castle, followed by their retinues. Chase's parents, and the King and Queen of Zamboulia, were escorted to their seats in the Royal Pavilion, especially created for this day.

Following those honored guests being seated, the music changed, and a spotlight played over the entrance to the castle. It seemed a little over-the-top to me since it was very bright and sunny. The Village wedding planner explained that it was for photos. I didn't argue.

I walked sedately down the path from the castle, with Tony at my side, to the wedding-cake dais where I would meet Chase. I knew he was walking from the Village Square.

"This is it," Tony whispered. "Run away while you still can!"

I laughed at him. "Not this time."

My bridesmaids followed me. A little girl, who was the daughter of one of the Lovely Laundry Ladies, was throwing flower petals on the ground in front of me.

The trumpets continued to blare as we walked. I couldn't hear the music that was being played by a symphony orchestra. It was hard to imagine that the music went well with the trumpets, but I kept my eyes on the prize: getting through the wedding.

“This corset is really uncomfortable,” Daisy growled from behind me.

“You shouldn’t have worn it.”

“Hey! I thought it went with the outfit.”

“Bart will like it.” I smiled.

“He already liked it a *few* times.” She laughed.

“You have to get married next.”

“No way. You fell for that. I’m not going there.”

We paused at the end of the walkway before ascending the ramp to the top of the dais. A loud voice read a prepared statement: “Please welcome our bride, Lady Jessie Morton, and our groom, Bailiff Chase Manhattan.”

There was thunderous applause. I gazed out over a sea of brides and grooms in various costumes, tuxedoes, and traditional white gowns. They looked so happy. A deep happiness welled up in me too, and I started crying.

“Keep it together,” Daisy said. “You’re not supposed to cry.”

“Tears of joy,” Adora said from behind her.

“Walk up the ramp,” the wedding planner said in my ear. Chase and I had both been fitted with two-way radios so we could hear their directions. They would also act as microphones when it came time for the vows.

Tony and I started up the ramp slowly, and I finally saw Chase.

He looked so handsome. For once, his dark hair was loose on his broad shoulders. I could see him searching for me too.

Bart and Phil were right behind him.

"There they are." Daisy waved to Bart. "I hope we're all gonna fit on that top thing without it falling down."

"I hope so too."

We reached the top of the dais where Chase and I were supposed to separate from our attendants.

Tony smiled and put my hand in Chase's. "Good luck you two." He even wiped a tear from his eye.

"Thanks." I kissed his cheek.

"Take good care of her, Chase." Tony shook his hand.

"You know I will."

Tony stepped aside to stand with the rest of the bridal party.

From the top of the dais, I could see all the pirates standing on the deck of the Queen's Revenge. The Templar Knights were out in force with their shields gleaming, and their horses fresh.

Knights from the Field of Honor were on their horses too. They saluted us with their swords and lances.

The cobblestones were filled with the residents of the Village. They all raised a tankard to us, and then spit on the ground to show their approval.

"Bet they didn't plan *that*!" I smiled at Chase.

"Probably not." He took my hand. "How are you doing?"

"Okay so far. You?"

"I'm good. Just ready for this to be over so we can go home."

"We have to make the rounds of all the parties, you know. Each guild is planning their own event."

"Five minutes each." He nodded. "I have more *important* plans."

A minister, dressed in fantastic Renaissance robes, approached the podium. He looked huge on the screens that were up around the Village. He was wearing an enormous sequined hat. I couldn't imagine how he kept it on his head.

I looked closer. "That's Merlin!"

"Yeah. Apparently, he's a minister of the Church of the Light," Chase explained. "Don't worry. I have a legal wedding license in my pocket."

"Of course you do!"

Merlin cleared his throat and began the vows. Most of them I couldn't understand. I said *'I do'* when the voice in my ear said to.

Chase put his ring on my finger. "I love you, Jessie. I always will."

That wasn't the line that he was supposed to say.

I didn't care. "I love you, Chase. I always will." I put my ring on his finger.

Merlin pronounced us man and wife. Fireworks were shot off of the top of the castle. Dancers from the Stage Caravan began gyrating in wild, colorful costumes that no Renaissance Faire of the past could ever claim.

The cannons were fired on the pirate ship until we were almost deafened by the sound.

Shakespeare recited the ode he'd written for us, but I'd have to ask him later what it said. His microphone wasn't working.

Master Archer Simmons and his men shot off their flaming arrows with no problems. It was a wonderful display.

But I barely saw it. I was dying to know what inscription Chase had put in my ring. I took it off and read it: *Forever and Always.*

"Couldn't you wait for that?" Chase asked.

"Have you looked at yours?"

He took off his ring. "*Always and forever*. Did you peek? Did the twins tell you?"

"No." I threw myself into his arms. "Guess this was meant to be, huh?"

"I guess so. Did he say kiss the bride yet?"

"He did. I was wondering when you were going to get around to it."

Chase kissed me, and I had the feeling that I was floating. It was amazing!

"Jessie?"

I opened my eyes and looked down. "We're floating! What the—?"

We looked at each other as screams erupted from the crowd below us. There were frantic commands in our ears as the wedding planner tried to decide what to do. Someone suggested calling the police.

"Wanda?" Chase asked

"In the ectoplasm!" Wanda appeared beside us. "Just my wedding present to the both of you on this fine day."

She dropped us right in the middle of the cold water of Mirror Lake. "Many happy returns!"

And so the final photo in our wedding book was that of us surfacing from the water and being dragged onboard the pirate ship.

All in all, a memorable day!

About the Authors

Joyce and Jim Lavene write bestselling mystery together. They have written and published more than 60 novels for Harlequin, Berkley and Gallery Books along with hundreds of non-fiction articles for national and regional publications.

Pseudonyms include J.J. Cook, Ellie Grant, Joye Ames and Elyssa Henry

They live in rural North Carolina with their family, their cat, Quincy, and their rescue dog, Rudi. They enjoy photography, watercolor, gardening, long drives, and going to our local Renaissance Fair.

Visit them at:

www.renaissancefairemysteries.com

www.joyceandjimlavene.com

www.Facebook.com/JoyceandJimLavene

Twitter: https://twitter.com/AuthorJLavene

Amazon Author Central Page:
http://amazon.com/author/jlavene

Upcoming!

Bewitching Boots

Book 7 in the Renaissance Faire Mysteries

A new shoemaker comes to live in Renaissance Faire Village after a successful weekend demonstration at the Arts and Crafts Museum. His boots are to-die for – literally. Jessie befriends and defends him when he is charged with killing a fairy. She knows that his shoes and boots are magical. She doesn't believe the gentle soul would hurt anyone. But when a second fairy is found dead wearing his shoes, it will take more than her belief in him to prove his innocence.

Other books in series

Book 1 – Wicked Weaves

Book 2 – Ghastly Glass

Book 3 – Deadly Daggers

Book 4 – Harrowing Hats

Book 5 – Treacherous Toys

Book 6 – Part I—Perilous Pranks—Novella

Book 6 – Part II—Murderous Matrimony

Made in the USA
San Bernardino, CA
19 July 2014